Nostradamus

The Real Story

This novel is dedicated to my beloved wife, Rosario, whose unwavering love and support inspire me every day. To my daughters, Patricia, Christy, and Alyssa, Your unwavering support has been the heart of this endeavor. To our wonderful sons-in-law, Devin and Brad, who have become cherished members of our family. And to our precious grandchildren, Braden, Maxine, Everett, Daphne and Ellison, whose laughter and curiosity remind me of life's greatest joys. Each of you has shaped my journey in ways words cannot fully express. This book is a testament to the love and strength of family, and I am forever grateful for each of you. Thank you for being the pillars of my creativity, bringing joy to every page written.
With gratitude and love.

Table of Contents

Preface

Michel de Nostradamus embarked on a journey that transcended the limits of ordinary existence. The tapestry of his life, woven with threads of astrology, medicine, and a mysterious clairvoyance, left an indelible mark on the pages of history.

As a physician, Nostradamus earned praise for his innovative approaches to treating the bubonic plague, a scourge that swept through Europe in the 16th century. However, it was his prophetic verses, expressed in a collection of quatrains, that immortalized him as a seer whose visions defied the confines of his time.

He was said to have gazed into a magic mirror that whispered secrets of centuries to come. In return, he wrote enigmatic verses that hinted at the unfolding tapestry of the future. His cryptic language, veiled in metaphors and symbolism, became a beacon for those seeking to decipher the enigma of time. It was amidst ancient scrolls and celestial reflections that Nostradamus, with his gaze fixed on the heavens, penned verses that seemed to predict events far beyond his era.

The 20th century—with its tumultuous upheavals and technological marvels—became a canvas upon which the words of Nostradamus appeared to cast their shadow. Anecdotes about his prophecies resonated through the annals of both the 20th and 21st centuries. Some pointed to verses hinting at the rise of Adolf Hitler, the dictator who plunged the world into war. Others whispered about quatrains that seemingly foretold the tragic events of September 11, 2001—a day etched forever in the collective memory of a global community.

After World War II, as the world grappled with the advent of nuclear energy, interpreters of Nostradamus' verses noted his ominous warnings of a third world war—a conflict that would unleash devastation on an unprecedented scale. The Cold War, with its geopolitical tensions, seemed to reflect prophetic echoes resonating through the pages of time.

However, skeptics pointed to the ambiguity of Nostradamus' language. Could his verses truly transcend the boundaries of time, or were they mere coincidences open to interpretation?

This is the true story...

Chapter 1: The Letter

The midday sun filtered through the blinds of Robert Michael Powell's crowded office, casting a warm glow over the books, papers, and half-finished experiments scattered across his desk. The room bore the unmistakable signs of a brilliant mind in action; its chaotic exterior reflected the intricate thoughts and theories swirling within. Robert, sat hunched over his desk, absorbed in the details of the envelope.

Robert stood at an even six feet, his lean, athletic frame a testament to years of discipline and focus. At 35, he carried himself with the quiet confidence of someone who had spent countless hours pushing both his body and mind to their limits. His broad shoulders and strong posture gave him an air of authority, though his movements were deliberate and precise, reflecting the meticulous nature of his work.

His face was angular, with high cheekbones and a well-defined jawline that hinted at a youthful vigor, though faint lines around his eyes suggested the toll of sleepless nights spent chasing impossible dreams. His piercing blue eyes were his most striking feature—sharp, intelligent, and always scanning his surroundings as if searching for answers hidden in plain sight. They carried both the intensity of his ambition and the weight of his doubts.

Robert's dark brown hair was thick but unruly, with streaks of gray beginning to thread through at the temples. It was a subtle reminder that time, even for him, marched forward. A neatly trimmed beard framed his face, adding a touch of ruggedness to his otherwise polished appearance. He dressed simply but sharply practical clothing that hinted at a man more focused on function than form.

The letter, clear and official, bore the seal of the United States Department of Defense. As he unfolded it, his eyes traced the carefully drafted lines announcing a fifty-million-dollar grant for the development of a time machine—a project that had consumed much of his career.

The weight of the letter settled in his hands. The paper crackled as he reread the words promising a major breakthrough. A surge of excitement coursed through him, mingled with the fatigue that had become a constant companion on his journey into the realm of theoretical physics and temporal dynamics.

Fifty million dollars. It wasn't just a sum; it was a lifeline—an opportunity to propel his work from the confines of theory into the tangible realm of experimentation. For over a decade, he had worked incessantly, driven by an unwavering belief in the possibility of time travel. His colleagues had dismissed his theories as fanciful and his pursuit of the unknown as quixotic at best. Yet here he was, holding in his hands recognition for a lifetime of work—an unexpected financial windfall that could shift the tide of skepticism and turn his dreams into reality.

The irony was not lost on Robert: an institution like the Department of Defense, dedicated to safeguarding the present and future, had now recognized the potential to rewrite the past. His gaze shifted from the letter to the cluttered shelves lining the walls of his office. Books on quantum mechanics, theoretical physics, and historical anomalies vied for space with notebooks filled with scribbled equations. The room, despite its disorder, was a sanctuary of knowledge—a testament to the relentless pursuit of understanding that had driven him since his early days as an aspiring scientist.

Leaning back in his creaky chair, the now-veteran scientist allowed himself a moment to absorb the magnitude of the opportunity before him.

The grant was not just a financial injection; it was a validation of his life's quest. It meant that others—powerful and influential—believed in the potential of his work to reshape the boundaries of human knowledge. Robert was a genius. He had graduated early from the Massachusetts Institute of Technology (MIT), completing his Ph.D. at just 23 years old.

Fascinated by the possibility of time travel, he had dedicated his career to uncovering the wonders hidden behind theoretical frameworks. Immediately after earning his master's degree, he won an award that allowed him to begin developing a machine that could one day enable humans to travel through time—once again proving Einstein's theories correct.

As he reflected on the implications, Robert's thoughts turned to the altruistic possibilities that lay ahead. The military had its reasons for investing in the project; perhaps visions of strategic advantages and tactical maneuvers danced in their minds.

However, for Robert, the potential of a time machine transcended military applications. He imagined a world where mistakes of the past could be revisited, examined, and—if possible—rectified. A world where lessons from history would no longer be confined to dusty tomes but could instead be witnessed firsthand.

The idea of changing the course of events—not for personal gain but for the betterment of humanity—resonated deeply within him. The crumpled letter lay forgotten on the desk, a mere physical representation of the transformation unfolding in his mind.

His gaze shifted to a chalkboard covered in complex equations—a visual representation of the labyrinthine paths he had traversed in search of temporal secrets. A whisper of doubt fluttered in the deepest recesses of his thoughts. The responsibility that came with such power was immense.

The potential consequences of meddling with the fabric of time weighed heavily on his conscience. But, as Robert often reminded himself, every scientific leap carried risks. It was the duty of an explorer to navigate the unknown, armed with knowledge and tempered by responsibility.

In the silence of his office, he found himself at a crossroads between ambition and ethics. The military grant was not just financial aid; it was a moral challenge. How would he wield this new power? Would he succumb to the allure of altering history for personal gain, or would he choose the path of altruism, seeking to mend the tapestry of time for the greater good?

The interplay of light and shadow danced around the room as Robert's mind churned with possibilities. The dusty volumes on his shelves seemed to call out to him, each one a repository of knowledge that might hold the key to unraveling time's mysteries.

With a determined gleam in his eyes, Robert rose from his cluttered desk. He looked out a window to the gardens that surrounded the lab. The evergreen trees and shrubs stood as steadfast sentinels, their deep greens vibrant even in the partly cloudy sky's filtered light. Towering cypress trees lined the edges of the property, their slender forms swaying gently in the breeze.

Closer to the building, mounded boxwoods and glossy-leaved hollies created a rhythm of shapes and textures that framed winding gravel paths. The garden was quiet, save for the occasional chirp of birds darting between the dense branches—a sanctuary of calm amidst the chaos of Robert's thoughts.

The ringing of his phone broke his reverie. He glanced at the screen and saw Richard's name. Picking up, he greeted his partner with a measured tone. "Richard."

"Robert," came Richard's voice, sharp with curiosity. "I've been waiting to hear from you. What's going on? Did you get something from them?"

Robert sighed, his gaze lingering on a cluster of arborvitae that shielded part of the garden from view. "Yes," he said after a pause. "A letter from The Pentagon arrived this morning."

"What does it say?" Richard pressed, urgency creeping into his voice.

"I can't discuss it over the phone," Robert replied firmly. "We need to meet in person."

"Robert," Richard protested, "you can't just drop that and leave me hanging. What's in the letter?"

"I'll explain everything when we meet," Robert insisted, his tone brooking no argument. "This isn't something I can risk discussing remotely."

Richard exhaled audibly on the other end of the line. "Fine," he said reluctantly. "Where and when?"

"The lab," Robert said simply. "Come as soon as you can."

"On my way," Richard replied before hanging up.

Robert put down the phone and turned back to the window, his mind racing even as his surroundings exuded tranquility. The evergreens outside stood resilient against winter's chill—an enduring reminder of constancy amidst change. But Robert knew that what lay ahead for him and Richard was anything but constant or predictable. Whatever was in that letter would shape their next move, and he needed to be prepared for whatever came next.

As he watched a sparrow flit between branches, Robert took a deep breath, steeling himself for the conversation to come. The path ahead was uncertain and riddled with challenges and ethical dilemmas, but the fifty million dollars represented not only an investment in technology but also a bet on the resilience of human consciousness. The future, it seemed, had arrived in an official envelope, and he was ready to seize it—armed with the power to shape time and an unwavering faith in the nobility of his cause.

Robert had grown up in the quiet town of Brooksville, Florida. In a place where time seemed to linger lazily in the air, young Robert Michael Powell discovered the enchantment of the night sky. Growing up in a family of modest means, he found solace and wonder in the cosmic tapestry above. His father, a mechanic, often regaled him with tales of celestial mysteries, planting the seeds of curiosity that would later define Robert's scientific journey.

As a child, Robert was drawn to books that transcended the boundaries of conventional understanding. His voracious appetite for knowledge led him to the dusty shelves of the town library, where he immersed himself in the works of Einstein, Hawking, Sagan and other luminaries of theoretical physics. The cosmos, with its unfathomable depths, beckoned to him, igniting a passion that would shape his destiny. He also loved reading fantastic novels that made him believe time travel was possible.

Robert's academic prowess became evident early on, casting a brilliant glow over the hallways of his elementary school in Brooksville. The humble town—a short drive from Tampa and close to the Gulf of Mexico—held within it a prodigious mind that would soon transcend the confines of conventional education.

Even in the early grades, Robert's love for numbers and patterns set him apart. His teachers, recognizing his unique talents, provided him with advanced coursework in an attempt to fulfill his insatiable appetite for knowledge. By the time he reached middle school, Robert's proficiency in mathematics had become legendary in the small community. He was only nine years old.

His teachers marveled at how effortlessly he grasped complex mathematical concepts, solving problems that left his peers scratching their heads. Algebra and geometry— typically reserved for older students—became Robert's playground. He approached each mathematical puzzle with the finesse of a seasoned mathematician, unraveling intricacies that seemed far beyond his years.

Word of Robert's mathematical genius spread beyond the confines of the school. Parents, educators, and even the local newspaper began to take notice of this prodigious talent emerging from their midst. The town's whispers carried tales of a young boy who saw the world through the lens of equations and formulas.

While mathematics captivated his mind, Robert's fascination with physics bloomed alongside it. His ability to comprehend the intricate dance of forces and particles impressed both teachers and visiting scholars who, intrigued by the stories of this young prodigy, made their way to Brooksville.

By the time Robert entered high school at just 11 years old, his status as a math and physics prodigy was firmly established. His reputation preceded him, creating an atmosphere of awe and anticipation as he stepped into the hallowed halls of Brooksville High. While many teenagers navigated the tumultuous waters of adolescence, Robert found solace in the elegant dance of numbers and the profound laws that governed the universe.

High school brought new challenges, but for Robert, it was a realm where his intellect thrived. He immersed himself in advanced physics courses, delving into the realms of relativity and quantum mechanics with a hunger for understanding that seemed boundless.

Recognizing his extraordinary potential, his teachers provided him with opportunities for independent study and research, nurturing his insatiable curiosity.

While his classmates grappled with the complexities of calculus, Robert explored the depths of theoretical physics. The dusty library shelves, often overlooked by his peers, became his sanctuary. There, he devoured works by scientific luminaries—from Newton's classical theories to Einstein's relativity and the cutting-edge ideas of contemporary physicists.

In the laboratory, where equations met experimentation, Robert's genius found tangible expression. He undertook projects that transcended the typical high school curriculum, constructing intricate apparatuses to explore principles gleaned from his voracious reading. His experiments often left teachers and visiting scientists in awe, showcasing a depth of understanding far beyond his years.

Robert's high school years were not only marked by academic accomplishments but also by his emergence as a mentor to his peers. Under his guidance, once-intimidating subjects like mathematics and physics became accessible and even exciting. His patient explanations and contagious enthusiasm ignited a passion for learning in students who had previously struggled with these disciplines.

The local community, recognizing the gem in their midst, rallied behind Robert. Scholarships and opportunities for advanced study poured in, including one from the prestigious Massachusetts Institute of Technology (MIT). This support paved the way for Robert's transition to a broader academic stage. The young genius from Brooksville was destined for greater heights, and the town took immense pride in nurturing the intellect that had blossomed within its embrace.

Robert's formative years, rooted in the rich soil of curiosity and supported by a community that believed in his potential, laid the foundation for the scientific luminary he would become. As he embarked on the journey beyond high school, the echoes of Robert's genius reverberated through the town, leaving an indelible mark on the place that had witnessed the early sparks of his intellectual fire.

The next chapter of his academic odyssey unfolded at M.I.T., where Robert's brilliance found a stage befitting its magnitude. Sitting across from his assigned counselor, Dr. Evelyn Marks, in her modest yet welcoming office, Robert felt both anticipation and resolve. The room was lined with shelves of academic journals and books on physics, mathematics, and engineering—an environment that seemed to echo the intellectual rigor of the institution.

Dr. Marks studied Robert for a moment, her sharp eyes assessing him with a mixture of curiosity and warmth. "So, Robert," she began, leaning forward slightly, "what brings you to M.I.T.? What do you hope to achieve here?"

Robert hesitated briefly, then spoke with measured confidence. "I want to master quantum mechanics and explore temporal fluctuation theory," he said. "I believe understanding these fields is the key to unlocking the deeper mysteries of time."

Dr. Marks raised an eyebrow, intrigued. "Temporal fluctuation theory? That's quite specific—and ambitious. Most students would start with broader goals."

Robert nodded. "I've been studying quantum mechanics independently for years," he explained. "But I need the resources and guidance that M.I.T. can provide to take my work further. My ultimate goal is to understand how fluctuations in space-time could allow us to manipulate it."

Dr. Marks leaned back in her chair, impressed by his clarity of purpose. "You're not here to dabble," she remarked with a faint smile. "You're here to push boundaries."

"Exactly," Robert replied. "I know it won't be easy, but I'm ready for the challenge."

Dr. Marks tapped her pen thoughtfully against her notebook before responding. "Well, you've certainly chosen the right place for it. We have some of the best minds in quantum physics and theoretical mechanics here—and access to cutting-edge technology that could support your research."

She paused, then added, "But you should know that pursuing something as niche as temporal fluctuation theory will require more than just technical skill. You'll need resilience and creativity—and perhaps a willingness to face skepticism from others."

Robert met her gaze steadily. "I'm prepared for that," he said simply.

Dr. Marks smiled again, this time more warmly. "Good," she said. "Because I think you have the potential to make significant contributions—not just to science but to how we understand reality itself."

As their conversation continued, Dr. Marks asked about Robert's academic background and personal motivations, offering insights into how he could navigate M.I.T.'s rigorous environment while pursuing his unique goals.

By the end of their meeting, Robert felt both challenged and encouraged—ready to begin his journey into the unknown realms of quantum mechanics and temporal fluctuation theory under Dr. Marks' guidance.

MIT welcomed Robert into its hallowed halls, recognizing in him a prodigious mind poised to reshape the landscape of theoretical physics. The institution, renowned for nurturing trailblazers, provided the perfect environment for Robert to explore the frontiers of knowledge.

In his sophomore year, Robert's academic journey took an extraordinary turn when he found himself under the tutelage of Professor Finlay, a luminary in the field of space-time experiments. The alignment of mentor and mentee marked the beginning of an exceptional partnership that would propel Robert's contributions to unprecedented heights.

Under Professor Finlay's guidance, Robert delved into the intricacies of space-time theories, exploring the very fabric of the universe. Finlay, a seasoned physicist with a reputation for pushing boundaries, had taken an interest in Robert's bold ideas. During one of their regular meetings in Finlay's office—a space cluttered with equations scrawled on whiteboards and stacks of research papers—Robert presented his latest findings on temporal fluctuation theory. Finlay leaned back in his chair, his sharp eyes scanning the diagrams Robert had laid out. "You're onto something extraordinary here," he said, his voice calm but charged with conviction. "The way you're integrating quantum entanglement with temporal displacement is... ambitious, to say the least."

Robert nodded, his excitement tempered by caution. "It's theoretical for now," he admitted. "But if we can stabilize the entangled states long enough to manipulate their temporal coordinates, we could teleport an object—not just across space but across time."

Finlay tapped a pen against his desk thoughtfully. "You're proposing a closed timelike curve," he said. "Essentially folding space-time to create a shortcut between two points in time."

"Exactly," Robert replied. "The challenge is maintaining coherence during teleportation. Any instability could collapse the system."

Finlay smiled faintly. "You're thinking like a scientist—and that's good. But don't let the challenges deter you. This is uncharted territory, Robert. The fact that you've even conceptualized this experiment shows you're on the right path."

Robert hesitated before asking, "Do you really think it's possible?"

"Possible?" Finlay repeated, leaning forward. "Robert, everything we know about quantum mechanics and general relativity suggests that time travel and teleportation aren't just science fiction—they're theoretically allowed by the laws of physics. What you're doing is taking those theories and turning them into something tangible."

He gestured toward the diagrams on the desk. "This experiment you're designing—it could redefine how we understand time and causality. But more importantly, it could prove that time isn't linear in the way we perceive it."

Robert felt a surge of determination at Finlay's words. "I still need to refine the parameters," he said. "The fluctuations are unpredictable, and I'm not sure how to account for external variables."

"That's part of the process," Finlay assured him. "You'll encounter obstacles—every great experiment does. But don't lose sight of your goal." He paused, then added with a glint of encouragement in his eyes, "You're not just working on an experiment, Robert—you're pioneering a new frontier."

As Robert left Finlay's office that day, he carried with him not only his mentor's confidence but also a renewed sense of purpose. For the first time, he felt that his vision of teleporting objects through time wasn't just a dream—it was within reach. The laboratory became his second home—a realm where equations transcended abstraction and merged with tangible experiments. Theoretical musings transformed into empirical investigations as Robert navigated the labyrinth of temporal mysteries.

His work quickly caught the attention of the academic community, and soon Robert found himself at the forefront of cutting-edge research. The experiments he conducted under Professor Finlay's mentorship garnered widespread acclaim, opening new vistas in understanding space-time dynamics. The academic community no longer saw Robert merely as a prodigy but as a visionary capable of redefining the contours of theoretical physics.

The impact of Robert's work extended far beyond the laboratory walls. His research attracted significant attention from both private and public sectors, igniting widespread interest in the transformative possibilities his discoveries held. Endowments in the millions poured into M.I.T., a testament to the belief in Robert's ability to unravel the mysteries of the cosmos.

This financial influx enabled M.I.T. to establish state-of-the-art facilities dedicated to space-time research, further solidifying its reputation as a hub of scientific innovation. Robert's sophomore year became a watershed moment for the institute, with his name becoming synonymous with groundbreaking advancements in the field.

Yet, amidst the accolades and financial windfalls, Robert remained driven by an unyielding passion for knowledge. The laboratory, with its hum of equipment and the flickering glow of monitors, became a realm where the boundary between theory and practice blurred. Robert's mind, a crucible of ideas, synthesized theoretical constructs into tangible experiments that pushed the boundaries of human understanding.

Professor Finlay, recognizing the immense potential in his protégé, provided a nurturing environment where Robert's creativity could flourish. The two formed a symbiotic partnership—merging Finlay's seasoned wisdom with Robert's boundless curiosity and innovative thinking.

As word of Robert's achievements spread, the academic community clamored for insights into his groundbreaking research. Conferences and symposiums became platforms for Robert to share his discoveries, pushing discussions on space-time theories into uncharted territories. His presentations were more than academic exercises; they were invitations for others to join him in unraveling the mysteries of the cosmos.

The endowments flowing into M.I.T. fueled an ecosystem of collaboration and innovation. Surrounded by brilliant minds, Robert worked alongside researchers who each contributed pieces to the intricate puzzle of space-time dynamics.

This synergy of collective intellect propelled their research forward, unraveling layers of understanding that had previously eluded even the most seasoned physicists.

Robert's sophomore year at M.I.T. marked not only a turning point in his academic trajectory but also a pivotal moment for theoretical physics as a whole. His pioneering work laid the foundation for a new era of exploration—one where space and time were no longer insurmountable barriers but gateways to uncharted realms of knowledge.

As he navigated the corridors of M.I.T., Robert carried with him the humility that had characterized his journey from the small town of Brooksville to the halls of one of the world's foremost institutions. The genius that had once sparked whispers in the hallways of his elementary school had now become a beacon, illuminating the path to a future where the mysteries of the universe awaited discovery.

Robert's meteoric rise in the academic realm continued unabated. By the age of 19, he had already embarked on his master's degree, a journey that propelled him further into the frontiers of theoretical physics. His insatiable curiosity and unparalleled intellect became the driving force behind his pursuit of knowledge.

The corridors of higher education became Robert's domain, where he navigated the complexities of advanced theoretical concepts with ease. His peers and professors marveled at the depth of his understanding and the speed at which he absorbed and synthesized information. While most students were still finding their academic footing, Robert was charting unexplored territories.

As he delved into his master's program, Robert's focus began to crystallize around a singular fascination: time travel. It was during one particularly groundbreaking experiment that the seeds of his future endeavors were sown.

In collaboration with a select group of colleagues, Robert designed and executed a series of experiments to probe the fabric of temporal reality. The laboratory hummed with anticipation as the team meticulously calibrated their instruments. The objective was clear: to manipulate time, even if only on a minuscule scale.

The experiments involved manipulating quantum particles in a controlled environment. Robert's insight into the intricacies of quantum mechanics allowed him to conceive a methodology that, if successful, would mark a paradigm shift in understanding temporal dynamics.

The initial trials yielded inconclusive results, but failure only fueled Robert's determination. Each setback became a steppingstone, guiding him toward refining the experimental parameters. Late nights in the laboratory became routine as Robert immersed himself in the intricacies of quantum entanglement and the delicate dance of particles through the corridors of time.

Toward the end of one session, Vivian Alves, a promising senior physicist from Brazil, joined him at the lab bench. Her sharp mind and fresh perspective had quickly made her an invaluable collaborator on the project. As Robert reviewed the data from their latest trial, Vivian approached with a notebook in hand.

"Robert," she began, her voice steady but tinged with urgency, "I've been analyzing the interference patterns from our last run. I think we need to recalibrate the entanglement field before we attempt another teleportation cycle."

Robert glanced up, intrigued. "What are you suggesting?"

Vivian flipped open her notebook to reveal a series of equations and diagrams. "The temporal displacement is being disrupted by fluctuations in the quantum field. If we adjust the spin alignment of the entangled particles before initiating the sequence, we might stabilize the system long enough to achieve a successful transfer."

Robert studied her notes carefully, nodding as he processed her insights. "You're right," he said after a moment. "We've been focusing too much on the spatial coordinates and not enough on maintaining coherence during the temporal shift."

Vivian smiled faintly, encouraged by his agreement. "So, what's our next step?"

Robert leaned back in his chair, his mind already racing ahead. "We'll need to reconfigure the entanglement generator and run simulations to test your theory. If it works, we'll be one step closer to achieving true temporal teleportation."

Vivian's eyes lit up with excitement. "Let's do it," she said. As they began mapping out their adjustments, Robert felt a renewed sense of purpose. The road ahead was still uncertain, but with collaborators like Vivian by his side, he knew they were on the brink of something extraordinary.

One pivotal night brought a breakthrough. The instruments registered anomalies—minute fluctuations hinting at disruptions in temporal progression. The significance of these findings reverberated through the academic community, placing Robert at the forefront of a burgeoning field.

With his master's degree secured at just 20 years old, Robert transitioned seamlessly into doctoral studies. Pursuing a doctorate at such a young age positioned him as a prodigy whose intellect transcended conventional boundaries. His doctoral thesis—a masterpiece of theoretical brilliance—delved into temporal mechanics, laying the groundwork for what would become his life's magnum opus: developing a functional time travel machine.

The shift from theoretical conjectures to practical applications marked a pivotal moment in Robert's career. His research focus sharpened as he immersed himself in engineering a device capable of traversing time itself.

One seminal experiment involved creating a miniature time dilation chamber. Within this controlled environment, Robert sought to manipulate time on an observable scale. The successful execution of this experiment proved controlled time manipulation was feasible, opening new vistas for exploration.

As Robert refined his theories, he grew increasingly convinced that time travel was not merely theoretical but a tangible reality awaiting realization. The enormity of this undertaking fueled his determination rather than daunted him. The laboratory transformed from a space for contemplation into one buzzing with machinery and energy—the birthplace of revolutionary invention.

Robert collaborated with engineers, physicists, and specialists from diverse fields, forming a multidisciplinary effort to bring his vision to fruition. A pivotal experiment involved creating a temporal field generator based on Robert's groundbreaking theories. This device demonstrated localized disruptions in time's fabric, confirming their approach's viability.

The decision to focus on developing a full-fledged time travel machine became central to Robert's doctoral research. Translating theoretical constructs into functional prototypes required ingenuity, innovation, and unwavering commitment to exploring the unknown.

As momentum built around his project, skepticism lingered within academia regarding its audacious goals. However, Robert's belief in its feasibility transcended conventions, fueling purpose and resilience. The laboratory echoed with machinery's clangs and generators' hums as it evolved into an experimental crucible for groundbreaking achievements. In this crucible, Robert transitioned from prodigious scholar to pioneering scientist—a journey culminating in technology poised to rewrite existence's rules. The corridors of academia braced themselves for the seismic impact of Robert's magnum opus – a functional time travel machine.

Robert Powell was in the second year of his doctorate when he conducted the experiment that would change the course of history. The young physicist had always been fascinated by the concept of time travel, but he approached it with a rigorous scientific mind. His research into temporal mechanics and quantum fields had led him to develop a prototype he called the Miniature Chrono-Field Generator (MCFG). It was a small, unassuming device, no larger than a shoebox, but it held the potential to manipulate time itself. The experiment was simple in design but groundbreaking in its implications. Using a Hot Wheels Mustang GT as the test object, Powell and his team aimed to send the car three days into the future. The Mustang, chosen for its small size and durability, sat on a metal platform in the center of the lab. The MCFG was positioned nearby, surrounded by an array of sensors and monitors to capture every detail of the event.

Powell's lab buzzed with nervous energy as he prepared to activate the device. His colleagues, a mix of graduate students and sponsoring scientists from various institutions, watched intently.

"This is it," Powell said, his voice steady but tinged with excitement. "If this works, we'll have taken the first step toward proving that time travel is possible."

He flipped a series of switches on the control panel, and the MCFG hummed to life. A faint blue glow emanated from the device as it began generating a localized chrono-field around the Mustang. The air in the room seemed to shimmer as if reality itself were bending.

"Activating chrono-field in three... two... one," Powell announced.

With a flash of light and a faint pop, the Mustang vanished. The room fell silent as everyone stared at the now-empty platform. Monitors displayed spikes in energy readings, confirming that something extraordinary had occurred.

"It's gone," one of Powell's colleagues whispered.

Powell exhaled slowly, his eyes fixed on the data streaming across the screens. "It worked," he said softly, then louder: "It worked!"

The team erupted into cheers and applause, but Powell remained focused. "Mark this moment," he instructed. "We'll know if it truly worked in three days."

The following days were filled with anticipation and scrutiny. News of the experiment spread quickly through academic circles, drawing both praise and skepticism. Some dismissed it as a clever trick, while others hailed it as a breakthrough in physics.

On the third day, Powell's lab was packed with observers—scientists from sponsoring institutions, journalists eager for a scoop, and even representatives from government agencies curious about potential applications of time travel technology.

At precisely 3:00 PM, as scheduled, the MCFG activated automatically. The air shimmered once more, and with another flash of light, the Hot Wheels Mustang GT reappeared on the platform exactly where it had been three days earlier.

The room erupted into chaos—gasps of disbelief, shouts of excitement, and hurried scribbling as scientists took notes. Powell stepped forward to examine the car. It was unchanged, save for a faint layer of dust that hadn't been there before.

"It's back," he said simply, holding up his hands to quiet the room. "Ladies and gentlemen, we've just witnessed an object successfully transported through time."

The implications were staggering. If a small object could be sent into the future and retrieved intact, what else might be possible? Could living beings make such a journey? Could time travel be used to study historical events or even prevent catastrophes?

Over the next decade, Powell's experiment became the foundation for an entirely new field of study: temporal mechanics engineering. Governments and private companies poured funding into research inspired by his work. Teams around the world collaborated to refine chrono-field technology, eventually leading to larger-scale experiments.

But for Powell himself, the moment the Hot Wheels Mustang Gt reappeared remained pivotal—not just for science but for humanity's understanding of time itself. It was proof that time was not an unyielding river but something that could be bent and shaped by those daring enough to try.

And it all began with a toy car and an idea that refused to stay confined by conventional limits.

The sun began its descent into the horizon, casting shadows through the large windows of the laboratory. The air vibrated with the soft hum of machinery and the occasional beep of computers running simulations.

Amidst the organized chaos of scientific apparatus and boards filled with equations, Robert and Richard Anders, his colleague and friend, stood before the imposing figure of the time machine capsule. Robert's eyes, ablaze with a mix of excitement and fear, turned to Richard, who mirrored his intensity.

The Department of Defense letter lay on the table—a tangible symbol of the seismic change about to unfold in their lives.

"Richard," Robert began firmly, though his voice carried the weight of the moment. "We've just received fifty million dollars. This isn't just funding; it's a directive from the highest levels of the U.S. military to develop a functional time machine."

Richard's eyes widened as the gravity of the news settled in. "Fifty million dollars? That's... beyond anything we could have imagined. But why? Why now?"

Robert pointed to the letter. "The military sees potential in our work. They believe a functional time machine could provide strategic advantages, alter the course of history, or perhaps prevent catastrophic events. It's an investment in the unknown, Richard—an act of faith in uncharted waters of temporal exploration."

Richard's brow furrowed with concern. "But what do they expect from us in return? This isn't just a philanthropic donation. There must be expectations—demands even."

Robert nodded solemnly. "That's the crux of it. We no longer work in a vacuum. We operate under the umbrella of military interests, and that comes with responsibility. They will expect results—not just scientific advancements but a working machine for their own purposes."

A heavy silence hung in the air as the implications of their new partnership with the military settled between them.

Richard broke the silence, his voice tinged with skepticism. "What if they want to use the time machine for purposes far from altruistic? What if this becomes a tool for manipulation—rewriting history according to their interests?"

Robert ran a hand through his salt and pepper hair, betraying the weight on his shoulders. "That's a valid concern, Richard. We must acknowledge the potential for misuse. But we also have an opportunity here—to guide this technology's development in a direction that aligns with our principles. We can establish safeguards, set ethical limits, and ensure that when operational, this time machine is used responsibly."

The two men paced through the laboratory, their footsteps echoing against the hum of machinery.

"Our responsibility now goes beyond science," Robert continued. "It's about building an ethical framework around this technology. We must be guardians of the timeline—stewards of both the past and future."

Richard looked at Robert with a mix of admiration and uncertainty. "So, what's our first step? How do we navigate this new terrain?"

Robert took a deep breath, already charting a course in his mind. "First, we need to establish clear communication with the military. We can't be mere contractors; we need to be collaborators. We set terms for our involvement and make it clear that ethical considerations are non-negotiable."

Richard nodded thoughtfully. "And what about the technology itself? How do we ensure it isn't used as a weapon or for political purposes?"

A determined gleam shone in Robert's eyes. "We build security mechanisms into its design—limitations that prevent exploitation for destructive purposes. We can encode ethical guidelines into its very functionality."

As they spoke, energy filled the laboratory—the weighty energy of ideas taking form. The whiteboards around them transformed from abstract equations into sketches illustrating a moral compass guiding their invention's development.

"But what if," Richard asked hesitantly, leaning on a workstation, "despite our best efforts, they push back? What if they see power and control as too tempting and ignore ethical considerations?"

Robert's gaze hardened as resolve took hold within him. "Then we leave," he said firmly. "We shut down the project if necessary. We cannot compromise our principles—the pursuit of knowledge should never come at morality's expense."

The gravity of Robert's words lingered in the air—a testament to his unwavering ideals.

As they delved deeper into their plans, purpose overcame unease. The laboratory—once a haven for theoretical musings—became a battleground for safeguarding their invention's soul.

Hours passed as their conversation evolved from abstract principles to actionable strategies. They outlined proposals for ethical oversight, brainstormed security measures, and drafted a code of conduct to govern their collaboration with military officials.

The whiteboards became canvases for ideals—a visual tapestry representing their commitment to embedding ethics into every fiber of their work.

As night fell and shadows stretched across the room under fluorescent lights, Robert and Richard emerged from their discussion united by determination. The fifty-million-dollar grant was no longer just funding; it was responsibility incarnate.

They were not merely scientists anymore—they were architects of humanity's future.

The next steps were clear: negotiate terms with military officials; meticulously design every aspect of their invention with ethics at its core; and prepare to oppose any force attempting to exploit their work for nefarious purposes.

As they prepared to leave for home after hours spent shaping history's trajectory within those walls, one silent witness remained—the time machine capsule itself—a towering symbol embodying human ambition tempered by wisdom.

Their journey into uncharted realms had taken an unexpected detour into moral territory—but armed with shared principles acting as their compass—they stood ready for whatever lay ahead.

Chapter 2: Temporal Alchemy

The laboratory was a sanctuary of steel and glass, a haven where science and imagination converged. Fluorescent lights hummed overhead, casting a sterile glow over rows of stainless-steel workstations, each crowded with monitors, tools, and intricate machinery. At the center of this technological symphony stood Robert, facing the culmination of his life's work: the time machine. The air vibrated with anticipation as he meticulously adjusted the complex array of dials, switches, and panels adorning the sleek metal surface of the capsule.

The exterior of the capsule, composed of a light yet durable alloy, gleamed with a polished finish that captured sunlight like a reflection of the future. Its precision-engineered curvature allowed it to glide through the temporal fabric with minimal disturbance—a vessel navigating the invisible currents of history. Across its metallic casing, intricate circuit patterns glowed softly in response to commands from the internal control panel. These circuits, marvels of temporal engineering, formed a delicate dance of light—a visual representation of the complexities beneath the surface. A series of panels adorned the capsule, each serving a specific purpose in the intricacies of time travel.

At its core was the Chrono-Field Generator, a pulsating engine of temporal energy that fused elements of the past and future. This technological heart granted the capsule its ability to conceal itself within the folds of time, rendering it invisible to observers in any era it visited. When Robert stepped inside, the interior revealed itself as a harmonious blend of functionality and ergonomic design. Control panels with integrated holographic displays responded seamlessly to his touch.

The Chrono-Field Generator wasn't just a machine; it was a symphony of scientific principles working in perfect harmony.

At its core were three revolutionary components that made time travel possible: specially engineered crystals, a compact fusion energy core, and quantum algorithms capable of bending spacetime.

The crystals embedded within the generator were unlike anything found in nature. Grown in zero-gravity conditions aboard orbital labs, their molecular structure had been meticulously engineered to resonate at specific frequencies. These frequencies weren't random—they corresponded to the natural vibrations of spacetime itself.

Robert had discovered that these crystals could act as amplifiers for temporal energy. When charged with power from the fusion core, they emitted coherent waves capable of distorting spacetime on a localized scale. Each crystal was tuned to a unique temporal frequency, allowing precise control over where—and when—the capsule would emerge.

But their role didn't stop there. The crystals also served as anchors, maintaining a quantum entanglement link with Robert's present timeline. This ensured that no matter how far he traveled into the past or future, he could always find his way back.

The fusion engine—a compact yet powerful source of temporal energy—emitted a soft glow that bathed the capsule in an otherworldly light. Once sealed inside this metallic cocoon, Robert found himself aboard a vessel poised on the brink of temporal exploration.

The fusion core was another critical piece of the puzzle. Traditional power sources simply couldn't generate the energy required to manipulate spacetime; only nuclear fusion could provide the necessary output. But even then, Robert had faced challenges in miniaturizing such a reactor. Through years of trial and error, he had developed a compact fusion core capable of sustaining reactions at temperatures hotter than the sun's surface. Magnetic confinement technology kept the plasma stable within its chamber, while superconducting materials ensured efficient energy transfer.

The energy produced by this reactor wasn't just raw power—it was carefully modulated and directed into the crystals for conversion into temporal waves. Additionally, some of this energy was used to generate a stability field around the capsule, protecting it from external forces like gravitational tides or quantum fluctuations during transit.

If the crystals and fusion core provided the tools for time travel, quantum mechanics provided the roadmap. The generator relied on advanced quantum algorithms to calculate precise spacetime coordinates. These calculations accounted for everything from planetary motion to cosmic background radiation—variables that could otherwise throw off a temporal jump by centuries.

The key lay in exploiting quantum superposition—the ability of particles to exist in multiple states simultaneously. By creating a quantum bubble around the capsule, Robert could place it in two different points in time at once. Collapsing this superposition state allowed him to "jump" from one temporal location to another.

The generator also utilized Einstein-Rosen bridges— wormholes—as shortcuts through spacetime. By folding space around itself, the capsule could traverse vast stretches of history without physically traveling through space.

The elliptical shape of the capsule, a testament to futuristic design mastery, contained within its confines the power to traverse the corridors of time—a journey that challenged the limits of human understanding and beckoned toward the enigmatic unknown. Across its metal casing, intricate circuit patterns softly glowed in response to commands from the internal control panel. These circuits, a marvel of temporal engineering, formed a delicate dance of light—a visual representation of the complexities lying beneath the surface.

Surrounding the time machine were testing apparatuses, computer banks, and shelves filled with prototypes and spare parts. In one corner, a 3D printer whirred to life, building complex components with precision.

The hum of machinery and the soft glow of computer screens created an atmosphere of anticipation within the hidden laboratory.

The heart of the operation lay in a meticulously designed room within a stand-alone building adjacent to the testing area. This secured chamber housed a state-of-the-art data storage center—a clandestine repository for the wealth of information generated by the time machine experiments. Rows of high-performance servers lined the walls, their rhythmic hum echoing through the room. From the outside, the building appeared to be nothing more than a simple warehouse.

The data stored within was a tapestry of temporal insights and quantum calculations, meticulously organized into secure databases. Encrypted algorithms safeguarded this treasure trove of information, ensuring that the secrets of time travel remained confined to the laboratory's digital vault. Advanced cooling systems protected the servers from overheating—a testament to both the sensitivity and magnitude of the data being processed.

A team of dedicated technicians monitored the servers around the clock, their expertise ensuring the integrity and security of this invaluable information. Intricate security protocols—both digital and physical—encased the data center in an impenetrable fortress against unauthorized access.

To further fortify resilience, redundant backups were stored at remote and secure locations. Preserving this data became paramount, given its potential impact on history's trajectory and the ethical considerations surrounding its manipulation.

The laboratory's network was isolated from external connections, creating an air gap that shielded sensitive data from cyber threats. Firewalls, encryption algorithms, and biometric access controls formed layered defenses—a digital fortress rivaling even the physical security measures. Scientists and engineers working on time machine experiments were granted access to this data center only through a meticulously controlled authentication process. Every entry was logged, and every interaction with the data was traceable—ensuring accountability and transparency in handling this paradigm-shifting information.

The storage facility itself was concealed behind layers of reinforced concrete and sophisticated security systems. Access required biometric identification, retinal scans, and multiple clearance checks. Even within this inner sanctum, the servers were encased in secure housings to prevent physical tampering.

The importance of safeguarding this knowledge extended beyond mere technical considerations—it was an acknowledgment of its profound implications for humanity's future. The laboratory stood as both a beacon of innovation and a bastion of responsibility, where every step forward into temporal exploration was tempered by ethical foresight.

As the time machine experiments progressed, the volume of data generated grew exponentially. The storage infrastructure was designed to scale seamlessly, accommodating the expanding repository of temporal knowledge. Regular audits and integrity checks were conducted to maintain the reliability of the stored information.

The secrecy surrounding the data storage was paramount, aligning with the clandestine nature of time travel research. The scientists understood the profound implications of their work and took every precaution to prevent unintended consequences.

In the laboratory, beyond the visible apparatus and tangible components, the digital realm held the key to unlocking the mysteries of time. The carefully stored data, guarded by layers of technological fortifications, stood as a testament to the commitment of those who dared to venture into uncharted territories of temporal exploration.

The smell of ozone lingered in the air, a byproduct of the electric currents running through the intricate network of cables and ducts that traversed the room. As Robert adjusted a calibration knob, Richard entered the laboratory, his eyes wide with awe at what lay before him.

"Robert, this is incredible. It looks like something out of a science fiction novel," Richard exclaimed.

Robert looked up from his work with a slight smile. "It's taken years to reach this point, Richard—countless hours of research, experimentation, and collaboration. But we're standing on the threshold of the impossible."

Richard approached the time machine and ran his fingers over its smooth surface. "It's almost surreal. I never thought I'd see something like this in my lifetime."

"That's the beauty of scientific exploration," Robert replied. "It takes us to places we never imagined and challenges the limits of what we believe is possible."

The two men exchanged a moment of silent acknowledgment before Robert gestured toward the time machine capsule. Positioned at the center of the laboratory, it stood as a technological marvel—a capsule with a hinged door that seemed like an entrance to another dimension.

Robert guided Richard through its intricacies with the passion of an artist describing his masterpiece. He explained it repeatedly, as if rehearsing for a future presentation to investors or government officials. Richard listened patiently to every word.

"The outer layer is composed of a reinforced titanium alloy," Robert explained, his fingers sliding over its cold metal surface. "It's designed to withstand extreme conditions that may arise during temporal displacement." He pointed to its curved structure. "The curvature minimizes resistance as we traverse temporal currents."

Richard nodded thoughtfully as Robert continued, pointing to a series of embedded touchscreen panels on the capsule's access control surface. "These control navigation, destination coordinates, and temporal parameters. Think of it as the cockpit for time travel. We'll need to input our destination details with absolute precision."

As Robert spoke, Richard couldn't help but marvel at how seamlessly art and science had fused in this creation. Every line and component seemed purposeful—a testament to meticulous craftsmanship.

"Inside," Robert said reverently as he opened the capsule's hinged door, "we have the Chrono Field Generator. It's the heart of this machine—creating localized distortions in space-time that allow us to break through temporal barriers."

Richard stepped closer, peering inside at what seemed like an otherworldly fusion engine glowing softly in its metallic cocoon.

"This is more than just technology," Richard murmured. "It's... transformative."

Robert nodded in agreement but added cautiously, "Transformative—but also dangerous if misused."

The two men stood silently for a moment longer before returning their focus to finalizing preparations for their groundbreaking project—a journey into time itself.

The interior of the capsule was a symphony of bright consoles, holographic screens, and softly humming machinery. The Chrono-Field Generator, a complex arrangement of crystalline structures and pulsating energy conduits, occupied the central space, emitting a subtle hum that resonated throughout the room. Richard looked inside, captivated by the fascinating dance of lights and shadows.

"It's like taking a step into the future," Richard said, his voice tinged with awe.

"In a sense, we are," Robert responded, his gaze fixed on the intricate components. "The future we're about to explore is unknown and waiting to be shaped by our actions. But we must tread carefully, Richard. The slightest miscalculation could have unforeseen consequences."

Richard nodded, his eyes reflecting a mix of excitement and fear. "I understand, Robert. We're venturing into uncharted territory and must be prepared for anything we may encounter."

When Robert closed the hinged door, the room seemed to hold its breath, as if aware of the gravity of the undertaking. The time machine, with its elegant contours and enigmatic aura, stood as a symbol of human ingenuity and the audacity to challenge the very essence of existence.

The two scientists returned to the control station and resumed their adjustments. "Our test launch is approaching," Robert said, his tone measured but intense. "We need to ensure that all components work perfectly. The Chrono-Field Generator must reach optimal stability, and the navigation systems must be flawless."

Richard nodded, pulling up data on the acquisition program. "I've been reviewing the logs from our last simulation. The data acquisition program handled the temporal fluctuations well, but there's still a slight delay in processing the feedback loop during the return phase."

Robert frowned, leaning over Richard's screen. "How slight?"

"Milliseconds," Richard replied, "but at this scale, even that could destabilize the field during reintegration."

Robert exhaled sharply. "We'll need to recalibrate the algorithms for real-time synchronization. I'll review the code tonight."

Richard hesitated before continuing. "There's also the matter of external variables—unpredictable environmental factors during the temporal trip. We need to simulate those conditions more rigorously."

Robert nodded in agreement. "You're right. Let's expand the parameters for the next simulation and stress-test every subsystem. The goal is clear: no anomalies, no risks."

Richard leaned back in his chair, his expression determined. "This has to work, Robert."

"It will," Robert said firmly, his gaze fixed on the glowing monitors. "But only if we leave nothing to chance."

Richard watched as Robert manipulated the controls with practiced ease, his mind absorbed in the intricate dance of variables that would propel them through time.

The laboratory, with its dim lighting and the hum of machinery, felt like a cocoon of possibilities—a crucible where the dreams of two men interwove with the fabric of reality. As night fell, it became a haven of concentrated determination. Robert and Richard worked in tandem, their movements synchronized like a well-rehearsed ballet. The air was charged with purpose; every keystroke and calibration was a step closer to the culmination of years of research and unwavering belief in human curiosity.

As the clock advanced, projecting shadows that danced across the laboratory floor, the time machine stood at the nexus between past and future—an embodiment of humanity's relentless pursuit of knowledge and its daring ambition to rewrite time itself.

Richard's journey into the world of technology and quantum computing began with a simple yet transformative event— the gift of an Apple computer in 1990. Nestled under the Christmas tree, the unassuming box held the key to a future that would see Richard become a trailblazer in the realms of quantum computing and artificial intelligence.

As he unwrapped the package, the sleek design of the Apple Macintosh captivated Richard's imagination.

Little did he know that this seemingly ordinary present would serve as the portal to a realm where he would shape the future of technology. That initial encounter with the computer sparked an insatiable curiosity, and Richard found himself drawn into the intricate world of programming.

In the quiet hours of the night, Richard hunched over the glowing screen of his Macintosh, delving into the intricacies of coding. The rhythmic tapping of keys became a symphony of creation as he experimented with algorithms and explored the vast landscape of software development. What began as a hobby soon transformed into a passion, setting the stage for Richard's journey into the frontiers of computing.

His aptitude for programming did not go unnoticed. Richard's knack for unraveling the complexities of code earned him recognition among his peers and mentors. The academic realm beckoned, and Richard embarked on a trajectory that would see him not only master the art of programming but also delve into cutting-edge domains such as quantum computing and artificial intelligence.

In the hallowed halls of higher education, Richard's journey took a quantum leap. The foundation laid by his early experiences with the Macintosh provided him with a solid understanding of programming languages, paving the way for deeper explorations. His voracious appetite for knowledge led him to specialize in the nascent field of quantum computing.

Under the guidance of visionary mentors, Richard navigated uncharted waters in quantum mechanics and computational theory. The intricacies of qubits, entanglement, and superposition became the building blocks of his intellectual arsenal.

Quantum computing, with its promise of exponentially enhanced processing power, captured Richard's imagination and drove him to unravel its mysteries.

The acquisition and integration of data emerged as central themes in Richard's academic pursuits. His fascination with seamlessly incorporating data into quantum computing paradigms became a catalyst for his specialization.

He envisioned a future where quantum computers could not only process vast amounts of data but also acquire and interpret information in ways previously deemed impossible.

As Richard delved deeper into quantum computing, he recognized its symbiotic relationship with artificial intelligence. The synergy between these two groundbreaking fields became the focus of his doctoral research. System design—a critical facet in integrating quantum computing with artificial intelligence—became Richard's forte.

His doctoral journey unfolded against the backdrop of a rapidly evolving technological landscape. Richard's research explored designing systems that harnessed quantum computing's potential for artificial intelligence applications. The fusion of these cutting-edge technologies held transformative promise, and Richard stood at the forefront of this intellectual frontier.

The corridors of academia bore witness to Richard's ascent as a luminary in quantum computing and artificial intelligence. His publications garnered accolades, while his innovative approach to system design drew attention from both academic and industrial circles. The world recognized Richard as a visionary poised to redefine technological progress.

In this crucible of innovation, Richard's journey mirrored the exponential growth of the technologies he embraced. The once-nascent field of quantum computing matured under his stewardship, while artificial intelligence discovered new horizons through his pioneering efforts. As a doctor in quantum computing and artificial intelligence, Richard became an inspiration for aspiring technologists.

The acquisition and utilization of data evolved from an academic theme into a guiding philosophy that extended beyond research laboratories. Richard envisioned a world where data-driven insights illuminated paths to progress and discovery. His expertise became sought after not only in academic circles but also within an ever-expanding tech industry hungry for visionary leaders.

The impact of Richard's work extended beyond the theoretical realm. Practical applications emerged from his research, ushering in a new era where quantum computing and artificial intelligence collaborated to solve complex problems. From optimizing computational tasks to unraveling the mysteries of machine learning, Richard's contributions became integral to the evolving tapestry of technological innovation.

In the annals of quantum computing and artificial intelligence, Richard's name became synonymous with visionary thinking and pragmatic implementation. His journey, catalyzed by a Christmas present that opened the door to the digital realm, unfolded as a testament to the transformative power of curiosity, dedication, and the relentless pursuit of knowledge. Richard, the architect of quantum futures and artificial intelligence landscapes, stood at the nexus of technological evolution—a pioneer whose legacy echoed through the corridors of time.

Chapter 3: Real Possibilities

The full moon, now just above the horizon, cast long shadows over the serene local park. A gentle breeze rustled the leaves of the ancient oaks lining the paths, while the distant chatter of a boat at sea and the sound of a train horn provided a whimsical soundtrack. On a weathered wooden bench near the heart of the park, Robert and Richard were engrossed in conversation, their eyes aglow with excitement and anticipation.

Robert, his hair beginning to turn gray and his beard meticulously groomed, leaned forward, his gaze fixed on the notebook in his hands. Across from him sat Richard, a decade his senior, with unruly brown hair and a perpetually curious expression. He sipped coffee from a thermos while absorbing the intricate equations scrawled on the pages.

"We're on the brink of something monumental, Richard," Robert declared, his voice low but weighted with years of dedication. "This time travel machine is no longer just theoretical. The calculations are falling into place; the physics is aligning."

Richard nodded, his eyes gleaming with a mix of enthusiasm and disbelief. "I can't believe we're at this point. It's like a dream."

"More like a dream within a dream," Robert laughed as he closed the notebook and set it aside. "But we can't let ourselves get carried away. There's still work to do—tests to conduct and safety measures to implement."

The two men lapsed into thoughtful silence, gazing into the distance as if peering through the fabric of time itself. Possibilities hung in the air like the scent of blooming flowers—tempting yet elusive. Robert's thoughts drifted back to how they first met. In the sprawling corridors of a prestigious scientific conference sponsored by the U.S. military, Robert found himself immersed in a sea of intellects contributing to cutting-edge research.

The air buzzed with excitement, and ambition seemed to permeate every corner of academia. It was amidst this tapestry of scientific fervor that Robert first encountered Richard—a brilliant mind with an insatiable appetite for knowledge.

The conference, held in Washington, D.C., served as a crucible for ideas that transcended conventional science. Robert, already renowned for his groundbreaking work in space-time experiments, felt an immediate resonance with Richard's approach to quantum computing and artificial intelligence. Their shared curiosity became an invisible thread drawing them together.

As Robert perused various presentations, one session captivated his attention: an exploration of integrating quantum computing with artificial intelligence. The speaker—none other than Richard himself—eloquently expounded on the transformative potential of merging these two technological frontiers. Ever the visionary, Robert recognized in Richard a kindred spirit navigating uncharted waters.

After Richard's presentation ended, their conversation began—a dialogue that transcended the confines of the conference hall.

"Richard," Robert began, shaking his brother's hand firmly, "your work is remarkable. The way you're leveraging quantum computing to enhance AI optimization—it's groundbreaking."

Richard smiled, his enthusiasm evident. "Thanks, Robert. But your work in temporal mechanics is no less impressive. I've been following your research on temporal fluctuation theory—it's fascinating. Have you considered how quantum computing could accelerate your simulations?"

Robert nodded thoughtfully. "That's exactly what I wanted to discuss with you. My experiments with temporal displacement are limited by classical computational speed. The algorithms I'm using to stabilize the Chrono-Field Generator require immense processing power—far beyond what we currently have."

Richard's eyes lit up. "Quantum computing could be the key. With its ability to process multiple states simultaneously, we could model temporal fluctuations in real time and refine your algorithms for stabilization."

Robert leaned in, intrigued. "And what about AI? Could it help predict and manage the chaotic variables during a temporal jump?"

"Absolutely," Richard replied. "AI could analyze patterns in the data and adapt the system dynamically during the experiment. It's a perfect synergy."

Robert smiled, a sense of clarity washing over him. "Then it's settled—we need to join forces. Your expertise in quantum-enhanced AI and my work in temporal mechanics could push both fields forward."

Richard extended his hand again, sealing their agreement. "Let's do it."

The ideas flowed freely between them were like a river weaving together their disparate expertise. For Robert, who mastered space-time experiments, Richard represented the missing piece—the bridge between theoretical exploration and practical application.

Their animated discussion soon caught the attention of influential figures within the U.S. military. General Bradley—a visionary leader attuned to scientific innovation—saw in Robert and Richard two architects capable of reshaping humanity's understanding of time itself.

In a secluded meeting room adorned with emblems of national security, Robert and Richard met General Bradley face-to-face. The air hung heavy with possibilities as Bradley wasted no time expressing interest in their work. The clandestine nature of their meeting hinted at its covert potential.

"Gentlemen," Bradley began, leaning forward, his voice steady but commanding, "I've reviewed the preliminary reports on your Chrono-Field Generator. What you're developing has the potential to change everything—not just for science, but for national security."

Robert exchanged a glance with Richard before responding. "General, our work is focused on advancing temporal mechanics for scientific discovery. We're not interested in weaponizing it."

Bradley raised a hand to calm them. "I understand your concerns," he said smoothly. "But let me assure you, my interest lies in ensuring your research reaches its full potential. That requires resources—funding, equipment, and access to facilities that only we can provide."

Richard leaned forward, skeptical but curious. "And what would you expect in return?"

Bradley smiled faintly. "Only that we remain informed of your progress and that you consider how your discoveries might serve the greater good. With the Department of Defense's R&D budget exceeding $95 billion annually, I can ensure you have everything you need to succeed."

Robert hesitated, his mind racing through the implications. "We'll need time to discuss this," he said cautiously.

"Take all the time you need," Bradley replied, standing to leave. "But remember—opportunities like this don't come often.".

General Bradley—a stern but discerning figure—delved deeply into their research. He saw not just intellectual pursuit but also strategic opportunity: harnessing time travel could revolutionize geopolitics. Recognizing their potential value to national security, Bradley introduced them to General Christopher James Andrews' department within the Pentagon—a division specializing in non-traditional systems and methods.

Yet this collaboration raised ethical dilemmas that cast long shadows over their partnership. Against this backdrop of opportunity and moral complexity, Robert extended an invitation to Richard—one that would bind their destinies together.

"Richard," Robert began solemnly, his gaze unwavering, "what we're on the brink of is revolutionary—but it comes with responsibilities beyond science alone. The military wants to harness our discoveries for strategic advantage, which means navigating uncharted ethical territories. I can't tread this path alone; I need someone who shares my vision but can also act as a moral compass when temptation arises."

Richard listened intently as these words settled over him like an unspoken vow. This was more than an invitation to collaborate—it was a call to confront ethical challenges alongside scientific discovery.

Finally, after moments of reflection that felt timeless in themselves, Richard responded with quiet resolve.

"Robert," he said firmly, "I share your vision—not just for advancing science but for upholding our ethical responsibility along the way. If we embark on this journey together, I'll stand as your moral compass while we navigate these complexities—not merely as scientists but as guardians of our shared humanity."

The pact forged in that clandestine meeting room laid the foundation for a partnership that would weather the storms of temporal exploration. Robert and Richard, both scientists and stewards of ethical integrity, emerged from that meeting as a dynamic duo poised to unravel the mysteries of time while safeguarding the principles that defined their humanity.

Little did they know that their journey would intertwine scientific innovation, ethical dilemmas, and the inexorable march of time into a narrative transcending the boundaries of fiction and reality.

Robert broke the silence with a serious tone. "Richard, we've run the calculations hundreds of times, but it's crucial that we fully understand the science behind what we're attempting. Time travel isn't just a matter of hopping into a machine and pressing a button. It's a delicate dance with the fundamental laws of the universe."

Richard nodded, setting his coffee aside. "I've been reviewing the equations as well. The theory is sound, but we must account for every variable. The slightest miscalculation could send us into the unknown with no chance of return."

"You're right," Robert agreed. "We have to be meticulous. This isn't just about testing a concept; it's about rewriting the narrative of human existence."

With dusk upon them, the atmosphere in the park shifted. The distant laughter of children gradually faded away, leaving behind the symphony of crickets and the occasional hoot of an owl. The two men on the bench were enveloped in an intellectual bubble, oblivious to the outside world as they delved into the complexities of their groundbreaking project.

Robert pointed toward the night sky. "Have you ever wondered if time is like the stars up there? Unfathomable in its vastness yet connected in ways we are only beginning to grasp."

Richard followed Robert's gaze; his expression tinged with melancholy. "It's humbling, isn't it? The idea that we are just tiny specks in this cosmic ballet, yet we dare to challenge its essence."

Robert nodded thoughtfully and continued, "The launch of our experiment is approaching. We've set the date for six months from now. That should give us enough time to run simulations, fine-tune the machine, and prepare for every imaginable scenario."

A moment of contemplative silence passed between them before Richard broke it, squinting in thought. "What if we succeed, Robert? What if we break through the barriers of time and witness the past or future firsthand? The implications are staggering."

Robert leaned back slightly, a faint smile on his lips. "That, my friend, is the beauty of it. The unknown is what drives discovery. Imagine the knowledge we could gain—the mysteries we could unravel. The impact on science, history, philosophy... it's immeasurable."

The bench creaked under their weight as they shifted slightly, looking at each other with a shared sense of determination. The moon cast a silvery glow on their faces, emphasizing the gravity of their endeavor.

"But" Robert cautioned, "we must also consider the ethical implications. Time is fragile and manipulating it could have consequences we cannot foresee. We are not just scientists; we are stewards of the secrets of the universe."

Richard solemnly nodded. "I understand. We cannot let our ambition blind us to the responsibility we bear. If we succeed, we'll enter uncharted territory and must tread carefully."

As the night progressed, their conversation deepened— exploring not only the intricacies of time travel but also its profound potential impact on humanity. The bench beneath them seemed to absorb the weight of their words—a silent accomplice to their dreams and aspirations.

And so, beneath the star-studded canopy of the universe, Robert and Richard pressed on—minds burning with the fire of discovery and a shared vision propelling them toward a future where time itself was no longer an immutable force but a canvas waiting to be painted with strokes of human ingenuity.

Richard Alder's home in the Belmont neighborhood was a picture of suburban tranquility. Nestled in a quiet cul-de-sac, the modest two-story house was filled with warmth, laughter, and the occasional chaos that came with raising an eight-year-old. Richard had built a good life for himself after years of hard work in the field of Coding and development of quantum computers. Though his days were spent juggling research alongside his friend and partner, Robert, his evenings were devoted to his family—a life he cherished above all else.

His wife, Emily, was the heart of their home. A stay-at-home mom by choice, she poured her energy into creating a nurturing environment for their son, Richard Jr., and supporting her husband's demanding career. Emily's days were filled with school drop-offs, meal planning, and managing the endless stream of laundry and homework that came with parenting. She loved her role and took pride in the little things that made their house feel like a home.

Emily was a physicist of remarkable talent, known for her groundbreaking work at Lawrence Livermore National Laboratory (LLNL). Over the years, she had developed several advanced systems in the field of nuclear physics and energy research, earning her widespread respect among her colleagues. Her days at LLNL were filled with intense problem-solving, collaborating with brilliant minds, and pushing the boundaries of science. But everything changed when she met Richard Alder at a physics conference in San Francisco.

Richard was presenting his research on temporal mechanics and quantum computing applications, a field Emily had always found fascinating but distant from her own work. His passion for his subject was infectious, and Emily found herself drawn to his ideas—and to him. They spent hours talking after his presentation, sharing their thoughts on science, life, and the future. By the end of the conference, they both knew their connection was something special.

Their relationship blossomed quickly. Emily found in Richard a kindred spirit—someone who shared her intellectual curiosity but also valued the simple joys of life. When Richard proposed six months later, she didn't hesitate to say yes. Shortly after their wedding, Emily made a bold decision: she took a sabbatical from her position at LLNL to focus on building their life together.

For Emily, stepping away from her career was not an easy choice. Science had been her identity for so long that she feared losing herself without it. But as she settled into her new role as a wife and soon-to-be mother, she discovered a different kind of fulfillment. Their home became a sanctuary of love and creativity, where science still played a central role—just in a new way.

Their son, Richard Jr., was born two years into their marriage. From the moment he arrived, Emily's world shifted again. She embraced motherhood with the same determination and care she had once given to her research. Watching RJ grow into a curious and bright child brought her immense joy.

Though Emily missed the lab at times, she found ways to channel her scientific mind into their family life. She encouraged RJ's budding interest in coding and strategy games, often sitting with him as he worked on puzzles or tinkered with his tablet. Together with Richard, they created a household where learning and exploration were celebrated.

Emily's days were now filled with school drop-offs, helping RJ with his homework, and managing their home. But in the evenings, when the family gathered around the dinner table or worked on creative projects together, she felt no regrets about her decision to take a step back from LLNL. Her work had been important—but this life they were building together was priceless.

Richard Jr., or "RJ" as they often called him, was an exceptionally bright child with an insatiable curiosity. At just eight years old, he had already developed a love for strategy games and coding. His favorite pastime was working on creative projects with his dad, who encouraged his intellectual curiosity at every turn. Together, they were developing a game where the main character was a microbe navigating life inside an unknown animal—a world filled with challenges like battling bad bacteria and viruses while searching for nutrients to survive.

The Alder household came alive each morning with the sound of Richard Jr.'s footsteps thundering down the stairs. "Mom! What's for breakfast?" he would call out as he slid into the kitchen, his hair still messy from sleep.

"Pancakes," Emily would reply with a smile, flipping golden-brown circles onto a plate. "But only if you promise to brush your hair before school."

Richard would wander in moments later, coffee mug in hand, already dressed for work but not quite awake yet. "Morning," he'd mumble before kissing Emily on the cheek and ruffling RJ's hair. Breakfast was always a lively affair, filled with RJ's chatter about school projects or the latest update to his favorite game.

After dropping RJ off at school, Richard would head to the university while Emily returned home to tackle her daily tasks. By mid-afternoon, she'd pick RJ up and help him with homework before starting dinner. It was a routine they had settled into comfortably—a rhythm that balanced work, family time, and personal pursuits.

Dinner was sacred in the Alder household—a time when everyone came together to share stories from their day. The table was set simply but thoughtfully: plates of steaming food, glasses of water or juice, and an ever-present bowl of salad that Emily insisted on including.

"So," Emily began one evening as they dug into her homemade lasagna, "how was everyone's day?"

RJ spoke up first, as usual. "We learned about ecosystems in science today! Did you know that some animals have bacteria in their stomachs that help them digest food? It's kind of like our game!"

Richard smiled at his son's enthusiasm. "That's true! Symbiosis is fascinating. Maybe we can add that to our game—what do you think?"

RJ nodded eagerly. "Yeah! The microbe could find friendly bacteria to team up with! They could work together to fight off viruses."

Emily laughed softly as she watched them brainstorm. "You two are going to turn this game into a full-blown science lesson."

"That's the plan," Richard said with a grin.

As dinner continued, they talked about everything from RJ's coding progress to Richard's life at the lab with his partner, Robert. Emily shared updates about upcoming school events and funny anecdotes from her day at home. It was a time of connection—a chance to unwind and enjoy each other's company.

After dinner, Richard often spent time in RJ's room working on their game together. The room was a mix of childhood whimsy and budding intellect: shelves lined with books on science and history sat alongside action figures and board games. A small desk held RJ's tablet and notebook, where he sketched ideas for their game.

"Okay," RJ said one evening as they sat side by side on his bed, tablet in hand. "So the microbe starts out small and weak, right? But as it eats nutrients, it gets stronger."

"Exactly," Richard replied. "And what happens when it encounters bad bacteria?"

RJ thought for a moment before tapping on his tablet screen. "It could use enzymes to break them down! But only if it has enough energy."

Richard nodded approvingly. "That's a great idea! And maybe we can add levels where the microbe has to navigate different parts of the body—like the stomach or bloodstream."

RJ's eyes lit up at the suggestion. "Yeah! And there could be boss battles against really tough viruses!"

They worked late into the evening, bouncing ideas back and forth as they refined their game concept. For Richard, these moments were more than just creative collaboration—they were opportunities to bond with his son and nurture his love of learning.

As bedtime approached, Emily poked her head into the room. "Alright, you two," she said with mock sternness. "It's time for RJ to get some sleep."

"Just five more minutes!" RJ pleaded.

Emily raised an eyebrow but smiled indulgently. "Five minutes—and then lights out."

After she left, Richard leaned over and ruffled RJ's hair affectionately. "Your mom's right—you need your rest if you're going to keep coming up with these great ideas."

RJ grinned sleepily as he set his tablet aside. "Thanks for working on this with me, Dad."

"Anytime," Richard said softly. He tucked RJ in before turning off the light and heading downstairs.

For Richard Alder, life revolved around family—his wife Emily, who kept their home running smoothly; his son RJ, whose bright mind never ceased to amaze him; and the quiet moments they shared together each day.

As he sat on the couch that night beside Emily—her hand resting lightly on his—Richard felt grateful for all they had built together: a life filled with love, laughter, and endless possibilities for what lay ahead.

And somewhere deep down inside him lingered another thought—What effects would the time machine have on his life, long term? Would he be able to travel to different times and maybe take his wife and son along, like on a vacation? Only time would tell.

Chapter 4: A Jump to Tomorrow

The laboratory buzzed with anticipation as Robert and Richard stood before the culmination of years of tireless work: the time machine capsule. The metallic cocoon, gleaming under the sterile glow of the lab lights, exuded an otherworldly aura. Countless hours of research, funding from the Department of Defense, and ethical considerations woven into the very structure of the machine had led them to this moment.

Robert, dressed in a sleek, custom-designed suit equipped with state-of-the-art sensors, stood in front of the open door of the time capsule. His pulse quickened with a mix of excitement and nervous energy. Richard, stationed at the control panel in the lab, adjusted the final parameters on the touchscreen displays, ensuring every detail was in place for the first human time jump.

"Remember, Robert, this is just a test," Richard said, his voice projecting through the communication system in Robert's helmet. "One week into the future. Gather information, observe, and make sure to return as soon as possible. We're still navigating uncharted waters."

Robert nodded; his eyes focused on the complex controls inside the capsule. "Understood, Richard. I'll keep my observations concise and won't interfere with anything. One week into the future—and I'll be back before you know it."

With that, Robert stepped into the time machine capsule. The door closed behind him with a soft hiss, sealing him inside the elliptical chamber. Richard remained in the control room, his eyes fixed on an intricate array of screens and dials as he prepared to orchestrate this unprecedented temporal journey.

The interior of the time machine capsule was a marvel of cutting-edge technology and meticulous design. The elliptical chamber glowed softly with pulsating light, housing an ergonomic seat surrounded by holographic interfaces. Robert settled into his seat—a product of precision engineering designed for comfort during temporal transitions.

The walls were lined with intricate circuitry woven together like a master craftsman's tapestry. Metallic lattices interlaced with fiber-optic strands served as conduits for algorithms that governed spacetime manipulation. Every inch of the capsule reflected a convergence of scientific innovation and aesthetic sensibility.

At its core, the Chrono-Field Generator, a technological masterpiece born from Robert's experiments at M.I.T.—the linchpin of temporal manipulation. Its crystalline structure, infused with rare isotopes, resonated with energy capable of bending spacetime itself.

Robert's fingers trembled as they hovered over the final set of controls. The time capsule stood before him, a gleaming testament to human ingenuity and his own relentless pursuit of the impossible. The room was quiet except for the faint hum of the Chrono-Field Generator, its rhythmic pulse filling the air with a low vibration that seemed to resonate with time itself. This was the moment he had worked toward for decades—a moment that would either redefine humanity's understanding of existence or end in catastrophic failure.

The capsule's elliptical frame gleamed under the sterile lights of the laboratory. Its polished alloy surface reflected Robert's determined face, etched with lines of exhaustion and hope. The intricate circuit patterns etched into the metal pulsed faintly, glowing in hues of blue and gold, as if alive. These circuits weren't mere conduits for electricity; they were pathways for temporal energy, designed to manipulate the very fabric of spacetime.

Now, within the capsule, the gentle hum of the engine filled the capsule as it prepared to propel Robert across time's corridors. Holographic interfaces flickered to life around him, displaying equations and coordinates mapping out the temporal landscape awaiting exploration.

The Chrono-Field Generator wasn't just a machine; it was a symphony of scientific principles working in perfect harmony. At its core were three revolutionary components that made time travel possible: specially engineered crystals, a compact fusion energy core, and quantum algorithms capable of bending spacetime.

Robert had discovered that the crystals in the generator could act as amplifiers for temporal energy. When charged with power from the fusion core, they emitted coherent waves capable of distorting spacetime on a localized scale. Each crystal was tuned to a unique temporal frequency, allowing precise control over where—and when—the capsule would emerge.

Richard double-checked every parameter before glancing at the countdown on the main screen. "On my signal," he said firmly. "Three... two... one. Launch!"

As Richard's voice echoed through the lab, the sleek surface of the capsule began to pulsate with light as the Chrono Field Generator activated.

Inside, Robert felt a soft vibration—a subtle shift in reality itself. The ambient hum intensified into a rhythmic pulse as colors around him began to morph into an otherworldly kaleidoscope of temporal energy.

As the capsule delved deeper into the timestream, its surroundings transformed profoundly. Abstract patterns resembling waves of data rippled across its walls while glowing streams of energy—temporal currents—flowed in mesmerizing patterns laden with fragments of history and glimpses of potential futures.

The air crackled faintly with electric charge as Robert perceived time itself as something tangible—a force flowing around him. Historical moments played out like holographic projections: ancient civilizations rising and falling; futuristic landscapes shimmering on distant horizons. He marveled at this interconnected web of events—the ebb and flow of causality laid bare before him. Faint echoes—voices and distant sounds—reverberated within these temporal currents as if whispering secrets from across history's vast expanse. The capsule became both vessel and observer in this river of time; Robert was its intrepid navigator. Amidst this visual symphony, fragments from Robert's own life emerged—pivotal moments that had defined his journey as a scientist. These glimpses were humbling yet awe-inspiring reminders of how deeply intertwined past, present, and future truly were.

Yet, as the capsule hurtled through the temporal stream, Robert couldn't help but wonder: Was this real? The kaleidoscope of colors and sensations overwhelmed his senses, stretching the boundaries of perception. Was he truly traversing time, or was this an elaborate construct of his mind—a hallucination triggered by the immense energy coursing through the Chrono-Field Generator? He thought about theories he had once dismissed: that time existed only as a construct of human consciousness, that its flow could be altered simply by how it was perceived.

The capsule's instruments displayed data confirming the temporal displacement, but Robert's thoughts lingered. What if this is all in my head? he mused. The whispers of history felt so vivid, yet so intangible. He resolved to trust the science—the precision of his calculations and the algorithms that had guided him here. But a small part of him wondered if reality itself was bending under the weight of his experiment, leaving him suspended between what was real and what his mind wanted to believe.

As his perception shifted further into fluidity, Robert sensed not just events but their gravity—the weight of decisions made and their echoes reverberating through time's tapestry. This journey was more than spectacle; it was an immersive exploration into existence's profound intricacies. In that surreal space between moments, Robert glimpsed possibilities: rewriting history not for personal gain but for humanity's betterment. The Chrono Field Generator pulsed around him like a beacon—illuminating paths through spacetime yet unexplored.

The hum reached its crescendo as reality blurred briefly into swirling mosaics outside the lab walls. Then came a sudden jolt—and silence.

In the control room, Richard stared at the screens intently while anticipation and anxiety warred within him. On-screen indicators confirmed it: the digital countdown now displayed exponential values—a sign that Robert had theoretically arrived one week into the future

In the confines of the time machine capsule, Robert's surroundings shifted from the familiar laboratory to an unknown temporal landscape. The hatch opened, revealing a scene that mirrored the laboratory but with subtle differences. The air felt the same, the lighting was identical, but there was a subtle change in energy—a sensation that transcended the bounds of time itself.

"Richard, can you hear me?" Robert's voice crackled through the communication system.

"Loud and clear," Richard responded. "I hear you. How does it feel on the other side?"

"It's... indescribable," Robert replied, surveying his surroundings. "Everything looks the same, but there's a sense of displacement, as if I'm a visitor in my own reality."

Richard monitored data streams and ensured that the temporal displacement occurred without anomalies. "Remember, the main goal is observation. Gather data, take notes, and don't interact with anything or anyone. We don't know the repercussions of altering even the slightest detail."

Robert nodded, leaning over the console as they reviewed the parameters of the experiment. "We need to focus on verifiable data," he said. "I'll record lottery numbers drawn within the last seven days and weather patterns—things that can be confirmed when I return."

Richard tapped on his tablet, pulling up a list of key metrics. "Good. I've also programmed the system to monitor environmental conditions during your temporal displacement—temperature, atmospheric pressure, even electromagnetic fluctuations. We'll compare those readings against historical records."

Robert adjusted his notes, considering Richard's points. "We should also include social observations—major events or anomalies that align with this specific date in history. The more cross-referenced data we gather, the better we can validate the experiment."

Richard agreed but added a cautionary note. "Just remember, Robert, this isn't about proving you were there—it's about ensuring the system works as intended. Stay focused on observation, not interaction."

Robert smiled faintly. "I know, Richard. Trust me—I'm not here to rewrite history." He glanced at the countdown timer on the console. "Let's get everything calibrated. This has to be flawless."

Together, they finalized their checklist, their shared determination driving them toward a successful temporal leap.

Following Richard's instructions, Robert ventured into the future. He walked through the laboratory, noting any changes and examining details that could betray the passage of time. The familiar smell of ozone lingered in the air, and the hum of machinery provided a constant backdrop. Everything seemed eerily similar, yet there was an undeniable tension in the air—a sense that something monumental had occurred.

Robert approached the computer terminal in the corner of the lab, its screen glowing faintly in the dim light. He logged in using his credentials, which thankfully still worked. The system booted up quickly, and he navigated to the data logs from the last month. His heart pounded as he clicked through the files, searching for any record of his leap into the future.

And there it was—a detailed record of his entry into the capsule and the subsequent activation of the Chrono-Field Generator. The timestamp confirmed it: seven days ago, he had stepped into the machine and vanished. The data showed a spike in energy levels as the chrono-field stabilized, followed by a sudden drop as he disappeared from this timeline.

Robert leaned back in his chair, staring at the screen. It was surreal to see his actions documented so clinically, as though they were just another experiment. But what caught his attention next sent a chill down his spine: a folder labeled "Notes—Richard." He opened it and began reading. The notes were meticulous, written in Richard's unmistakable style—concise yet filled with curiosity and insight. The first entry read:

"3:19:06: Robert has successfully entered the chrono-field and transitioned to a temporal destination 7 days into the future. Initial readings suggest stability within expected parameters. Awaiting further data."

Robert scrolled through subsequent entries, each one detailing Richard's analysis of the data being transmitted back from the capsule. It seemed that even as Robert traveled through time, some form of communication had been established—data packets sent back to their original timeline as proof of his journey.

"3:19:15: Energy fluctuations detected within the chrono-field suggest temporal interference. Possible external factors influencing Robert's trajectory? Further analysis required."

The entries became increasingly speculative as Richard tried to piece together what might be happening on Robert's end. One note caught Robert's eye:

"3:19:55: Received anomalous data suggesting temporal feedback loop. Could this indicate an attempt by Robert to communicate? If so, what is he trying to tell us?"

Robert's mind raced as he read those words. He had no memory of attempting to communicate during his journey—had something happened that he couldn't recall? Or was Richard misinterpreting the data?

The final entry was dated just hours before Robert's reappearance:

"3:20:28: Chrono-field activity reaching critical levels. Preparing for potential reintegration event. If successful, this will confirm our hypothesis about temporal elasticity and pave the way for further exploration."

Robert exhaled slowly, his hands trembling slightly as he closed the file. Richard had been tracking every moment of his journey with unwavering focus, trying to understand what had happened and what it meant for their work.

But now that Robert was back, new questions arose: What had he experienced during those seven days? Why did he feel as though something important was missing from his memory? And most importantly—what would they do next?

He turned away from the computer and looked around the lab once more. The equipment hummed softly, waiting for its next command. For a moment, he felt a pang of doubt—had they gone too far? Was humanity ready for what they were uncovering?

But then he thought of Richard's notes—the passion and determination behind every word—and felt a renewed sense of purpose. They weren't just scientists; they were explorers charting unknown territory.

Robert stood up and walked over to a whiteboard covered in equations and diagrams. He picked up his tablet and began writing furiously, capturing every fragment of memory he could recall from his journey into the future.

When Robert returned to the lab later that day, they would have much to discuss. Together, they would unravel the mysteries of time itself—and perhaps discover what lay beyond its veil.

For now, Robert focused on one thought: this was only the beginning..

After thoroughly exploring the laboratory, he decided to venture beyond its limits. Stepping into the hallway, he noticed a subtle alteration in ambient lighting—a slight change in color temperature suggesting the passage of time.

"Richard, I'm going beyond the laboratory. Everything seems... subtly different. I'll explore the immediate surroundings and report back."

"Proceed with caution, Robert," Richard advised. "We're treading unknown ground. Stay alert and avoid unnecessary interactions."

As Robert continued his exploration, he encountered familiar faces—colleagues and researchers he had known for years. Interactions were brief and uneventful, a testament to the delicate balance of temporal observation. He made mental notes to ensure he did not disturb the natural flow of events.

Exiting the laboratory, he found himself on the university campus. Students walked along paved sidewalks, rushing to their next classes. Some sat on grassy areas, chatting about their day or recounting adventures from the night before.

As Robert walked past them, one student recognized him and called out, "Hi Dr. Powell! Do you have a minute to spare?"

Robert stopped briefly and replied, "Hi! I don't have much time. Do you have a question for me?"

"Yes," said the student. "When will you be reviewing applications for this spring's internship program?"

Robert answered, "We should be done with the review process within two weeks. Then we'll schedule interviews. Be alert—we'll notify those moving forward via email. I hope to see you soon."

"Thank you, Dr. Powell! I'll be on the lookout—I hope to see you soon as well."

Robert continued his walk around campus. Everything appeared normal: classes were in session, sunlight illuminated familiar paths, and the sky was its usual shade of blue. Yet something about this ordinary scene felt extraordinary.

Returning to the lab, Robert's gaze fell on a screen mounted on the wall displaying the current date—exactly one week in advance. Understanding hit him with a jolt: he was in the future, witnessing events that had not yet occurred in his own time.

"Richard," he reported through his communicator, "I've reached the one-week mark. The date matches our expected temporal displacement. I'm ready to return now. I think we have enough data to analyze once I'm back."

"Copy that," Richard replied calmly. "I've logged all data. Robert entered the capsule-initiated return sequence... Three... two... one."

The Chrono Field Generator hummed as it synchronized with temporal recalibration protocols to initiate reentry. The soft vibration beneath Robert intensified as his capsule began its trajectory back to the present.

Holographic interfaces displayed temporal coordinates aligning perfectly with those of his original spatial location in the laboratory.

As Robert traversed spacetime at speeds exceeding light itself, he reflected on this surreal journey—the boundaries of conventional physics seemed to dissolve under temporal exploration's demands.

Moments blurred into streaks of light as time compressed around him; reality stretched and bent like fabric under strain.

Occasionally, Robert glimpsed divergences hinting at parallel universes—realities echoing familiar events yet shaped by alternate choices. It felt like walking along diverging paths at a cosmic crossroads where each decision manifested unique outcomes.

These glimpses profoundly shifted his perspective: cause-and-effect relationships unfolded nonlinearly across infinite possibilities.

Navigating this delicate balance between exceeding light-speed travel and exploring parallel universes left Robert marveling at their interconnectedness—phenomena transcending scientific understanding challenged preconceptions about time's nature or multiverse intricacies.

Meanwhile—in real-time—Richard monitored quantum fluctuations alongside gravitational currents critical toward ensuring successful synchronization during reentry sequences.

Finally breaching temporal thresholds—the capsule materialized inside the lab awaiting its return. The door of the capsule opened with a hiss, revealing Robert, now a temporal voyager returned to the present. Richard, a mix of relief and awe evident on his face, approached the capsule. The success of the journey was clear in Robert's expression—a blend of satisfaction and wonder at the possibilities unlocked by the Chrono Field Generator.

Richard, absorbing the implications of their groundbreaking achievement, nodded in agreement. The temporal voyage had not only provided valuable data but also offered a glimpse into the delicate dance of existence. The partnership between Robert and Richard, solidified by their mastery of time, stood at the forefront of scientific achievement.

"Welcome back Robert! What did you observe? Any changes, anomalies?" Richard asked eagerly.

Robert recounted his observations, describing subtle changes in the lab environment and mundane interactions with his colleagues. "It's like looking through a window into a parallel reality—one that's just a step ahead of ours. The structure of time is delicate, Richard, but it seems to hold firm under our scrutiny."

In the echoing hum of the time machine capsule, Robert reflected on the fragility of the temporal fabric and the profound implications of his explorations. The choice between surpassing the speed of light or venturing into parallel universes presented a dichotomy that underscored the boundless mysteries awaiting discovery within the uncharted territories of spacetime.

"Excellent work, Robert," Richard said. "Now let's run a diagnostic on the time machine systems to ensure everything is functioning correctly. We need to analyze the data you've collected and compare it to our predictions."

As the partners delved into post-test analysis, a sense of accomplishment filled the lab. Digital screens displayed graphs and tables confirming the success of the temporal displacement. The air vibrated with the excitement of scientific triumph, but a lingering question floated in the background.

Unable to contain his curiosity, Richard broached the subject. "Robert, while you were in the future, did you get the winning lottery numbers? It would be a practical way to test our time machine's predictive capabilities."

A wry smile appeared on Robert's lips. "I must admit, I checked the numbers for the upcoming state lottery. I'll retrieve them now."

Robert accessed the information he had gathered during his time in the future and relayed the lottery's winning numbers to Richard.

A few days later, as the state lottery numbers were revealed on local television, Robert and Richard sat in amazement, writing down each number as it was announced. Richard's eyes widened as he processed what he saw. "This is incredible. It worked! We have the winning numbers for the state lottery a week before the draw. This is a game-changer."

But Robert's expression remained thoughtful, a hint of concern shadowing his features. "Richard," he began cautiously, "we must be careful with this knowledge. Using the time machine for personal gain—even something seemingly harmless like winning the lottery—could have far-reaching consequences. We have an ethical responsibility to use this technology wisely."

Richard nodded solemnly, understanding the gravity of their situation. "You're right, Robert. We must tread carefully. The line between scientific exploration and ethical considerations is a fine one."

Chapter 5: Looking to Yesterday

Robert, reviewing the data from the trip to the future on his screen, said "I've been thinking about the destination for this next test," he began. "What if I visited your hometown? Specifically, when you were a child?"

Richard raised an eyebrow, intrigued but cautious. "Why my hometown?"

"It's personal enough to make the data meaningful," Robert explained. "We can compare my observations with what you remember, and we'll have verifiable points—like weather patterns, local news events, or even something as simple as the type of clothes you wore back then."

Richard leaned back in his chair, considering the idea. "It does make sense," he admitted. "But you'll need to be extremely careful. If you're spotted or leave any trace behind…"

"I won't," Robert assured him. "This is strictly observation. I'll record everything—details about the neighborhood, the people I see, even small environmental factors like cloud cover or temperature."

Richard nodded slowly. "Fine. But let's add a layer of verification. I'll cross-reference your notes with historical records once you're back to confirm accuracy."

"Agreed," Robert said firmly. "Let's finalize the parameters and lock in the date."

As they worked together, their shared determination solidified—the past would soon become their proving ground.

The time machine capsule hummed with potential as Robert prepared for another leap through the temporal fabric. The previous test had been a success, but now the duo was ready for a more personal exploration. The destination: December 25, 1990—forty-five years ago.

At the system control display, Richard Anders adjusted the settings, ensuring precise temporal coordinates for Robert's journey. The air vibrated with a mix of excitement and nervous energy.

The time capsule, now a vessel of nostalgia and curiosity, was ready for its next leap into time.

"Richard, this is a more personal test," explained Robert, his voice resonating through the communication system. "My goal is to observe without altering anything and gather information about the past."

Richard nodded, acknowledging the importance of the test. "Understood. Proceed with caution and remember—don't do anything that would change who I am today."

Robert remembered the time he conducted a lecture visiting all the possible ramifications of the Time Paradox. He recalled it in this way…

He stood at the front of the lecture hall, his tall frame silhouetted against the glowing holographic display behind him. The room was packed with eager students, their faces a blend of curiosity and skepticism. They had come to hear the man who had built the world's first functional time machine explain one of the most perplexing challenges of temporal mechanics: the Temporal Paradox.

Robert adjusted his glasses and cleared his throat. "Good afternoon, everyone. Today, we're going to discuss one of the most fascinating—and dangerous—concepts in time travel: temporal paradoxes. These are not just theoretical puzzles; they are very real challenges that my team and I have faced in our work."

He paused, letting his words sink in. The room was silent, save for the faint hum of the holographic projector.

"To understand paradoxes," he continued, "we must first understand what happens when you manipulate time. Time travel is not just about moving from one point in history to another.

It's about interacting with causality itself—the chain of cause and effect that governs everything in our universe."

The hologram shifted, displaying a glowing timeline stretching from left to right. Events were marked along it like beads on a string.

"Now," Robert said, pointing to a specific point on the timeline, "imagine you travel back to this moment in 2000. Let's say you accidentally interfere with a seemingly trivial event—perhaps you knock over a glass of water at a dinner party. That small action could ripple outward, altering events in ways you can't predict."

The timeline on the hologram began to distort, branching into multiple paths.

"This is what we call the Butterfly Effect," he explained. "A minor change in the past can lead to massive consequences in the future. But that's just the beginning. Let's talk about true paradoxes."

The hologram shifted again, this time displaying two interlocking loops.

"The first type of paradox we'll discuss is perhaps the most famous: the Grandfather Paradox," Robert said. "Imagine you travel back in time and accidentally—or intentionally—prevent your grandfather from meeting your grandmother. If they never meet, your parent is never born, and therefore you are never born."

He let that thought hang in the air for a moment before continuing.

"But if you were never born, how could you have traveled back in time to prevent their meeting? This creates a logical contradiction—a paradox where cause and effect collapse into impossibility."

One student raised her hand hesitantly. "Dr. Powell, does that mean time travel to the past is impossible?"

Robert smiled faintly. "Not necessarily. There are theories that attempt to resolve this paradox. One is called the Novikov Self-Consistency Principle." He gestured toward the hologram, which now displayed a looped timeline.

"This principle suggests that even if you travel back in time, your actions are already part of history. In other words, you can't change anything because whatever you do has already happened."

He glanced at the students' faces and added, "It's like being trapped in a movie where no matter what choices you think you're making, the ending remains the same."

Another student raised his hand. "But what about free will? Doesn't that mean we're just following a script?"

"That's one interpretation," Robert admitted. "Others argue that free will still exists but is constrained within certain boundaries—boundaries defined by causality itself."

The hologram shifted again, this time displaying an image of a book appearing out of thin air.

"Next," Robert said, "we have the Bootstrap Paradox, also known as an ontological paradox. This occurs when an object or piece of information exists without any clear origin."

He gestured toward the hologram as it zoomed in on the book.

"Imagine you travel back in time with a copy of Shakespeare's Hamlet. You give it to Shakespeare before he writes it. He then uses your copy as inspiration to write Hamlet. But here's the problem: where did Hamlet originally come from? It seems to exist without ever being created."

The students murmured among themselves as they tried to wrap their heads around it.

"This paradox challenges our understanding of causality," Robert said. "It suggests that some events might exist outside our conventional notions of cause and effect—a closed causal loop where something simply is because it always has been."

The hologram now displayed two billiard balls on a table.

"Let's move on to Polchinski's Paradox," Robert said. "This one involves physical objects rather than people or information."

He pointed at one ball as it rolled toward a wormhole depicted on the table.

"Imagine a billiard ball enters a wormhole and emerges from it moments earlier—just in time to collide with its past self and prevent itself from entering the wormhole in the first place."

The students leaned forward, intrigued by this mind-bending scenario.

"This paradox highlights how physical interactions can create logical contradictions," Robert explained. "If the ball prevents itself from entering the wormhole, how did it emerge from it? And if it didn't emerge from it, how could it prevent itself?"

One student raised her hand eagerly. "Is there any way to resolve that?"

"Yes," Robert replied. "One possible solution is Novikov's Self-Consistency Principle again—it suggests that any interaction must be self-consistent with history. In this case, perhaps the collision only deflects the ball slightly so that it still enters the wormhole but at a different angle."

Robert stepped away from the hologram as it displayed branching timelines once more.

"One way to avoid these paradoxes altogether is through parallel universes or multiverse theory," he said. "This theory suggests that every time you make a change in the past, you create an entirely new timeline—a separate universe where those changes take effect."

He paused for emphasis before adding, "In this model, there are no paradoxes because your actions don't affect your original timeline—they simply create an alternate reality."

The students seemed both fascinated and unsettled by this idea.

"But" Robert cautioned, "this raises its own questions: If every decision creates a new universe, how do we define 'reality'? And what happens if these universes interact?"

As he wrapped up his lecture, Robert turned serious. "Paradoxes aren't just intellectual exercises—they have real implications for how we approach time travel ethically," he said. "If even small actions can ripple outward unpredictably—or if alternate timelines can be created—how do we ensure we don't cause harm?"

He looked out at his audience, his voice steady but grave.

"Time travel isn't just about exploring history or satisfying curiosity—it's about responsibility. Every step we take into the past carries consequences we may not fully understand until it's too late."

The room was silent as Robert concluded his lecture.

"So," he said finally, "as future scientists—or perhaps future time travelers—I urge you to think carefully about these questions: What should we do with this power? And more importantly... what shouldn't we do?"

With that, he stepped away from the podium as applause filled the hall—a mix of admiration for his brilliance and awe at the daunting challenges he had laid before them.

The Chrono-Field Generator came to life, enveloping Robert in a cocoon of temporal energy. The familiar sensation of displacement overtook him, and as the laboratory blurred into a mosaic of colors, he prepared to venture into the heart of Richard's yesteryears. The hum of the generator deepened into a resonant vibration that seemed to synchronize with his heartbeat, creating an almost meditative rhythm. Time itself felt malleable, as though the fabric of reality was being stretched and folded around him.

As the capsule accelerated through spacetime, Robert experienced a profound shift in perception. The boundaries of his physical body seemed to dissolve, replaced by an awareness that extended beyond his immediate surroundings. Quantum decoherence—the process by which quantum systems lose their superposition states—appeared to manifest visually as streaks of light and shadow danced across his vision.

These were not ordinary lights; they shimmered with an iridescence that defied description, pulsating in patterns that hinted at the underlying quantum fluctuations governing spacetime itself.

The soundscape within the capsule was equally surreal. The hum of the Chrono-Field Generator transformed into a symphony of harmonic overtones, each note resonating with the frequencies of the quantum field. It was as if Robert were hearing the "music" of spacetime—the vibrations of strings at the Planck scale, where reality itself is woven. Occasionally, sharp pops and crackles punctuated this symphony, reminiscent of static interference but far more profound, as though they were echoes from alternate timelines brushing against his own.

Physically, the journey was both exhilarating and disorienting. The sensation of acceleration was paradoxical: while his mind registered movement at velocities exceeding the speed of light, his body felt weightless, suspended in a state of perfect equilibrium. This phenomenon could be attributed to the Einstein-Rosen bridge effect—the theoretical "shortcut" through spacetime created by the Chrono-Field Generator. Within this wormhole-like construct, traditional notions of inertia and momentum ceased to apply.

As Robert's journey progressed, he became aware of subtle distortions in his perception of time. Moments seemed to stretch and contract unpredictably, a direct consequence of time dilation as described by Einstein's theory of relativity. At one point, he felt as though hours had passed; at another, mere seconds.

This temporal fluidity was accompanied by fleeting glimpses into alternate realities—parallel universes where events had unfolded differently. These visions appeared as translucent overlays on his surroundings: a version of himself standing in a different laboratory, or Richard speaking with someone unfamiliar.

Emotionally, the experience was overwhelming. Awe and wonder coursed through Robert as he contemplated the enormity of what he was witnessing. The realization that he was traversing not just time but also the multiverse filled him with a sense of profound humility. Yet there was also an undercurrent of fear—an awareness that tampering with such forces could have unforeseen consequences. He thought about the concept of quantum entanglement, where particles remain connected across vast distances, influencing each other instantaneously. What if his actions here created ripples that entangled with events in other timelines?

As the capsule began to decelerate, signaling its approach to December 25, 1990, Robert's surroundings shifted once more. The kaleidoscope of colors resolved into recognizable shapes: snow-covered trees, children playing in a park, and festive decorations adorning houses. The transition from the abstract realm of quantum phenomena back into tangible reality was jarring yet comforting—a reminder that despite its complexities, time ultimately grounded itself in moments like these.

Stepping out of the capsule into Richard's childhood neighborhood felt like stepping into a living memory. The air carried a crispness unique to winter mornings, mingled with the faint scent of pine and wood smoke.

Sounds were sharper here: the crunch of snow underfoot, the distant laughter of children, and the melodic strains of Christmas carols wafting through the air. Light seemed softer yet more vivid than he remembered—perhaps an artifact of his heightened awareness after traversing spacetime.

The park near Richard's childhood home materialized around Robert. It was a crisp winter day. Children bundled up in winter coats and scarves played merrily in the snow. Bicycles whizzed by, and cheerful laughter echoed in the chilly air. Discreetly dressed in period-appropriate clothing, Robert took a moment to absorb the scene. The surroundings were both familiar and strange—a testament to the timeless nature of childhood joy. The park seemed untouched by the years that had passed.

Robert's emotional state shifted again as he observed young Richard interacting with his friends. There was an innocence to these moments that transcended time—a purity untainted by future complexities or regrets. Watching this scene unfold filled Robert with a bittersweet longing for simpler times while deepening his appreciation for the intricate web of experiences that shape a person's life.

With determination, Robert walked toward the children riding their bicycles on the streets surrounding the park.

"Who is Richard?" Robert asked the group of children with an air of innocent curiosity.

A young boy, wide-eyed with wonder, stepped forward. "I'm Richard. Who are you? And what do you want?"

Robert smiled, realizing he had found the younger version of his partner. "I'm a friend," he said gently. "I work at your school. I was wondering if you could tell me about your Christmas—did you get what you were hoping for? What did you receive this year?"

The boy beamed with pride. "I got a new bike! It's red and has these cool racing stripes—I can go really fast on it!"

As young Richard spoke excitedly about his gift, Robert observed the scene around him: other children chattered about their presents—remote-control cars, dolls, board games—and their faces lit up with joy. The air was filled with the magic of Christmas morning—a timeless reminder of innocence that transcends time itself.

After bidding goodbye to the children, Robert continued his journey through the past.

For a while, he explored the neighborhood, taking note of details: familiar faces of neighbors, decorations adorning houses, and Christmas carol sounds emanating from the homes in the festive wonderland.

The scene was a tableau of Christmas warmth, frozen in time yet alive with motion. Snow blanketed the ground, muffling footsteps and creating a soft crunch under Robert's boots as he walked. Each house seemed to tell its own story through its decorations: strings of multicolored lights framed windows and rooftops, glowing warmly against the crisp winter air. Some homes had elaborate displays—a life-sized Santa Claus with reindeer perched on a lawn or glowing nativity scenes nestled among bushes dusted with snow.

The smell of wood smoke wafted through the air, rising from chimneys that emitted thin streams of gray smoke curling into the pale morning sky. The scent mingled with the faint aroma of breakfast cooking—bacon sizzling, coffee brewing, and perhaps pancakes or freshly baked bread. These smells carried a sense of comfort and familiarity, grounding Robert in the humanity of this moment.

As he walked past one home, a man in a plaid robe stepped onto his front porch to retrieve the morning paper. The man paused briefly to take in the scene—a quiet moment of reflection as he surveyed the snow-covered street before retreating inside. Robert noted how ordinary yet profound this act seemed; it was a snapshot of life untouched by time's relentless march.

Children's laughter echoed from nearby yards as they played in the snow, their voices blending with the faint strains of Christmas carols coming from an unseen radio. The neighborhood exuded a sense of togetherness and joy, each detail reinforcing the timelessness of these simple moments.

An hour later, as he approached the Anders' residence, a wave of nostalgia washed over him. The house—adorned with festive lights and a wreath on its door—exuded warmth and familial love. Through its windows, Robert glimpsed a bustling Christmas morning: gift wrap scattered across the living room floor and holiday aromas wafting through the air.

Standing in the shadows of the past, Robert felt deeply connected to these people and moments that had shaped Richard's childhood. This trial wasn't just about gathering data; it was a journey into the heart of human experience.

Inside the house, young Richard reveled among the unwrapped gifts beneath a gleaming Christmas tree adorned with twinkling lights. Laughter echoed through the room as a couple, possibly his grandparents, shared in his excitement. From his vantage point outside, Robert observed silently—a spectator to a moment frozen in time.

While marveling at this scene, Robert noticed one particular gift: a rectangular box—a package that promised something special. Intrigued but careful not to interfere with events, he decided to approach Richard's parents, who were sitting on a bench on their porch, enjoying warm drinks and watching the children play.

"Hi, Merry Christmas!" Robert said warmly as he approached them. "I'm a friend of Richard's teacher from school. I was wondering—looks like your Christmas is a complete success! Could you share with me what kind of gifts Richard received this year? He seems completely immersed in that one."

The door to the house was ajar, allowing a clear view of Richard playing in the living room. The boy was busy trying to figure out what appeared to be some kind of computer— a gift that clearly captured his full attention.

Richard's parents exchanged a glance before smiling proudly. "That's his first computer," his mother said. "We thought it would be a good educational tool for him. He's always been fascinated by technology."

Robert nodded thoughtfully, appreciating the significance of this moment. The computer wasn't just a gift—it was the spark that would ignite Richard's lifelong passion for science and innovation.

As Christmas morning unfolded before him, Robert mentally noted the details: the laughter, warmth, and love permeating the house. The task was not just about gathering information; it was about understanding the essence of a moment that had shaped Richard's life trajectory.

The hours of the past passed like a fleeting dream. The images, sounds, and emotions of a bygone era enveloped him in a tapestry of memories. As he bid farewell to the Anders' residence and retraced his steps through the snowy streets, a sense of gratitude washed over him.

The journey into the past had offered not only data but also a glimpse into the human experience—a reminder that the threads of our lives are woven with the moments we cherish. Robert approached the sleek surface of the capsule, its elliptical form shrouded in stealth mode, rendering it invisible. As he neared it, his hand brushed against its surface, activating the touch-sensitive control panel. A soft glow emanated from the interface, revealing hidden buttons and holographic displays.

With a series of deliberate gestures, he initiated the process to deactivate stealth mode. The once-concealed capsule gradually materialized, blending seamlessly into its surroundings. The ambient hum of machinery within signaled its readiness for Robert's return journey.

In the laboratory, Richard monitored the capsule from his control station and noted its change in visibility. The countdown continued, ticking away the seconds until Robert's reentry. The atmosphere in the lab hummed with anticipation—a palpable tension as they awaited their temporal explorer's return to the present.

Inside the capsule, Robert began his own countdown. The journey into the past had offered more than just data; it had provided a profound reminder of life's cherished moments. Meanwhile, in the laboratory, Richard anxiously followed every second of progress.

As Robert initiated the temporal sequence, a subtle vibration coursed through the capsule. The ambient hum of machinery intensified, resonating through its elliptical chamber. The sleek surface pulsated with rhythmic light—a visual manifestation of temporal currents enveloping it.

In this heart of temporal transition, Robert closed his eyes and surrendered to sensations beyond ordinary perception. Time itself seemed to embrace him in a dance of continuity and flux. The air inside crackled with energy—a fusion of historical echoes and future possibilities.

Fleeting glimpses of his past and potential futures flickered across his mind like fragments from a kaleidoscope. Each second felt like an eternity as he traveled through corridors of time with indescribable fluidity.

The trip reached its crescendo as temporal energies surged around him. Disorientation gripped him briefly—a sensation akin to being caught in a cosmic whirlwind. He "saw" time's fabric folding and unfolding—a visual symphony of chronological dynamics that defied comprehension.

A final pulse marked reentry as light flooded his vision. Vibrations subsided, and Robert opened his eyes to find himself back in the familiar confines of their laboratory. His temporal journey had enriched not only his understanding of history but also his perception of time's intricate tapestry. As he took in the experience just lived, Robert synchronized his movements with the arrival. With a final tap on the control panel, the capsule's door hissed open, revealing its enigmatic interior. Robert exited the capsule, his face reflecting both exhaustion and exhilaration. The door sealed behind him as the capsule emitted a pulsating glow.

Richard glanced at digital readouts. The lab seemed to hold its breath—caught between echoes of the past and the imminent return of a man who had dared to navigate time itself. Success depended not only on technical precision but also on Robert's ability to traverse history with sensitivity and respect.

Removing his helmet, he spoke with awe and solemnity: "I visited your childhood home, Richard—Christmas Day in 1990. You received a computer—your first one—and I saw how much it meant to you."

Richard's eyes widened with surprise and nostalgia. "A computer? I remember! It was a Macintosh," he said with a smile tinged by memory. "I spent countless hours exploring it—that gift set me on my path to where I am today."

Robert nodded knowingly; satisfaction softened his expression as he replied: "This wasn't just an experiment—it was a reminder that human stories are woven into time itself. Every decision we make or gift we receive contributes to life's intricate tapestry."

The two scientists stood amidst their laboratory's technological marvels for a moment of shared understanding. Their time machine had become more than an instrument for scientific discovery—it was now a vessel for introspection and connection to humanity's defining moments.

As they prepared to analyze data from Robert's journey into Richard's past, both men felt renewed purpose coursing through them. Their machine held potential far beyond unraveling history—it could illuminate humanity's shared experiences while offering glimpses into uncharted futures.

The laboratory—once merely theoretical—had become an arena where science met humanity head-on: proof that exploration across time could deepen our understanding not only of history but also ourselves.

Chapter 6: Conflicting Agendas

The rhythmic hum of the time machine's capsule echoed softly in the laboratory as Robert and Richard immersed themselves in the meticulous analysis of their recent temporal excursions. The glow from computer screens bathed the room in ambient light, while equations sprawled across chalkboards—a testament to their relentless quest to unravel the mysteries of time.

Amid their scientific fervor, a shrill ring shattered the concentrated atmosphere. Robert, startled by the unexpected interruption, glanced at his phone. The caller ID displayed an unknown number, but beneath it were the words: Pentagon - General Andrews. A sense of anticipation and unease filled the room as he answered.

"Dr. Powell," came a commanding voice on the other end, "this is General Andrews from the Pentagon. I trust I'm not interrupting anything crucial?"

Robert exchanged a quick glance with Richard, silently acknowledging the gravity of the call. "No, General. What can I do for you?" he replied cautiously.

"I would like you and Dr. Anders to meet with me in Washington for a briefing," General Andrews continued, his tone formal and deliberate. "There are matters we need to discuss regarding the development of your time machine."

A hint of suspicion crept into Robert's voice. "What kind of matters, General?"

"I would prefer to discuss it in person," Andrews responded carefully. "Let's just say that the capabilities of your machine have piqued the interest of some high-level officials, and we need to ensure that its potential aligns with national interests."

Robert hesitated for a moment before replying. "Understood. We'll be there."

When the call ended, Robert turned to Richard with a furrowed brow. "We have to be cautious, Richard. Government involvement could change everything—the trajectory of our project, our control over its use... everything."

Richard nodded solemnly. "We've come this far on our own terms," he said firmly. "We can't compromise our principles now."

General Christopher James Andrews was a distinguished figure in the United States Marine Corps, known for his exemplary leadership, strategic acumen, and commitment to service. Born in 1972 in Annapolis, Maryland, Andrews grew up in a military family, with his father serving as a naval officer. This upbringing instilled in him a deep sense of duty and discipline. Following his graduation from the United States Naval Academy in 1994, where he earned a degree in International Relations, Andrews was commissioned as a Second Lieutenant in the Marine Corps. Andrews began his career as an infantry officer, quickly distinguishing himself during his early deployments. His first major assignment was with the 1st Battalion, 5th Marines, where he served as a platoon commander during peacekeeping operations in the Balkans in the late 1990s. His ability to lead under pressure earned him recognition and set the stage for his rapid ascent through the ranks. By the early 2000s, Andrews had completed advanced training at the Marine Corps Command and Staff College and was deployed to Iraq during Operation Iraqi Freedom.

As a battalion commander, he led over 1,000 Marines during pivotal urban combat operations in Fallujah, earning him the Silver Star for gallantry.

Throughout his career, Andrews demonstrated a unique ability to adapt to evolving threats. In Afghanistan, he spearheaded counterinsurgency efforts as part of NATO's International Security Assistance Force (ISAF), focusing on building local partnerships and stabilizing volatile regions.

His innovative approaches to asymmetric warfare earned him accolades and further cemented his reputation as a forward-thinking leader.

Promoted to Brigadier General in 2015, Andrews transitioned into roles that emphasized strategic planning and international collaboration. He served as the Deputy Director of Operations at U.S. Central Command (CENTCOM), where he coordinated multi-national efforts against emerging global threats. During this time, he was instrumental in developing strategies to combat terrorism and cyber warfare, showcasing his ability to address complex challenges on a global scale.

In 2021, Andrews was appointed Commanding General of Marine Forces Europe and Africa, where he oversaw joint operations with NATO allies and strengthened partnerships across two continents. His tenure was marked by successful large-scale exercises designed to enhance readiness and interoperability among allied forces.

Recognizing his expertise in risk assessment and global security, Andrews was selected in 2023 to lead the newly established International Risk Assessment Task Force (IRATF). This high-profile position placed him at the helm of a multidisciplinary team tasked with identifying and mitigating emerging threats to global stability.

Under his leadership, the IRATF has focused on addressing challenges such as climate-driven conflicts, cyber threats, and geopolitical instability.

General Andrews' career was defined by his unwavering dedication to service and his ability to navigate the complexities of modern warfare. His leadership of the IRATF reflected not only his military achievements but also his commitment to fostering international cooperation in an increasingly interconnected world. A decorated Marine with numerous awards—including the Silver Star, Legion of Merit, and Defense Superior Service Medal—Andrews continued to exemplify the highest standards of military excellence.

Days later, they found themselves in a nondescript conference room in the heart of Washington, D.C. The jet touched down smoothly at Ronald Reagan Washington National Airport, the late afternoon sun casting a golden glow over the Potomac River. Dr. Robert Powell and Richard Anders, his partner and trusted confidant, stepped off the plane into the crisp Washington air. The hum of activity at the airport was constant, a mix of travelers hurrying to their destinations and military personnel moving with purpose. Waiting for them on the tarmac was a black GMC SUV, its sleek exterior polished to a mirror finish. The vehicle exuded authority, its tinted windows concealing the occupants within.

A tall man in a sharply pressed military uniform stepped forward as they approached. His name tag read "Major Carter," and his posture was as rigid as his demeanor.

"Dr. Powell, Mr. Anders," he greeted them with a curt nod. "Welcome to Washington, D.C. General Andrews has arranged for me to escort you directly to the Pentagon."

Robert returned the nod, his expression neutral but alert. "Thank you, Major. We appreciate the arrangement."

The major opened the rear door of the SUV and gestured for them to enter. Inside, the vehicle was outfitted with all the trappings of government luxury—plush leather seats, a secure communications system embedded in the console, and reinforced glass designed to withstand almost any threat.

As they pulled away from the airport, Richard leaned back in his seat, glancing out at the view. The route from Reagan National Airport to the Pentagon offered glimpses of iconic landmarks that seemed to embody both history and power. Gravelly Point Park came into view first, its open spaces offering stunning views of planes taking off and landing against the backdrop of the Washington Monument.

"Every time I'm here, it feels like stepping into a history book," Richard remarked, his eyes fixed on the towering obelisk in the distance.

Robert didn't respond immediately; his mind was already focused on their upcoming meeting with General Andrews. The general had requested their presence to discuss potential military applications of Robert's groundbreaking Chrono-Field Generator—a prospect that filled him with equal parts excitement and unease.

The SUV merged onto George Washington Memorial Parkway, running parallel to the Potomac River. To their left, Arlington National Cemetery stretched out in solemn rows of white headstones—a stark reminder of the sacrifices that had shaped the nation's history.

The Air Force Memorial rose nearby, its three stainless steel spires reaching skyward like contrails frozen in time.

Major Carter broke the silence from the driver's seat. "We'll be passing by some notable landmarks on our way to the Pentagon," he said, his tone professional but slightly perfunctory. "To your left is Arlington National Cemetery, and just ahead is Memorial Bridge."

As they crossed Memorial Bridge, Richard caught sight of more iconic structures—the Lincoln Memorial stood resolute at one end of the National Mall while further down loomed the stately dome of the U.S. Capitol Building. Between them, the Washington Monument pierced the sky like an exclamation point on America's story.

"This city really knows how to make an impression," Richard said with a low whistle.

Robert finally turned from his thoughts and gave a small smile. "It's designed to," he replied. "Every building here is a symbol—of power, resilience, or sacrifice."

The SUV veered off onto Route 27 as they approached their destination. The Pentagon came into view—a massive five-sided fortress that seemed both imposing and impenetrable. Its sheer scale was overwhelming even for those who had seen it before; it wasn't just a building but an institution unto itself.

As they neared one of the secured entrances, Major Carter slowed to a stop at a checkpoint manned by armed guards. After presenting credentials, they were waved through.

Inside the Pentagon's sprawling complex, Major Carter parked near an entrance reserved for high-level visitors. He stepped out first before opening their door.

"General Andrews is expecting you in Conference Room Delta," he informed them as they exited. Robert adjusted his coat against the chill before glancing at Richard. "Ready?"

Richard nodded but couldn't suppress a wry grin. "As ready as I'll ever be for something like this."

They followed Major Carter through a labyrinth of corridors lined with portraits and plaques commemorating key moments in military history. The air inside was cool and faintly sterile, carrying with it an undercurrent of urgency that seemed to permeate every corner of this place.

When they finally reached Conference Room Delta, Major Carter opened the door and gestured for them to enter. Inside waited General Andrews—a grizzled man with sharp eyes that seemed to take in everything at once—and several other high-ranking officers seated around a long table. The air in the room was charged with a sense of formality, and the polished wood of the conference table seemed to bear the weight of countless high-stakes discussions. General Andrews, a stern figure clad in military attire, stood with purpose. He exchanged brief pleasantries before getting straight to the point.

"Gentlemen, I appreciate your promptness. The matter at hand is delicate and urgent," he began.

Seated across from the general, Robert and Richard exchanged a glance that conveyed a shared understanding: their scientific endeavors were about to intersect with a new and potentially perilous agenda.

"Your time machine has the potential to change the rules of the game for national security," General Andrews continued, fixing his gaze on Robert. "We have identified several problematic areas around the world—regions plagued by dictators and tyrants. With your technology, we could send specialists back in time to eliminate these threats before they gain power."

General Andrews leaned forward, his hands clasped on the polished table, his voice steady but charged with urgency. "Gentlemen," he began, fixing Robert and Richard with a piercing gaze, "the world is unraveling faster than we can contain it. The geopolitical landscape is a minefield—Ukraine remains a flashpoint, with no end in sight to the conflict. In the Middle East, tensions escalate daily, and now there's talk of broader regional involvement from powers like Iran and Turkey. These aren't isolated incidents—they're part of a larger pattern of destabilization."

Robert exchanged a glance with Richard but remained silent as Andrews continued, his tone growing heavier. "And it's not just war. Trade wars and economic decoupling are reshaping alliances. The United States is pulling back from globalization while China doubles down on its influence in Asia and Africa. We're seeing the formation of trade blocs that could fracture the global economy entirely."

Richard leaned forward slightly. "And you think our work could help address these issues?"

Andrews nodded. "Absolutely. The ability to observe past events in real-time or even predict future outcomes could give us an unprecedented advantage—whether it's identifying vulnerabilities in supply chains or understanding the root causes of conflicts before they spiral out of control." He paused, his eyes narrowing. "And then there's climate change. Record temperatures last year pushed global systems to their limits—floods, droughts, wildfires. Natural disasters are becoming more frequent and more devastating. We're losing ground every day."

Robert frowned. "But how does our work fit into that? We're not solving climate change with time travel."

Andrews raised a hand. "Not directly, no. But imagine being able to study historical weather patterns in detail—seeing how ecosystems adapted or failed under similar conditions centuries ago. That kind of data could inform strategies for mitigation today."

Richard nodded slowly but remained cautious. "You're talking about using our technology as a tool for global stability."

"Exactly," Andrews said firmly. "But let's not sugarcoat this—it's also about power. Whoever controls this technology controls the future, literally and figuratively. And right now, we can't afford to let it fall into anyone else's hands."

Robert leaned back in his chair, his mind racing with the implications of Andrews' words. The general wasn't just describing problems; he was laying out a vision—one where their work became a linchpin in navigating an increasingly fractured world.

"I understand your concerns," Robert said finally. "But this kind of power comes with risks—risks we can't fully predict yet."

Andrews nodded gravely. "I'm not asking for blind trust, Dr. Powell. I'm asking for partnership—to use this technology wisely and responsibly to address challenges that no one nation can tackle alone."

The room fell silent as Robert and Richard exchanged another glance, each weighing the enormity of what lay ahead.

Richard's eyes narrowed as his suspicions solidified: this wasn't just scientific curiosity on the government's part—it was about harnessing their time machine as a tool for strategic advantage. "Eliminate threats, General?" Richard interjected sharply. "Do you mean assassinate?"

General Andrews met Richard's gaze steadily. "I mean neutralize," he clarified. "Imagine a world where certain leaders never come to power—where atrocities are prevented before they occur. Your time machine offers us an unprecedented ability to reshape history for global stability."

Robert leaned forward; his voice measured but firm. "General, altering history in that way is fraught with ethical and moral implications. It's a slippery slope. How can we be certain such interventions won't have catastrophic unintended consequences?"

General Andrews sighed deeply, acknowledging the gravity of their concerns. "Dr. Powell, Dr. Anders," he said solemnly, "we face unprecedented challenges in today's world. Traditional methods of diplomacy and intervention often fall short. Your time machine offers us an opportunity to address these challenges at their roots—saving countless lives and preventing conflicts before they begin."

The weight of his words hung heavily in the air as Robert mulled over the implications. His thoughts turned immediately to temporal paradoxes—the intricate dilemmas that arise when time travel disrupts causality, creating contradictory scenarios that defy logic. He remembered the lecture he presented years earlier, where he discussed classic examples like the "grandfather paradox," where altering past events could prevent one's own existence, challenging fundamental understandings of time's coherence.

The potential for abuse loomed large in Robert's mind: manipulating history to fit political agendas was a risk too significant to ignore.

"General Andrews, we need time to consider this," Robert said firmly. "The ethical considerations are immense, and we cannot rush into a decision of such magnitude."

General Andrews nodded, reluctantly acknowledging the complexities at play. "I understand your concerns, Dr. Powell. However, time is of the essence. We face crises that demand immediate attention. I'll give you 90 days to complete the time machine and begin training specialists for these missions. Then we'll reconvene."

As the meeting concluded, Robert and Richard left the Pentagon with a weighty decision hanging over them. The government's interest had transformed their scientific endeavor into a potential tool of geopolitics, and the responsibility of wielding such power loomed heavily before them.

The ride back to the airport was somber, the air was charged with tension. Richard broke the silence, his voice reflecting the gravity of their situation. "Robert, we can't allow the government to turn our invention into a weapon. We started this project with the goal of expanding human knowledge— not becoming pawns in political games."

Robert nodded solemnly. "I couldn't agree more, Richard. We must proceed with caution. Let's continue our work but also explore ways to ensure that the time machine is used responsibly. We must establish safeguards to prevent its abuse."

Robert thought long and hard about leaders and tyrants throughout history. The black GMC SUV hummed softly as it navigated the streets of Washington, D.C., but Robert's mind was elsewhere, lost in the corridors of time. The meeting with General Andrews had gone as expected—one sided, and laden with the weight of moral ambiguity. The military's interest in his Chrono-Field Generator was no surprise, but it had left him grappling with the question that always haunted him: What is the true cost of altering history?

His thoughts turned to historical figures whose actions had irrevocably shaped the world. Some had brought progress and enlightenment, while others had plunged humanity into darkness. What if their paths could have been changed? What if one moment, one decision, could have rewritten entire chapters of history?

The first figure who came to mind was Julius Caesar, a man whose ambition and brilliance had forever altered the course of Western civilization. Caesar's crossing of the Rubicon in 49 BCE—a single, defiant act—had set in motion the fall of the Roman Republic and the rise of the Roman Empire.

Robert imagined standing on that riverbank, watching as Caesar's legions marched forward. Could he have stopped Caesar? Should he have? Without Caesar's empire, would Europe have developed differently? Perhaps democracy would have flourished earlier—or perhaps chaos would have reigned for centuries longer.

Then there was Napoleon Bonaparte, another towering figure whose actions reshaped continents. Robert pictured him at the height of his power, standing over maps of Europe with his generals, plotting campaigns that would redraw borders and topple monarchies. Napoleon's rise had brought revolutionary ideals to much of Europe but at an immense cost—millions dead in wars that spanned decades. Could Napoleon's ambitions have been tempered? What if someone had intervened before his disastrous invasion of Russia in 1812? Would Europe have avoided years of bloodshed, or would another figure have risen to fill his place?

Robert's thoughts darkened as he considered Adolf Hitler, perhaps the most infamous figure in modern history. He thought about Hitler's early years—his rejection from art school, his time as a struggling young man in Vienna—and wondered how different things might have been if someone had reached him before his ideology took root. Could a single conversation or event have derailed Hitler's path to power? Or was his rise an inevitability born from the social and economic conditions of post-World War I Germany? The atrocities of the Holocaust and the devastation of World War II weighed heavily on Robert's mind as he considered the ethical implications of interfering with such a pivotal figure.

Finally, Robert thought about Martin Luther King Jr., a leader whose courage and vision had inspired millions to fight for justice and equality. King's actions during the Civil Rights Movement had changed the trajectory of American history for the better, but his life had been tragically cut short by an assassin's bullet.

What if someone could have prevented King's death? Would his continued leadership have accelerated progress toward racial equality, or would it have provoked even greater resistance from those who opposed him?

As these figures swirled in his mind, Robert felt a deep sense of responsibility—and unease. Each action they had taken, each decision they had made, had rippled outward through time, shaping not only their own eras but also the world that followed. To intervene in any one of their lives would be to risk unraveling those ripples, creating unintended consequences that could be far worse than what history already held.

The SUV slowed as it approached Reagan National Airport, but Robert barely noticed. His thoughts were consumed by one overriding question: Was it ever right to change history? Leaders like Caesar and Napoleon had wielded immense power; tyrants like Hitler had caused unimaginable suffering; visionaries like King had inspired hope and progress. Each represented a thread in humanity's vast tapestry—a tapestry that was fragile and complex beyond comprehension.

As they pulled into the airport parking area, Richard glanced over at him. "You've been quiet," he said.

Robert managed a faint smile but didn't elaborate. How could he explain what was on his mind? The weight of history—and the potential to alter it—wasn't something easily shared.

Instead, he stepped out of the SUV and looked up at the sky, where planes roared overhead like fleeting moments passing through time. He knew one thing for certain: no matter how advanced his technology became or how tempting it might be to intervene in history's darkest moments, time itself was not something to be wielded lightly. It was a force far greater than any individual—a force that demanded humility above all else.

Chapter 7: Ethical Dilemma

The hum of jet engines provided a constant backdrop as the scientists flew back to Cambridge, across the Charles River in Boston, Massachusetts. The private jet provided for Robert and Richard's journey to the Pentagon was a C-37B Gulfstream 550, a military variant of Gulfstream Aerospace's renowned business jet. Chosen by the Pentagon for its VIP transport needs, the C-37B exemplified the perfect combination of advanced technology, comfort, and security, making it the preferred choice for high-ranking officials and critical missions. Its sleek, aerodynamic design allowed for high-altitude, intercontinental flights with a range of 6,700 miles, ensuring non-stop travel between distant locations. Powered by two BMW/Rolls Royce BR710C4-11 turbofan engines, the jet delivered exceptional performance with a cruising speed of Mach 0.85 and a maximum altitude of 51,000 feet.

Inside, the C-37B was outfitted with state-of-the-art avionics, including an enhanced flight management system and advanced communications technology. The aircraft was equipped with encrypted satellite communication systems, allowing secure real-time discussions and data sharing during flights. This "office in the sky" capability ensured that passengers could remain productive even at 40,000 feet.

The interior reflected both luxury and functionality. Plush leather seating accommodated up to 12 passengers in a spacious layout, with fully reclining seats that converted into beds for long-haul flights. A polished wood conference table sat at the heart of the cabin, surrounded by ergonomic chairs designed for extended meetings. Ambient lighting complemented the sleek furnishings, creating an atmosphere of understated elegance.

Additional amenities included a fully equipped galley for gourmet meals, a private lavatory, and ample storage space. The cabin's soundproofing minimized engine noise, providing a serene environment for work or rest.

The Pentagon selected the C-37B not only for its technological sophistication but also for its ability to transport VIPs in unparalleled comfort and security— qualities befitting the gravity of Robert and Richard's mission.

The luxurious seats and polished interior of the private plane starkly contrasted with the intense discussions that had unfolded at the Pentagon. The fate of their time machine, once a beacon of scientific achievement, now hung in the balance as they grappled with the ethical complexities of General Andrews' vision.

Sitting across from each other, Robert and Richard exchanged contemplative glances. The atmosphere in the cabin was charged with residual tension from their Pentagon meeting. The plane pierced through the clouds, its trajectory paralleling the divergent paths that lay before them.

"We cannot allow the government to use the time machine as a tool for manipulation," Richard said, breaking the silence that had settled between them.

Robert nodded firmly. "The potential for abuse is too great. We started this project with the goal of expanding knowledge—not becoming enablers of political agendas. We need to establish safeguards and fail-safe systems to ensure responsible use of this technology."

As the plane soared above the clouds, the two scientists delved into a discussion that would shape the future of their invention. The implications of government interest had laid bare the moral and ethical dilemmas inherent in wielding the power to alter history.

"The question is," Richard reflected, his gaze fixed on the distant horizon visible through the plane's windows, "how do we ensure that the time machine isn't misused?"

Robert reclined in his seat, his mind already formulating a plan. "We need fail-safe mechanisms—controls and checks that prevent the time machine from being used for nefarious purposes. Relying solely on ethical considerations isn't enough; we must incorporate safeguards into the very fabric of its design."

The discussion unfolded with a meticulous exploration of possible fail-safe systems. Their laboratory whiteboards— now a distant memory as they flew above the clouds— would soon bear sketches and equations outlining ethical boundaries and technological limitations.

"Biometric authentication," Richard suggested, leaning forward in his seat. "We could link access to specific individuals, ensuring that only those with proper authorization can operate it."

Robert nodded thoughtfully. "That's a good start. But biometric systems alone can be compromised. What if we implemented a decentralized control system? Something requiring multiple layers of authorization—like a keyholder model where no single person has full access."

Richard's eyes lit up. "A distributed safeguard. That could work. We'd need at least three independent verifications for any significant temporal displacement. Maybe one for the Chrono-Field Generator activation, one for navigation input, and another for final execution."

"Exactly," Robert said. "And we should also consider embedding an AI oversight system. Something that monitors ethical compliance in real-time and flags any potential misuse."

Richard hesitated, then added, "What about limiting destinations? We could pre-program the machine to only allow observation in specific time periods—no pivotal moments in history, no major events that could risk paradoxes."

"That's smart," Robert agreed. "And we could add a feature to log every trip—date, destination, purpose. Full transparency."

They sat in silence for a moment, the hum of the plane's engines filling the space as they both considered the weight of their decisions.

"We also need to think about external pressures," Richard said finally. "What happens if someone tries to force us— or whoever controls this—to use it unethically?"

Robert sighed, his expression serious. "Then we build in an emergency shutdown protocol—a way to disable the machine entirely if it's ever at risk of falling into the wrong hands."

Richard leaned back, nodding slowly. "A self-destruct mechanism?"

"Not destruction," Robert clarified. "But something irreversible—like wiping all critical systems and data so it can't be rebuilt or used again."

Richard frowned but conceded the point. "It's drastic, but I see your reasoning."

Robert looked out the window at the endless expanse of clouds below them. "This machine has the potential to change everything—for better or worse. If we're going to build it, we have to make sure it can't be misused."

Richard met his gaze with quiet determination. "Agreed. Let's make sure we leave nothing to chance."

As the plane descended toward Logan International Airport, their ideas began to take shape. It wasn't just about preventing misuse—it was about ensuring that their time machine remained a tool for humanity's improvement rather than a pawn for hidden motives.

"We need to thoroughly document these security systems," Richard emphasized. "This isn't just for us; it's for future generations. If the time machine ever falls into the wrong hands, these safeguards will be our last line of defense."

Robert agreed, a sense of purpose settling within him. "Our responsibility goes beyond scientific advancement," he said resolutely. "It's about creating a legacy of responsible innovation—a legacy that stands the test of time."

The plane landed in Boston, and as Robert and Richard disembarked, the weight of their decisions hung heavily in the air. Their laboratory—with its whiteboards and time machine capsule—awaited them like a sanctuary filled with possibilities. But they were unaware that their sanctuary had already been compromised.

Unbeknownst to them, covert operatives from the Pentagon had orchestrated a secret operation to gather intelligence on their advancements in temporal technology and its potential applications. Silent and invisible, elite agents infiltrated their lab under cover of darkness with calculated precision designed to avoid detection.

With unparalleled expertise, these operatives planted cameras and microphones invisible to human eyes. Tiny devices camouflaged within intricate machinery recorded every conversation, scrutinized every equation scrawled on whiteboards, and silently observed each temporal experiment conducted by Robert and Richard.

The sanctity of their work had become an unwitting stage for clandestine surveillance.

These hidden devices captured discussions about ethical implications of time travel, nuances of altering historical events, and potential consequences tied to their groundbreaking technology. The Pentagon sought not only to understand how their time machine worked but also to gauge Robert and Richard's motivations—the intentions behind wielding such unprecedented power.

As the partners delved deeper into their research, the hidden cameras documented the ebb and flow of their collaboration. The Pentagon's spy teams, equipped with state-of-the-art technology, monitored the emotional and intellectual journey of the scientists as they navigated the uncharted waters of time travel.

The invisible surveillance extended beyond the laboratory walls. The spies sought to capture moments of vulnerability, indecision, and conviction as Robert and Richard grappled with the moral quandaries inherent in manipulating the fabric of time. The clandestine operation aimed to provide a comprehensive portrait of the scientists, revealing not just their scientific prowess but also the very essence of their characters.

When they entered the laboratory, a sense of familiarity mixed with the urgency of their mission. Fail-safe systems had to be implemented rapidly, and the chalkboards—once again filled with scribbles of scientific research—bore witness to the convergence of ethics and innovation. Unbeknownst to them, General Andrews had already taken steps to stay ahead. The private conversation they believed secure had been eavesdropped upon. The walls had ears, and the hidden microphones on their plane had captured every word.

In a dimly lit intelligence facility, General Andrews sat before a bank of monitors. The audio signal from the plane echoed through the room as a cold smile spread across his lips. "They think they can defy orders and forge their own destiny," he muttered to himself. "But they forget who they're dealing with."

Back in the lab, Robert and Richard continued their work, unaware that their discussions about fail-safe systems were already known to the Pentagon. The ethical considerations driving their journey now faced harsh scrutiny under an unrelenting gaze.

Days passed quickly as the laboratory became a hive of activity. The government-imposed deadline loomed over them, but they were determined to retain control over their invention.

Tirelessly, they worked to perfect the time machine while debating its ethical implications late into the night. They wrestled with questions of morality and responsibility— grappling with what it meant to act as arbiters of history. The chalkboards, once filled with equations, now bore scribbles of ethical dilemmas and philosophical quandaries.

As the 90-day deadline approached, Robert and Richard found themselves at the intersection of science and ethics. Their time machine—a marvel of technological achievement—carried with it the potential to reshape history itself. Every decision they made would determine not only its fate but also that of humanity's future.

A knock on the laboratory door interrupted their focus. General Andrews entered with an air of authority that unsettled both scientists. "Gentlemen," General Andrews greeted them formally, his tone laced with a veiled threat that was impossible to miss. His sharp eyes moved between Robert and Richard, assessing them like a predator sizing up its prey. "I trust you've been making good progress on our project."

Robert exchanged a glance with Richard, whose jaw was set in quiet defiance. Taking a measured breath, Robert responded carefully. "General, we've made significant progress on the time machine," he said evenly. "However, we must insist on implementing safeguards to prevent misuse."

Feigning interest, Andrews leaned back in his chair and nodded curtly. "Of course, Dr. Powell," he replied smoothly. "We want responsible use of this technology as well—but time is of the essence. What we need are results, not delays."

Richard couldn't hold back any longer. "With all due respect, General," he said sharply, "this isn't just another piece of military equipment you can deploy at will. We're talking about time itself—history, causality—things that can't be undone once they're tampered with."

Andrews' expression darkened slightly, but he maintained his composure. "Mr. Anders," he said in a tone that was both condescending and authoritative, "I understand your concerns. But let me remind you that this is not just about science—it's about national security. If we don't develop this technology first, someone else will. And do you think they'll hesitate to use it?"

Robert interjected before Richard could escalate further. "General Andrews," he said firmly, "we're not disputing the importance of ensuring this technology doesn't fall into the wrong hands. But the risks of using it irresponsibly are just as great—if not greater."

Andrews leaned forward slightly, his presence filling the room like a storm cloud. "Robert. Can I call you Robert?" he said slowly, his voice low and deliberate, "you're a brilliant man. But let me make one thing clear: the world we live in is not governed by idealism—it's governed by power and pragmatism. The ability to observe or even influence historical events could give us an advantage no enemy could match."

Robert's stomach churned at the implication, but he kept his voice steady. "And what happens when that power is abused? What happens when someone decides to rewrite history for their own gain?"

Andrews smirked faintly, as if amused by the question. "You're assuming we'd allow that to happen," he said smoothly. "This project would be under strict oversight— every mission carefully planned and executed with precision."

Richard scoffed audibly this time. "Strict oversight? By whom? Politicians? Generals? People who see history as nothing more than a chessboard?"

The tension in the room thickened as Andrews fixed Richard with a cold stare. For a moment, it seemed as though the general might lash out, but instead, he smiled—a thin, calculated expression that didn't reach his eyes.

"Mr. Anders," Andrews said evenly, "I understand your skepticism. But let me assure you, this isn't about playing God or rewriting history for personal gain. This is about protecting our nation—our way of life—from threats both past and future."

Richard shook his head slightly, refusing to be swayed by the general's polished rhetoric. "General Andrews," he said carefully, "you're asking us to hand over a tool that could destabilize everything we know about reality itself. Even observation carries risks—what happens if someone inadvertently changes something? Or worse—what if someone deliberately does?"

Andrews' smile faded as his expression turned serious again. "That's why we need people like you involved in this project," he said earnestly—or at least pretending to be earnest. "To ensure those risks are minimized."

Richard leaned forward now; his voice laced with frustration. "You keep saying 'minimized,' General—but what about eliminated? What guarantees can you give us that this technology won't be used recklessly?"

Andrews paused for a moment before responding—a calculated move designed to project thoughtfulness rather than evasion.

"Gentlemen," he began slowly, his tone softening just enough to seem genuine, "I understand your concerns better than you might think." He gestured toward the table as if inviting them into confidence. "This isn't just another weapon or tool—it's something unprecedented in human history. That's why I've personally ensured that any use of this technology will go through rigorous review processes involving experts like yourselves."

Robert's eyes narrowed slightly; the words were carefully chosen but rang hollow.

"We're not asking you to relinquish control entirely," Andrews continued smoothly. "In fact, I envision this project as a partnership—scientists and military working together to ensure its responsible use."

Richard opened his mouth to argue further, but Robert placed a hand on his arm—a silent signal to let it go for now.

"General," Robert said after a pause, his tone measured but firm, "we'll continue our work on the machine—but only under the condition that safeguards are implemented from the outset."

Andrews inclined his head slightly in acknowledgment but didn't commit outright—a subtle evasion that didn't go unnoticed by either scientist.

"Of course," Andrews said finally with an air of finality that suggested the conversation was over—for now at least. He stood and extended his hand first to Robert and then to Richard.

"Thank you for your candor," he said warmly—or at least as warmly as someone like Andrews could manage. "I hope I've set your minds at ease."

As they left the lab room and walked down the hallway toward General Andrews' waiting SUV, Richard muttered under his breath: "He's lying through his teeth."

Robert didn't respond immediately but finally said quietly: "I know."

They both fell silent as they exited into the cold January air outside—a silence filled with unspoken fears about what their creation might become in hands they couldn't trust...

As General Andrews left with a false sense of control, Robert and Richard exchanged knowing looks beneath a facade of compliance. Their true safeguards remained concealed within their labyrinthine designs—a testament to their resolve to protect their invention from misuse.

Meanwhile, days earlier in a secure facility shrouded in secrecy, General Andrews met with Agent Mitchell—the leader of his clandestine operations team—to discuss the progress of their covert mission.

The room was dimly lit, its walls lined with monitors displaying live feeds from surveillance cameras, encrypted communications, and classified dossiers. The faint hum of sophisticated equipment filled the air, punctuated by the occasional murmur of operatives working in the background.

Andrews paced restlessly, his polished boots clicking against the tiled floor. His face was a mask of controlled frustration, but his tone betrayed the sharp edge of his impatience. "Their principles could jeopardize everything," he said sharply, gesturing toward a file on the table marked Top Secret. "If they discover our true intentions, they might sabotage this mission—or worse."

Agent Mitchell leaned back in his chair, his demeanor calm and calculating. A man of few words, Mitchell had built a reputation for handling delicate operations with ruthless efficiency.

He steepled his fingers as he regarded Andrews. "Dr. Powell and his partner are intelligent," he said evenly. "But intelligence can be manipulated. They believe they're in control of this project—let's keep it that way."

Andrews stopped pacing and turned to face Mitchell directly. "And if they start asking too many questions? If they begin to suspect what we're really planning?"

Mitchell's lips curled into a faint smirk. "Then we give them answers—just not the whole truth." He tapped a folder on the table containing fabricated mission reports and doctored timelines. "We've already prepared contingencies to steer them in the direction we need. They'll think they're safeguarding history while we ensure it serves our interests."

Andrews frowned but nodded reluctantly. "I don't like leaving so much to chance," he muttered. "This isn't just about controlling history—it's about securing our future. If Powell or his partner decide to pull the plug on this project, we lose everything."

Mitchell's expression hardened slightly. "Then we make sure they don't have that option."

Andrews raised an eyebrow, intrigued but cautious. "Go on."

Mitchell leaned forward, lowering his voice even further despite the room's secure environment. "We've already embedded operatives within their research team—people who report directly to me. If Powell or Richard become a liability, we'll neutralize them before they can do any damage."

Andrews' jaw tightened as he considered the implications of Mitchell's words. He wasn't one to shy away from hard decisions—his career had been built on them—but even he understood the risks involved in taking such drastic measures.

"And if it comes to that?" Andrews asked quietly.

Mitchell's eyes were cold and unflinching. "Then we proceed without them," he said simply. "The machine is nearly operational—we have access to the data so we can move forward if necessary."

Andrews exhaled slowly, running a hand over his face as he weighed their options. "I'd prefer not to resort to that," he admitted finally. "Powell is too valuable—his expertise is irreplaceable."

"Agreed," Mitchell said with a nod. "But value only goes so far when it becomes a threat."

As contingency plans were outlined in meticulous detail, both men had agreed that success depended not only on technological precision but also on controlling those who had unlocked its secrets. In this high-stakes game where power clashed with conscience, nations' fates hung precariously in balance—a gamble where temporal integrity collided with ambition.

There was a moment where neither man spoke as the weight of their conversation settled over them like a shroud. Finally, Andrews straightened and adjusted his uniform, regaining his composure.

"Keep me updated on their progress," he ordered curtly. "And make sure your people stay close—they're our insurance policy."

Mitchell inclined his head slightly in acknowledgment before standing as well. "Understood, General."

As Andrews left the room, his mind churned with conflicting thoughts—ambition and pragmatism clashing against the faint echoes of doubt that lingered in the back of his mind.

Meanwhile, Mitchell remained seated for a moment longer, his gaze fixed on one of the monitors displaying live footage from Powell's lab. He didn't believe in doubt or hesitation; for him, there was only the mission—and ensuring its success at any cost.

With a final glance at the screen, he rose and exited through a side door, disappearing into the shadows like a ghost—a man whose presence was felt more than seen, guiding events from behind the scenes with an iron grip and an unyielding resolve.

Every move at the lab was being monitored closely through hidden cameras and microphones embedded in the machinery. Intelligence gathered revealed heated debates between Robert and Richard over ethical concerns about using time travel for military purposes.

"Their reservations are clear," Mitchell thought calmly. "But if they step out of line or attempt sabotage, we'll intervene immediately."

Chapter 8: Shadows of Sacrifice

The morning sun cast a golden glow over the harbor, illuminating the expanse of water as Robert and Richard embarked on their morning routine. The rhythmic sound of their footsteps echoed against the bridge pavement, blending with the symphony of port life: the distant hum of ships, the creaking of rigging, and the lively chatter of dockworkers. When they reached the center of the bridge, the harbor stretched out before them, a panorama of bustling activity.

Cargo vessels loomed in the distance; their massive hulls silhouetted against the rising sun. Seagulls circled overhead, their cries adding to the ambient soundtrack of maritime industry. Amidst the hustle and bustle, the pair found a moment of respite. The familiar routine of their morning run provided a semblance of normalcy—a stark contrast to the weighty decisions and clandestine conversations that had defined their recent days.

Boston's maritime industry has always been deeply intertwined with the city's identity, economy, and innovation. From its early days as a bustling port for colonial trade to its modern role as a hub for global shipping and technology, Boston Harbor has been a vital artery of commerce and progress. For Robert and Richard, the harbor's rich history and cutting-edge facilities represented more than just a link to the past—they saw it as a potential lifeline for their groundbreaking work on the Chrono-Field Generator. If ever their lab equipment needed to be moved discreetly, Boston's maritime infrastructure offered a unique avenue to safeguard their research.

Boston's relationship with the sea stretched back nearly 400 years. The harbor's natural depth and strategic location made it an early center for shipbuilding and trade. By the mid-19th century, Boston had become one of America's most important ports, exporting goods like textiles, lumber, and iron while importing spices, tea, and other commodities from Europe and Asia.

Shipyards like McKay's in East Boston produced legendary clipper ships that revolutionized maritime travel with their speed and efficiency.

Even as industries evolved, the harbor remained a focal point for innovation. During World War II, the Charlestown Navy Yard became a critical site for building and repairing naval vessels. Today, Boston Harbor generates over $8 billion annually in economic impact, supporting industries ranging from shipping to tourism. Its modern facilities include container terminals, cruise ship docks, and specialized research vessels that reflect the city's ongoing commitment to maritime excellence.

Boston's maritime legacy isn't just about trade—it's also about science and technology. Institutions like MIT have long leveraged the harbor as a testing ground for cutting-edge research in ocean engineering, naval architecture, and marine robotics. The MIT Sea Grant Program has been instrumental in designing advanced propulsion systems, hydrodynamic structures, and sustainable energy solutions for ships. Collaborations with organizations like Oldendorff Carriers have pushed the boundaries of ship design, integrating digital fabrication techniques and alternative energy sources to meet modern environmental standards.

One of the most intriguing aspects of Boston's maritime innovation is its fleet of research vessels. These ships are floating laboratories equipped with state-of-the-art technology for studying everything from climate change to underwater acoustics.

Some vessels are used to test military applications like stealth systems or autonomous navigation; others focus on environmental monitoring or renewable energy projects. For Robert and Richard Powell, these ships represented more than just scientific tools—they were potential sanctuaries for their work.

As Robert and Richard delved deeper into their time travel research at MIT, they became increasingly aware of the risks involved. The Chrono-Field Generator was not just a scientific marvel—it was a potential target for those who sought to exploit its power. Government agencies like General Andrews' team had already shown interest in using the technology for military purposes, raising ethical concerns about how it might be weaponized.

In private discussions late at night in their Cambridge lab, Robert brought up an idea that had been simmering in his mind: "If we ever need to move the equipment—if things get too dangerous—we could use one of the research vessels in Boston Harbor."

Richard frowned but nodded thoughtfully. "It makes sense," he admitted. "A ship is mobile, self-contained, and secure—especially if it's outfitted for classified research."

Robert elaborated on his vision: "Imagine loading the generator onto a vessel designed for oceanographic studies or naval testing. It could operate as a mobile lab while staying under the radar. And if we needed to relocate quickly, we'd already be at sea."

The scientists began researching specific ships that might suit their needs. They identified several possibilities through MIT's connections with the Center for Ocean Engineering and the Sea Grant Program. One vessel stood out—a retrofitted military research ship equipped with advanced sensors and secure communication systems. Originally designed for testing underwater drones, it had ample space for their equipment and could operate autonomously if necessary.

Moving sensitive lab equipment through Boston presented logistical challenges but also opportunities. The city's dense network of roads connecting MIT to the harbor included key routes that could be monitored or concealed depending on their needs. The Ted Williams Tunnel provided direct access between Cambridge and South Boston's Conley Terminal—a facility capable of handling large cargo discreetly.

Once at the harbor, their chosen vessel could be loaded under cover of night using cranes designed for heavy machinery. From there, it could slip out into international waters or remain anchored in one of Boston Harbor's many secluded coves.

The idea of using a ship as a mobile lab also aligned with Robert's broader vision for time travel research. "A vessel gives us freedom," he explained to Richard during one of their planning sessions. "We're not tied to any one location or jurisdiction. We can conduct experiments without interference—whether it's from governments or anyone else."

Richard added another layer to the plan: "And if we're ever cornered? A ship gives us an escape route."

Their discussions often circled back to Boston Harbor itself—a place where history met innovation at every turn. From its storied past as a center of trade to its modern role as a hub for cutting-edge technology, the harbor embodied resilience and adaptability—qualities that mirrored their own journey as scientists navigating uncharted waters.

Despite its practicality, the idea of relocating their lab raised ethical questions that weighed heavily on Robert's mind. Could they justify hiding their work if it meant denying humanity access to potentially life-saving discoveries? Or was secrecy necessary to protect against those who would misuse their technology?

As they gazed out over Boston Harbor, Richard voiced what they were both thinking: "This place has always been about connections—between people, places, ideas. Maybe that's what we need right now—a way to stay connected while staying safe."

Robert nodded silently; his eyes fixed on the horizon where ships moved steadily toward distant destinations. In that moment, he realized that whether on land or sea, their mission would always be about navigating uncertainty—charting a course through history while protecting its fragile balance.

Boston Harbor had seen centuries of change—wars fought and won, industries rise and fall—but its spirit endured: a testament to human ingenuity and perseverance. For Robert and Richard Powell, it was both an inspiration and a reminder that even in turbulent times, there was always a way forward—if only they had the courage to find it.

The revelation of the Pentagon's intrusion came as a shock to Robert and Richard, altering their perception of trust within what had once been their private sanctuary. The covert surveillance added an unforeseen layer of complexity to their already intricate journey, raising questions about the ethical boundaries of those seeking to control time travel for geopolitical agendas. Their laboratory, once a haven for scientific discovery, now bore witness to a clash between innovation and those who sought to exploit it for power.

"I can't believe we're being watched," Richard said, his voice low but tense, carried away by the morning breeze. "The government's interest in the time machine has put us under a microscope."

Robert glanced around instinctively, his eyes scanning the bustling harbor below. The rhythmic clang of distant sound of ship horns filled the air. "We can't underestimate General Andrews," he said grimly. "He has resources far beyond our lab. Surveillance, infiltration—every move we make could be scrutinized."

Their sneakers tapped rhythmically against the pavement as they continued their run across the bridge, a steady counterpoint to the symphony of port activity below. Richard's brow furrowed as he spoke again, his tone somber. "It's come to this. Government interest isn't just a threat to the time machine—it's a threat to us. We need to make a decision soon."

Robert nodded, his gaze fixed ahead as if searching for answers on the horizon. The weight of impending decisions settled heavily on him. "We can't allow the time machine to become a tool for manipulation," he said firmly. "Our security systems will only buy us so much time. We need a drastic solution—something that eliminates temptation altogether."

Standing at the top of the bridge, they paused briefly to take in the view: seagulls circling overhead, waves splashing against the riverbank below, and ships moving steadily through the harbor. The vastness of it all felt both grounding and overwhelming.

"I've been thinking," Richard began cautiously after catching his breath. "One of us needs to disappear with the time machine—take it to a moment and place only they know. Sacrifice one for the greater good."

Robert slowed his pace, his gaze fixed on the horizon as he absorbed Richard's suggestion. The gravity of his words hung in the air; this was no small decision.

"I have a wife and children," Richard continued in a hushed tone, breaking the silence. "Responsibilities I can't abandon. You're single—no family ties. It makes sense for you to take this risk."

Robert stopped running altogether, turning to face Richard fully. His friend's words hit him like a wave, heavy with truth and inevitability. Sacrifice: one of them would vanish with the time machine, leaving behind everything they knew for humanity's future.

"You're right," Robert said sincerely after a long pause. "I can't ask you to make that sacrifice—your family needs you." He hesitated before adding, "But one of us must take this responsibility for the common good."

Richard nodded but pressed further, his voice tinged with worry. "If you're going to do this, we need safeguards in place—ways for you to contact me if something goes wrong or if you need help."

"I'll choose a time when I can return safely," Robert replied, his tone resolute but measured. "I'll make contact when it's right."

Richard exhaled deeply but didn't look relieved. Instead, he glanced over his shoulder at their surroundings before speaking again in an even quieter voice. "We also need to assume we're being surveilled right now—even here." He gestured subtly toward a parked car near the base of the bridge where two figures sat motionless inside.

Robert followed his gaze and frowned slightly but didn't react outwardly. "You're probably right," he said softly. "Which means we need to move quickly before Andrews tightens his grip."

"Agreed," Richard said firmly. "But we also need misdirection—something that throws them off your trail once you're gone."

"I've already thought about that," Robert admitted after a moment's hesitation. "I'll leave false leads behind—encrypted data files pointing to decoy destinations and fabricated experiments."

Richard raised an eyebrow, impressed despite himself. "You've been planning this longer than I realized."

"Not planning," Robert corrected gently, "preparing—for when it became inevitable."

They stood in silence for a moment longer, the enormity of their decision pressing down on them like the weight of history itself.

Finally, Richard broke the quiet with one last plea. "Promise me one thing: wherever you go, whatever happens… don't lose yourself in it."

Robert met his gaze steadily and nodded. "I promise."

The bridge—symbolic of connection—became an unlikely stage for a decision that would ripple through history itself. Partners united by science and ethics now faced an unimaginable sacrifice.

"We need to choose carefully," Richard cautioned as they resumed running along the harbor path. "The destination must be precise—a safeguard against external influence or manipulation."

The bustling port masked their conversation with its cacophony of sound: ship horns, waves crashing against docks, and seagulls crying overhead drowned out any possibility of eavesdropping by General Andrews' team.

As they descended from the bridge into shadows cast by the trees and bushes that lined the trail, Robert made his decision clear: "We'll meet in the lab tonight at 8:00 p.m." His voice was steady but resolute. "By midnight, one of us will be gone—and so will the time machine."

Unbeknownst to them, outside their laboratory preparations were already underway for another kind of intervention. General Andrews convened with Agent Mitchell in a dimly lit room filled with blueprints and surveillance monitors.

"Time is running out," Andrews muttered as he paced restlessly in his military uniform, its insignias gleaming under harsh fluorescent light.

Agent Mitchell outlined his plan with precision: an operation designed not just to seize control but also to compel Robert and Richard into activating and testing their invention under duress.

"The scientists are unpredictable," Mitchell warned grimly. "Their principles could jeopardize everything if they sabotage or expose our mission."

Andrews nodded sharply but remained resolute. "Then we'll ensure compliance—whatever it takes."

As shadows deepened over Boston Harbor that evening, two parallel plans had unfolded almost simultaneously: one driven by sacrifice and ethics; another by power and manipulation.

The plan involved deploying a specialized team of operatives skilled in covert operations. Under the shroud of darkness, these agents would infiltrate the lab, swiftly securing Robert and Richard without raising alarm. Their expertise in such missions ensured that the abduction would be seamless, leaving no room for resistance.

Once sequestered, the scientists would be coerced into activating the time machine. General Andrews emphasized the urgency of the mission: to eliminate a would-be dictator in Southeast Asia. Agent Mitchell's operatives, trained for such high-stakes assignments, would serve as the temporal agents sent back to alter the course of history.

As the general and the clandestine leader fine-tuned the details, the gravity of their actions settled upon them. The plan to forcibly initiate time travel raised ethical concerns, but the urgency of geopolitical maneuvers prevailed. The balance between power and morality tilted as they embraced the Machiavellian necessity of their mission.

The hours passed as General Andrews and Agent Mitchell parted ways, armed with a clandestine strategy that would set their plan in motion. The fate of nations now hinged on the convergence of temporal exploration and covert military operations, where the pursuit of power blurred the lines between calculated manipulation of time and unpredictable consequences.

In sharp contrast to General Andrews's meeting, a somber decision awaited Robert and Richard. The decision had been made; the sacrifice accepted. The port, with its ebb and flow of life, bore witness to a pact that transcended the boundaries of time.

The day unfolded with a sense of calm urgency. The partners, each immersed in their respective responsibilities, prepared for the night that would redefine their shared journey. The port, now bathed in soft hues of twilight, served as the backdrop for final preparations for the impending sacrifice. As the sun sank on the horizon, painting the sky in shades of orange and purple, Robert and Richard converged in the laboratory.

The time machine capsule, a silent witness to their scientific efforts, stood ready for a journey that would transcend the limits of temporal understanding. The air was heavy with anticipation, but also with caution—they knew General Andrews' team was likely watching and listening. Every move they made could be under surveillance, and they needed to act carefully.

Richard plugged his phone into the lab's sound system, scrolling through his playlist until he found something loud and chaotic. Moments later, the pounding bass of a rock anthem filled the room. Robert adjusted a set of strobe lights they had hastily rigged up earlier, ensuring they flashed erratically enough to distort any surveillance footage.

The combination of noise and light created an environment designed to overwhelm both cameras and microphones.

"This should buy us some privacy," Richard said, raising his voice over the music as he double-checked the strobe settings.

Robert nodded, glancing at the capsule. "Let's hope it works. If Andrews' team gets wind of what we're about to do..."

"They won't," Richard interrupted firmly. "We've planned for this."

The two moved quickly but methodically, setting up the program that would guide the time machine on this crucial voyage. Robert leaned over the console, entering coordinates and parameters while Richard monitored external systems for any signs of interference.

"Are you sure about your destination?" Richard asked, his tone serious despite the music blaring around them.

Robert paused briefly before replying. "It's the safest option. A quiet point in history where I can observe without drawing attention—and where I can hide if necessary."

Richard frowned but didn't argue. "Just remember, you can't stay too long. The longer you're there, the greater the risk of being noticed—or worse."

"I know," Robert said quietly. He glanced at his friend, a flicker of gratitude crossing his face. "Thank you for trusting me with this."

Richard smirked faintly. "I don't have much choice, do I? I truly appreciate the sacrifice you are making."

They shared a fist bump before returning to their work. As Richard ran diagnostics on the Chrono-Field Generator, Robert reviewed the program one last time.

"Everything checks out," Richard said after a few minutes. "The generator is stable, and the navigation system is locked in."

Robert exhaled slowly, feeling the weight of what was about to happen settle on his shoulders. "This is it," he said softly.

"Are you sure about this, Robert?" Richard's voice carried a mix of concern and resignation. "Once you enter that capsule, there's no turning back. The past is relentless."

Robert nodded; determination etched in his eyes. "We made this decision for the greater good, Richard. It's a sacrifice, yes, but it's also an opportunity to protect the time machine from misuse. The responsibility now falls on my shoulders."

Richard placed a hand on his shoulder. "You've got this," he said firmly. "Just remember—check in with me from time to time."

"I will," Robert promised. He stepped toward Richard, and the two men—who had spent so many years sacrificing their personal lives, their time, and their relationships—embraced. It was a rare gesture for them, something they did not practice often, but in that moment, it carried the weight of unspoken gratitude and mutual respect.

It was time. They activated the final sequence, their faces illuminated by the glow of the console as the capsule hummed to life behind them. The music continued to blare, masking their voices as they exchanged one last look—a silent acknowledgment of everything at stake.

As Robert stepped into the capsule and prepared for departure, he couldn't help but feel both exhilaration and trepidation. This wasn't just a scientific experiment—it was a leap into the unknown.

"We cannot predict what awaits the traveler," Richard said, his voice heavy with the weight of imminent farewell. "But we have made this decision for the common good. Whatever happens, we will face the consequences."

Robert nodded, a mix of determination and resignation in his eyes. "The time machine will be hidden, and its secrets safeguarded. The sacrifice, though painful, is a testament to our commitment to ethical innovation. The future of humanity depends on it."

As the laboratory clock struck 11:20 p.m., the partners exchanged a final glance. The lab, the bridge, the port, and bustling life outside seemed to hold their breath in anticipation. The decision—etched into the fabric of their collaboration—was irreversible. At 11:33 p.m., Robert and Richard initiated the time travel sequence.

The hum of the Chrono Field Generator filled the laboratory—a sound that resonated through both present hallways and past realms. The time machine capsule glowed with temporal energy as seconds passed; their partnership faced its deepest test yet. The night enveloped the laboratory in a cocoon of uncertainty. Outside its walls, the port continued its rhythmic dance with history's tides.

As the temporal shift reached its zenith, reality itself seemed to undulate under the weight of their unfolding sacrifice. What they did not know was that their decision's consequences would echo through time—carrying with them traces of sacrifice, innovation, and humanity's enduring quest for an ethically shaped future. Boston, its universities, its people, and its port—with its ships and seagulls—witnessed a moment that transcended present boundaries and ventured into uncharted territories of history.

Chapter 9: Echoes Through Time

The laboratory, bathed in the ethereal glow of the Chrono Field Generator, stood as a silent witness to the culmination of a journey that had transcended the boundaries of scientific exploration. The time machine capsule, a vessel of temporal possibilities, hummed with energy as Robert prepared to embark on a journey that would redefine the very fabric of his existence.

Richard, his friend and partner in this quest for knowledge, stood by the control panel. The weight of their decision—the sacrifice hanging in the air like an unspoken farewell—pressed heavily upon them. The control room, with its monitors and instruments, resembled a sanctuary of scientific endeavor.

"I'll encrypt all our work," Richard promised, his fingers dancing over the keyboard. "The government won't be able to access the machine's specifications, construction plans, or operational details. Even if it costs me my life, I'll protect our legacy." They agreed on the story they would tell General Andrews: a failed experiment in which both Robert and the machine were lost forever. The exact location of their disappearance would remain unrecoverable. Together they wondered—would this be enough?

Robert glanced at the displays in the capsule. He quickly did a final check of the system. "Thank you, Richard. You've been more than a friend; you've been a partner in every sense. Protecting our work is about safeguarding not only our vision but also humanity's future."

As Robert prepared to initiate the temporal displacement sequence, Richard initiated the encryption process, the laboratory transformed into a tapestry of technological activity. Lines of code scrolled across screens; algorithms danced in the digital realm as their scientific endeavors transmuted into encrypted layers of protection.

The Chrono-Field Generator emitted a subtle hum, signaling that the time machine was ready to operate. The moment had arrived: an intersection of science, sacrifice, and unexplored territories of time.

Anticipation reached its crescendo. "I'll see you on the other side," said Richard firmly despite the emotional undercurrents swirling in the room.

Robert nodded; his gaze fixed on the gleaming door to the past. "Thank you for everything," he said softly. "I'll carry our legacy with me—even into the unknown." With that, the capsule's door closed, sealing him within a cocoon of temporal energy.

The hum of the Chrono-Field Generator intensified as reality itself seemed to ripple under the strain of temporal displacement. Outside the capsule, Richard watched with a mix of pride and sadness while finalizing encryption protocols that would ensure their work remained hidden from prying eyes.

The clock read 11:26 p.m. Richard stood before the sealed capsule containing their greatest creation—and Robert's greatest sacrifice. Once encryption was complete, the laboratory became a testament to ethical resilience in scientific innovation. Sacrifice—embodied in Robert's journey to the past—resonated through every corner of their shared space.

In silent solitude within the laboratory walls, Richard felt an unexpected sense of closure.

In a kaleidoscope of light bouncing around the laboratory, Richard silently vowed to protect their vision at all costs. The government—with its ambitions and agendas—would find no entry into this sanctuary of discovery. Outside, it was just another night in Boston, where people rested, most of them asleep at this hour, awaiting the arrival of a new day.

Richard—the guardian of their temporal secrets—stood firm amidst it all. Their shared legacy was now engraved within encrypted files: echoes through time that testified to ethical resolve and human ingenuity in confronting an uncertain future.

Two hours earlier, General Andrews' clandestine strike force had received warnings emanating from the lab's surveillance equipment that altered the trajectory of their mission. As the scientists, Robert Powell and Richard Alders, were reportedly preparing to 'destroy' the time machine—a device central to Andrews' ambitions for geopolitical dominance. This revelation triggered an immediate and decisive response. Mobilizing the covert operations team trained in rapid deployment and surgical precision, General Andrews ordered the strike force to intercept the scientists before they could sabotage the machine.

The team, composed of elite operatives from Andrews' paramilitary division, was already on standby at a nearby staging area. Equipped with state-of-the-art weaponry and surveillance technology, they moved swiftly into action. Their orders were clear: secure the laboratory, prevent any destruction of the time machine, and detain Powell and Alders for interrogation. Failure was not an option.

Within minutes, the operatives boarded unmarked tactical vehicles designed for speed and discretion. An encrypted communication channel buzzed with updates as the team leader coordinated movements with Andrews' command center. Satellite imagery provided real-time visuals of the lab's perimeter, while drones equipped with thermal imaging scanned for potential threats.

The strike force adopted a multi-pronged approach. A reconnaissance unit was dispatched ahead to assess entry points and monitor activity within the lab. Meanwhile, the main assault team prepared for a rapid breach-and-clear operation. Time was of the essence; every second brought them closer to losing control over the situation.

As General Andrews' task force approached the laboratory—bathed in the soft glow of computer screens and filled with the persistent hum of machinery—it became clear that this was a gateway to the unknown. Inside,

Robert, now settled into its ergonomic seat. The interior was as sleek as its exterior—holographic displays floated before him, responding instantly to his touch. Data streamed across them: crystal resonance frequencies, fusion core output levels, and quantum probability fields—all stable.

He reached out and activated the primary sequence. The Chrono-Field Generator roared to life, its hum deepening into a resonant thrum that seemed to shake reality itself. Outside the capsule's transparent viewport, space began to ripple and distort like water disturbed by an unseen force.

"Temporal anchor engaged," announced an automated voice from the control panel.

Robert took one last look at his lab—a place that had been both sanctuary and prison for so many years—and verified his destination: "May 3, 1519" as it glowed on the screen—a portal to a bygone era and a pivotal chapter in human history.

With resolve, Robert typed in coordinates "43.6402° N, 5.0970° E" a small field near Salon-de-Provence—a town where Michel Nostradamus had once lived and worked. Nestled between Saint-Rémy-de-Provence to the northwest and Marseille to the southeast of France, it was a deliberate choice: a chance to immerse himself in history while safeguarding his legacy from those who sought to exploit it. As he activated the Chrono-Field Generator, Robert felt time's currents envelop him. The capsule—a vessel traversing history's corridors—carried him toward an unknown destination. The laboratory's sights and sounds faded into echoes as he disappeared into another era

Meanwhile, tension mounted as Andrews' convoy neared its destination. The laboratory loomed ahead, its exterior bathed in an unfamiliar glow from residual energy emitted by Powell's departure. The reconnaissance unit reported back: one heat signature remained inside—presumably Richard Alders—while another had vanished moments earlier.

The strike force disembarked silently, their movements synchronized and deliberate. Using night-vision goggles and sound-suppressed weapons, they advanced toward the lab's entrances. The team split into two groups: one positioned at the main entrance while another secured a rear access point.

"Alpha Team in position," whispered the leader of the first group into his comms, his voice barely audible over the faint crackle of static. "No movement at the main door. Awaiting orders."

"Bravo Team in position," came another voice, this time from the rear of the building. "Rear access secured. No signs of external security measures."

The team leader, a seasoned operative named Carter, surveyed the scene from his vantage point near the main entrance. "Intel confirms Alders is still inside," he said quietly over the comms channel.

Carter continued, "Coordinating time. I read 11:35 p.m. We breach on my mark. Alpha takes the front; Bravo sweeps from the rear. Secure the target and retrieve any critical data or equipment."

"Copy that," replied Bravo's leader, a sharp-eyed operative named Langley. "We'll cover all exits to ensure no one slips through."

Carter turned to his team, his voice low but commanding. "Remember—this is a high-priority asset retrieval mission. Minimize damage to equipment, but don't hesitate if Alders resists. Andrews wants him alive, but we can't afford delays."

One of Alpha's operatives adjusted his grip on his weapon and muttered under his breath, "Bet Alders knows we're coming."

"Doesn't matter," Carter replied curtly, catching the comment. "He's not going anywhere without Powell."

Inside Bravo's channel, Langley gave similar instructions to his team as they prepared to breach the rear entrance. "Keep it tight and quiet," he said firmly. "We don't know what kind of traps they might've set up in there—or what kind of tech we're dealing with."

Another operative chimed in skeptically, "You think this 'time machine' stuff is real? Or just some smoke-and-mirrors project?"

Langley's response was sharp. "Doesn't matter what I think. Andrews believes it's real—and that's all that matters for us."

As both teams finalized their positions, Carter gave the signal: "Alpha and Bravo teams—breach on three... two... one... Mark!"

With practiced precision, Alpha Team forced open the main entrance while Bravo Team simultaneously entered through the rear access point. The lab's interior was dimly lit, its corridors eerily silent except for the faint hum of machinery still active from Powell's recent departure.

"Alpha moving in," Carter reported as his team advanced cautiously down the central hallway.

"Bravo sweeping left," Langley added as his team fanned out through adjacent rooms

The comms crackled briefly before Carter spoke again: "Eyes open—this place is more than it seems."

Inside the lab, Richard Alders worked with frantic precision as chaos unfolded around him. He knew time was running out. The encryption process for safeguarding data on the Chrono Field Generator—its blueprints, operational protocols, and research—was nearly complete. But merely encrypting it wasn't enough; he needed to hide it where no one would think to look.

Richard thought of his son's. It contained a simple game he had developed for Richard Jr.—a puzzle-solving adventure filled with colorful characters and intricate mazes. It was perfect. No one would suspect that humanity's most powerful invention was hidden within a child's game.

He quickly embedded encrypted files into the game's code, disguising them as harmless assets like background textures and character animations. To ensure further security, he added a unique cipher only he could decode before transmitting it back onto his son's tablet at home. The entire process took less than two minutes but felt like an eternity.

As explosive charges detonated at both entrances moments later, smoke filled the air as armed operatives poured into the lab with weapons drawn.

"Hands in the air! Step away from the controls!" barked one operative as they surrounded Richard. He hesitated briefly before complying, raising trembling hands above his head.

While one team restrained him in handcuffs, another focused on stabilizing the Control Panel computer, which emitted erratic energy signatures following Powell's departure.

"Sir," came a voice over Andrews' secure channel, "Powell is gone. It looks like he activated the machine just before we arrived."

Andrews' voice crackled back through their earpieces: "Do not let that machine be destroyed under any circumstances! Secure it immediately."

Richard was dragged into a makeshift interrogation area nearby while technicians worked feverishly to analyze remaining systems in hopes of recovering operational data.

"You don't understand what you've done," Richard spat at his captors during questioning. "That machine is too dangerous—it should never have existed."

The lead interrogator leaned closer with icy resolve: "What we understand is that you tried to destroy something vital to national security—and you will tell us everything you know."

Richard remained silent; his gaze fixed on some distant point as though contemplating events already set in motion. General Andrews arrived at the scene at 11:40 p.m. to oversee operations personally. Surveying Richard with disdain, he barked orders: "We may have lost Powell for now, but this machine's secrets are still ours—and so is our future! Take every computer and hard drive back to my office!"

The strike team moved with mechanical precision, their boots thudding against the lab's concrete floor as they secured the facility. Armed operatives fanned out, sweeping every corner for hidden devices or threats. The Chrono-Field Generator's signature, still humming with residual energy from Robert Powell's recent departure, stood at the center of their attention.

A team of technicians, clad in tactical gear, began dismantling peripheral systems for transport. Cables were carefully disconnected, hard drives removed, and sensitive components packed into reinforced cases. Every piece of equipment was cataloged and tagged under General Andrews' orders to ensure nothing was left behind.

Richard Alders, restrained in a corner of the room under heavy guard, watched the scene unfold with a mix of dread and determination. His mind raced as he replayed the encryption process he had completed just moments before the breach. Had he missed anything? Was there a single program or file left vulnerable to their probing? He clenched his fists, his heart pounding as he saw the operatives handling the machinery that had consumed years of his and Robert's lives.

The technicians turned their attention to the lab's servers, extracting data drives and connecting them to portable decryption units. Richard's stomach churned at the sight. He knew they would try to break through his algorithms—layers of encryption designed to reflect the complexity of time itself.

Robert Powell's journey through history was under way—a journey destined to ripple through time in ways none of them could predict.

Back at his Pentagon office, General Andrews began drafting contingencies for tracking Powell across temporal dimensions while consolidating control over his newfound power source. For now, though victory seemed within reach, shadows of uncertainty loomed large over what lay ahead.

The first contingency involved developing a system to monitor Powell's movements through time. Andrews had already tasked his clandestine operations team, led by the unflinching Agent Mitchell, with exploring methods of temporal surveillance. If Powell was using the Chrono-Field Generator to traverse history, they needed a way to track him.

"Agent Mitchell," Andrews had said during their last meeting, "we need eyes in every era he might visit. I don't care if it means deploying autonomous surveillance drones or using the Quantum Computer Artificial Intelligence Project we have been developing at Quantico—we must know where he is and what he's doing."

Mitchell had nodded curtly, already considering the logistics. The team had begun experimenting with quantum entangled particles that could act as temporal beacons. These particles would remain linked across time, allowing them to triangulate Powell's location whenever he activated the generator.

But there were risks. Deploying such technology into the past could leave traces that future historians—or worse, rival nations—might discover. Still, Andrews was willing to take that gamble. "We'll clean up the mess later," he had said dismissively.

If surveillance failed to contain Powell, Andrews knew they would need a more aggressive approach: temporal interdiction. The idea was simple in theory but staggeringly complex in execution—send nano robots back in time to locate and intercept Powell before he could complete his objectives.

This plan required precision. Any interference with Powell's actions would have to be carefully calibrated to avoid creating paradoxes or destabilizing the timeline entirely.

Andrews envisioned a specialized nano robotic force equipped with Micro-chrono-devices—versions similar of Powell's generator—capable of short-range temporal jumps.

These were miracles of science. Derived from Powell's M.I.T. Doctoral experiments, the Technology Intelligence Development Project had developed molecule size detectors that were successfully teleported to future and past events. Using quantum computer knowledge, they could 'travel' to many events in history in very little 'present time'.

"Think of it as tactical time travel," Andrews had explained to his advisors during a classified briefing. "We're not rewriting history; we're managing it."

To prepare for this contingency, Andrews ordered extensive training for his operatives in historical accuracy and cultural immersion. They would need to ensure that the nano robots would blend seamlessly into any era they entered, whether it was ancient Rome or the Cold War.

Andrews also considered the possibility that Powell might attempt to destroy the generator or render it unusable to prevent its exploitation. To counter this, he devised a plan for temporal containment—a strategy aimed at isolating Powell and his technology within a specific point in time.

The concept involved creating a "temporal quarantine zone," an area where time itself would be locked in stasis. Using advanced quantum field manipulation techniques developed by DARPA, Andrews hoped to trap Powell and the generator in a closed loop of time from which they could not escape.

"This is our last resort," Andrews had told Mitchell gravely. "If we can't control him—or if he becomes too dangerous— we'll seal him away forever."

Mitchell had raised an eyebrow but said nothing. He understood that such measures came with enormous risks; tampering with time on such a scale could have unforeseen consequences for the entire timeline.

To accomplish this, Andrews' team would have to locate Powell and the Chrono-field generator first. That was a daunting task in itself.

Despite his mistrust of Powell's principles, Andrews recognized that outright conflict might not be the best approach. As a contingency, he considered attempting to co-opt Powell through covert collaboration.

Once we locate him, we will establish contact. "We'll make him believe we're on his side," Andrews mused aloud during one late-night strategy session with Mitchell. "Offer him resources, support—whatever it takes to keep him close." If he made it to wherever and whenever he is, we will find him. Then, we will appeal to his altruism and sense of human benevolence.

The goal was not genuine partnership but manipulation. By gaining Powell's trust, they could monitor his actions more closely and potentially steer him toward objectives aligned with their interests.

Mitchell had been skeptical of this approach but agreed to explore it nonetheless. "Scientists like Powell are idealists," he had said dryly. "They want to believe they're doing the right thing. We just must convince him our way is right."

As Andrews finalized his plans late into the night, doubts gnawed at the edges of his resolve. Time travel was an uncharted frontier fraught with ethical dilemmas and existential risks. What if their actions created paradoxes that unraveled reality itself? What if Powell's warnings about unintended consequences proved true?

But Andrews dismissed these thoughts as weakness—a luxury he could not afford. The stakes were too high; America's dominance depended on securing control over this technology before anyone else could exploit it.

He extinguished his cigarette and leaned back in his chair, staring at the ceiling as if seeking answers from above. For all his confidence in his contingencies, one truth remained unshakable: Robert Powell was an enigma—a man whose intellect and morality made him both an asset and a threat.

Andrews knew that controlling such a man would be no easy task. But as he stared into the shadows of uncertainty that loomed over what lay ahead, one thing was clear: failure was not an option.

Unbeknownst to him, however, Robert Powell was already several steps ahead charting a course through history that would challenge everything Andrews thought he knew about power, control, and the nature of time itself.

Richard thought to himself, "I won't let our sacrifice be in vain, Robert," his fists clenched. The files, encrypted with algorithms as intricate as temporal currents, had become a digital fortress against intrusion.

Chapter 10: Whispers Of The Past

From childhood, Robert had always been captivated by the enigmatic life and extraordinary achievements of Nostradamus. The 16th-century seer's ability to predict the future with astonishing precision had been a constant source of intrigue for him. He delved into Nostradamus' quatrains, fascinated by the poetic verses that seemed to reveal glimpses of events yet to unfold. The question lingered in Robert's mind like a persistent echo: How could a man from centuries past possess such extraordinary foresight? The intricacies of Nostradamus's predictions, shrouded in cryptic language, fueled his curiosity, prompting him to embark on a journey of exploration and discovery.

As Robert examined Nostradamus's life, he sought to unravel the layers of mystique surrounding the seer. What inspired this Renaissance figure to gaze into the fabric of time and paint vivid images of the future? The connection between Robert and Nostradamus, separated by the vast expanse of history, became a bridge that transcended the boundaries of centuries, as if two minds were intricately linked in the quest to unlock the hidden secrets in the tapestry of time.

He hesitated for a moment; eyes fixed on the screen. The anticipation, the weight of responsibility, and echoes of Robert's sacrifice resonated throughout the laboratory.

He replayed in his mind how this had begun. With a decisive strike, Robert had initiated the sequence, and the Chrono-Field Generator had become alive. The laboratory, bathed in the subtle glow of temporal energy, underwent a transformation. The very fabric of reality seemed to ripple as the time machine capsule began its journey into the past. Richard, a silent observer of the temporal shift, knew that their legacy was now intertwined with the annals of history. Inside the Chrono-Field Generator, Robert Powell had experienced a phenomenon that defied ordinary perception. As the machine initiated its temporal displacement sequence, the capsule became enveloped in a shimmering field of quantum energy. The hum of the generator intensified, resonating with a frequency that seemed to vibrate through his very being.

The air inside the capsule grew dense, as if time itself were compressing around him. This was not merely a journey through space—it was a traversal of the very fabric of reality.

The journey was governed by principles derived from Robert's doctoral research on quantum teleportation and space-time curvature. During his PhD years, Robert had conducted groundbreaking experiments on the manipulation of quantum entanglement to achieve instantaneous transfer of information across spatial distances. He had theorized that by extending these principles to the macro scale and combining them with Einstein's equations on space-time curvature, it would be possible to create a stable conduit through time. This conduit relied on bending the fabric of space-time into a closed time like curve, effectively linking two points in history.

As the Chrono-Field Generator activated, it manipulated gravitational and quantum forces to create this curve. The capsule became a self-contained bubble within the warped space-time continuum, shielded from external influences. Robert observed faint distortions in his surroundings—light bending unnaturally, colors shifting into hues he had never seen before. These were manifestations of what he had once described in his research as "quantum foam," the chaotic fluctuations at the Planck scale where classical physics broke down.

Within this bubble, time ceased to flow linearly. Seconds stretched into what felt like minutes, while other moments seemed to collapse into an instant. Robert's instruments displayed erratic readings: gravitational fields spiked and ebbed unpredictably, and temporal coordinates flickered as if struggling to stabilize.

This was consistent with his earlier simulations, which predicted that traveling through a warped space-time conduit would temporarily disrupt local chronons—the theoretical "time particles" he had studied extensively

The sensation of movement was unlike anything Robert had ever experienced. It was not physical motion but rather a shift in existence itself. He felt as though he were both stationary and hurtling forward at unimaginable speeds simultaneously—a paradox explained by the duality of quantum mechanics and relativity at play within the generator.

Robert's thoughts drifted to his early experiments with tele-transportation during his PhD candidacy. Back then, he had successfully demonstrated the transfer of simple atomic structures across short distances using entangled particle pairs as carriers. Those experiments had laid the foundation for understanding how information—and eventually matter—could be transmitted without traversing intervening space. Now, years later, those principles were being applied on an unprecedented scale: not just across space but through time itself.

As the capsule neared its destination, Robert noticed a gradual stabilization of his instruments. The chaotic quantum fluctuations began to subside, replaced by a steady hum that signaled the convergence of temporal coordinates. Outside the capsule's window, faint images of medieval France began to materialize—a patchwork of fields and forests bathed in twilight.

Despite the awe-inspiring nature of his journey, Robert remained acutely aware of its stakes. The Chrono-Field Generator represented not just scientific achievement but also immense power—power that could reshape history or destroy it entirely if misused. As he prepared for arrival, he resolved to honor the sacrifices made to safeguard this technology and ensure it would never fall into the wrong hands.

The capsule slowed its descent through time, and with a final pulse of energy, it came to rest in 1519 near Salon-de-Provence. The hum subsided, leaving only silence—a silence heavy with both triumph and uncertainty about what lay ahead in this uncharted chapter of human history.

Now, in the past, the time machine capsule materialized in a field near Salon-de-Provence. The hum of temporal displacement echoed across the serene expanse, and as the energy dissipated, Robert found himself at the crossroads of history.

Inside the sleek, elliptical capsule of the time machine, Robert Powell worked with steady precision. The hum of the Chrono-Field Generator filled the confined space, a low, resonant sound that seemed to vibrate through his very bones. The capsule was a masterpiece of engineering, its interior a symphony of cutting-edge technology and ergonomic design. But today, Robert's focus was on one specific system: the cloaking mechanism—a critical feature designed to render the time machine undetectable.

The capsule's invisibility shield was not a mere afterthought; it was a necessity. Robert had always known that traveling through time carried risks beyond the scientific challenges. The possibility of being seen by people in the past or present could lead to catastrophic consequences—paradoxes, disruptions in causality, or even exposure to hostile forces in his own timeline. To mitigate these risks, he had designed an advanced cloaking system that combined quantum mechanics, light manipulation, and electromagnetic field distortion.

At the heart of the cloaking system was a specialized array of quantum light-bending modules embedded into the capsule's outer shell. These modules were connected to a central control unit located on the main console inside the capsule. The modules worked by manipulating photons in real-time, bending light around the capsule to create the illusion of invisibility. To an outside observer—or even sophisticated detection equipment—the capsule would appear as nothing more than empty space.

Robert activated the system from a holographic display on the console. His fingers moved deftly over the interface, inputting commands and calibrating parameters with practiced ease. The display projected a three-dimensional model of the capsule surrounded by a shimmering field of energy—the visual representation of the cloaking mechanism at work.

"Initializing photon redirection matrix," Robert murmured to himself as he tapped another command. The modules on the capsule's exterior began to emit faint pulses of energy, their synchronized operation creating a seamless distortion field.

The system relied on advanced algorithms to analyze incoming light and electromagnetic waves from every angle. By calculating their trajectories in nanoseconds, the modules redirected these waves around the capsule, effectively making it invisible to both human eyes and electronic sensors. The process was so precise that even thermal imaging systems would detect nothing but ambient background radiation.

A key component of the cloaking mechanism was its use of quantum entanglement. Each module contained entangled particles that communicated instantaneously with one another, regardless of distance. This allowed the system to maintain perfect synchronization across all modules, ensuring that no gaps or distortions appeared in the cloaking field.

The entangled particles also served another purpose: they acted as sensors, detecting any changes in environmental conditions that might compromise the cloak's effectiveness. If someone attempted to scan for anomalies or if unexpected atmospheric conditions arose—such as heavy fog or electromagnetic interference—the system would automatically adjust its parameters to compensate.

In addition to bending light, the cloaking mechanism employed an electromagnetic field distortion generator housed beneath the capsule's floor panels. This generator emitted low-frequency electromagnetic waves that disrupted radar and sonar signals. Any attempt to detect the capsule using conventional methods would yield false readings—an empty blip on a radar screen or silence on a sonar display.

Robert checked the generator's output levels on another holographic display. The readings were stable, but he adjusted them slightly to account for fluctuations in Earth's magnetic field—a variable that could vary depending on his temporal destination.

"Field distortion at optimal levels," he noted aloud before turning his attention back to the main console.

The entire cloaking system was overseen by an artificial intelligence program integrated into the capsule's operating system. The AI monitored all aspects of the cloak's performance in real-time and could make split-second adjustments as needed. It also analyzed potential threats—such as nearby aircraft or surveillance drones—and adapted the cloak accordingly.

"Ai status?" Robert asked aloud.

A soft voice emanated from the console speakers: "Cloaking mechanism operating at 99.8% efficiency. All systems nominal."

Satisfied with this response, Robert leaned back slightly in his chair and exhaled slowly. The cloaking mechanism was one of his proudest achievements—a testament to what humanity could accomplish when science and imagination worked in harmony.

As he sat there, watching streams of data flow across the holographic displays, Robert reflected on why this system mattered so much. It wasn't just about avoiding detection; it was about preserving history itself. If someone in 18th-century London or 1st-century Rome spotted an otherworldly machine materializing out of thin air, it could alter their perception of reality—and by extension, history—in ways he couldn't predict or control.

Then there were modern threats: governments like General Andrews' team back at the Pentagon would stop at nothing to seize control of this technology if they discovered its location during a temporal jump. The cloak wasn't just protection against curious eyes from centuries past—it was a shield against those who sought power at any cost.

Robert glanced at one final diagnostic readout before initiating a full-system test. The capsule vibrated slightly as energy coursed through its circuits, powering up every subsystem simultaneously.

Onscreen, a simulation showed how the cloaking mechanism would perform under various conditions—bright sunlight, dense urban environments, even high-altitude storms. "Perfect," Robert said quietly as he reviewed the results.

As reality warped around him and colors blurred into incomprehensible shapes, he felt a familiar rush of anticipation mixed with apprehension. Moments later, he checked his external cameras and saw nothing but trees and sky reflected back at him—a perfect illusion created by his cloak.

For now, his invention was safe. Hidden. Not just across time, but also from those who might misuse it. However, Robert knew this was only one step in a much larger journey—a journey where invisibility might be his greatest weapon against forces he could not yet fully understand.

The field, bathed in the gentle light of dawn, stretched before him. Distant hills, adorned with the vibrant colors of spring, whispered stories of centuries past. The air, fragrant with blooming flowers, carried echoes of a world waiting to be rediscovered. Inside the capsule, Robert changed into attire meticulously prepared for this journey into the unknown.

He donned simple garments reflective of 16th-century France—worn fabric chosen for its ability to blend seamlessly into the historical tapestry. His clothing bore the authenticity of the era, complete with intricate embroidery and accessories that mirrored the fashion sensibilities of Provence in the 1500s.

To further enhance his integration, Robert carried a satchel filled with carefully curated items. Among them was an intricately designed leather-bound journal with aged, weathered pages containing notes on local customs and language to help him navigate social intricacies. A quill and inkwell accompanied the journal, lending authenticity to his scholarly persona.

The satchel also contained coins from the period to facilitate transactions without arousing suspicion. A small vial of locally sourced perfume added a sensory dimension, immersing him in the olfactory nuances of 16th-century Provence. These items became his temporal toolkit, enabling him not only to observe but also to participate in the vibrant life of the past.

Robert Powell had always known where he wanted to go if circumstances forced him to take the time machine and disappear. Long before he and Richard had their tense conversation on the bridge by Boston Harbor, Robert had been preparing for this possibility. He understood that stepping into another era required more than just a time machine—it demanded meticulous planning, historical knowledge, and practical tools for survival.

The "go bag" he had assembled was a product of years of research and foresight. It was compact yet comprehensive, containing everything he would need to blend into 16th-century France without drawing undue attention. Each item was chosen with care, reflecting his deep understanding of both history and human behavior.

Robert's garments were not hastily thrown together; they were the result of careful study and collaboration with experts in historical costuming. During his time at MIT, Robert had cultivated relationships with reenactors and costume historians who specialized in creating authentic period attire. Through these connections, he obtained clothing that adhered to the styles and materials of 16th-century France.

The outfit included a linen chemise as an underlayer, a woolen doublet with padded shoulders for warmth and style, and breeches made from sturdy fabric appropriate for a middle-class scholar or merchant. The ensemble was completed with leather boots, a felt cap, and a cloak lined with simple embroidery—a touch that suggested modest refinement without signaling wealth.

To ensure authenticity, Robert also consulted historical sources such as paintings, fashion plates, and texts describing daily life in Renaissance France. He even practiced wearing the garments in private to familiarize himself with their weight and movement.

One of Robert's most significant challenges was acquiring coins and artifacts that would pass scrutiny in 16th-century Provence. Modern currency or poorly made replicas could easily expose him as an outsider. To address this, Robert turned to reputable dealers who specialized in historical artifacts.

He sourced coins like the écu d'or and teston, which were commonly used in France during the Renaissance. These coins were authenticated by numismatists to ensure their accuracy in weight, design, and composition.

Robert also included small trinkets such as a wooden rosary, a brass compass (a rare but plausible possession for a scholar), and a simple leather pouch for carrying them.

To avoid suspicion about their pristine condition, Robert carefully aged these items using techniques learned from conservators—subtle scuffing on coins and slight wear on leather straps gave them the appearance of having been used over time.

Robert knew that surviving in another era required more than just blending in physically; he needed a convincing backstory. His journal became central to this effort. Inside its weathered pages were notes written in French using period-appropriate penmanship—a skill he had practiced extensively.

The journal contained observations on local customs, key phrases in Provençal dialects, and sketches of landmarks he might encounter. It also included fabricated literature establishing him as an itinerant scholar traveling through Provence to study its culture and natural history.

This scholarly persona gave him plausible reasons to ask questions or visit unfamiliar places without arousing suspicion. It also allowed him to carry tools like quills, ink, and parchment without standing out—they were essential instruments for someone in his supposed profession.

Beyond clothing and artifacts, Robert's go bag included practical supplies for survival and adaptability. Drawing inspiration from modern survival kits—often referred to as bug-out bags—he packed items that could serve multiple purposes while remaining inconspicuous.

A small tin containing herbs commonly used for medicinal purposes during the Renaissance (such as lavender for wounds or chamomile for calming) was tucked into his bag. Hidden within this tin were modern antibiotics concealed in wax-paper wrappers designed to look like herbal remedies. Dried fruits, nuts, and hard biscuits supplemented his provisions until he could acquire food locally.

A small knife with a bone handle served both practical needs (such as cutting rope) and social ones (it was common for men of his station to carry such tools). A flint-and-steel fire starter was another essential item disguised as period-appropriate equipment.

Much of Robert's preparation was made possible by MIT's extensive resources. The university's libraries provided access to rare manuscripts detailing life in Renaissance France, while its connections with museums allowed him to study authentic artifacts up close.

Robert also collaborated with colleagues specializing in archaeology and anthropology to refine his understanding of material culture from the period. Their insights helped him anticipate challenges he might face—such as how to barter effectively or avoid offending local customs—and prepare accordingly.

Before leaving his apartment for what might be the last time, Robert carefully reviewed every item in his go bag one final time. Each piece represented months—or even years—of preparation: garments tailored to historical accuracy; coins polished but not pristine; tools selected for their utility and plausibility.

As he zipped up the bag and slung it over his shoulder, Robert felt a mixture of anxiety and resolve. He knew that once he stepped into the time machine, there would be no turning back. Every detail mattered; every choice could mean the difference between success and failure.

After activating the concealment mechanism on the time machine to ensure it remained hidden from prying eyes, Robert felt a mix of anticipation and fear. His decision to plunge into an era he could never return from was both a sacrifice and an opportunity: an opportunity to safeguard his work's legacy and protect it from temporal manipulation. Now camouflaged within its surroundings, the time machine stood as a silent sentinel in the field. The hills, fields, and distant villages remained untouched by its enigmatic presence.

Emerging into the morning light, Robert felt the gentle caress of a breeze carrying with it the weight of history. The covert time machine blended seamlessly with its surroundings like a mirage. As he surveyed his environment, he realized he had become a silent observer in a world beyond time's currents.

Meanwhile, back in his laboratory far into the future, banks of computers encrypted files and recorded data from Robert's temporal shift with relentless vigilance. The responsibility for protecting their shared legacy weighed heavily on Richard Alders' shoulders as he prepared for relocation under General Andrews' orders. The looming threat of government interests exploiting their work remained ever-present.

The encrypted files—guarded by layers of sophisticated digital security—stood as a fortress against external intrusion. Committed to his promise to Robert, Richard resolved to protect their work at all costs.

Chapter 11: Salon-de-Provence

The cobblestone streets of Salon-de-Provence echoed with the muffled sounds of everyday life. The town, nestled against the backdrop of rolling hills and embraced by the warmth of the Provençal sun, was a canvas of rustic charm and simplicity. With a population of around 1,500 souls, it thrived in a world untouched by the relentless march of time. Robert—now adopting the persona of Michel— entered the town with the casual gait of a local. His attire, carefully chosen to match 16th-century fashion, allowed him to move seamlessly through the narrow alleyways and bustling market squares.

The air carried the fragrance of freshly baked bread mingled with the subtle scents of herbs and flowers adorning windowsills. As he wandered through the heart of the town, Michel observed locals going about their daily routines. Merchants sold their wares in open-air markets, their stalls adorned with colorful fabrics, spices, and handmade goods. Children played in the streets, their laughter blending with the distant hum of conversations. The church, a dominant presence in the town square, bore witness to the spiritual heartbeat of Salon-de-Provence. Its spire reached toward the sky, a symbol of unwavering faith anchoring the community.

Michel paused for a moment, contemplating the intricate architecture and tranquil serenity surrounding this sacred space. Continuing his exploration, he was drawn to a lively tavern on the north side of the square. The aroma of freshly made wine and beer wafted through the air as he entered. Locals gathered around wooden tables, engaging in animated conversations and laughter that resonated with the camaraderie of a tightly knit community.

Michel sat at a table and observed his surroundings with curiosity. The tavern keeper, a robust figure with a hearty laugh, served drinks with practiced efficiency.

Robert's French was passable—thanks to his mother's insistence that he master it as a child. Her parents, French immigrants who had arrived in the United States after World War I, had carried their language and culture with them like treasures from the old world. Growing up in a household where French was spoken daily, Robert's mother had inherited not only the language but also a deep reverence for her heritage. She passed that reverence on to her son, ensuring that he would never forget the roots that stretched across the Atlantic to Provence.

Robert's early exposure to French came in the form of bedtime stories. His mother would read to him from books she had brought from her parents' collection—tales of knights and castles, of bustling Parisian streets and quiet countryside villages. At first, young Robert struggled with the unfamiliar sounds and rhythms of the language, but his mother was patient. She would repeat phrases slowly, encouraging him to mimic her pronunciation until it felt natural. By the time he was six, Robert could hold conversations in French, much to his grandparents' delight.

As he grew older, his mother's lessons became more structured. She insisted that he study French grammar and vocabulary alongside his schoolwork, often quizzing him at the dinner table or during car rides. "You'll thank me one day," she would say whenever he complained about conjugating verbs or memorizing irregular forms. And she was right—though Robert didn't realize it at the time.

His fluency deepened during summer visits to his grandparents' home in New York City. They lived in a vibrant immigrant neighborhood where French-speaking neighbors gathered at cafés and bakeries reminiscent of those in their homeland. Robert spent hours listening to their conversations, picking up idioms and colloquialisms that textbooks couldn't teach. His grandfather, a retired tailor with a penchant for storytelling, would regale him with tales of life in Provence before the war, weaving history and culture into every anecdote.

By the time Robert reached high school, he was fluent enough to excel in advanced French classes. His teachers were impressed by his near-native accent and grasp of idiomatic expressions—skills that set him apart from his peers. But it wasn't just academic success that drove him; Robert had developed a genuine love for the language and its connection to his family's history.

At MIT, where he pursued his groundbreaking research on time travel, Robert's fluency in French became an unexpected asset. His studies often required him to delve into historical texts and documents written in Old French— a task that would have been daunting without his linguistic background. He also formed friendships with international colleagues who appreciated his ability to converse effortlessly in their native tongue.

When Robert began preparing for his journey into 16th-century France, he realized just how invaluable his mother's lessons had been. The ability to speak French fluently wasn't just a convenience; it was a lifeline—a way to navigate an unfamiliar world without drawing suspicion. He knew that even minor linguistic mistakes could betray him as an outsider, so he spent weeks refining his pronunciation and studying regional dialects specific to Provence during the Renaissance.

His preparation extended beyond language. Drawing on what he had learned from his grandparents and years of independent study, Robert immersed himself in the cultural nuances of 16th-century France. He memorized common greetings and gestures, practiced writing with quills on parchment, and familiarized himself with social hierarchies and etiquette.

He ordered a beer in fluent but slightly accented tones. As he sipped his drink, Michel studied his fellow patrons: weathered faces marked by sun and time exchanging stories that echoed through time-worn walls. In this medieval tapestry of life, Michel felt an unexpected sense of belonging. Immersing himself in 16th-century life had become his gateway to a world free from modern complexities.

The customs and way of life in Salon-de-Provence unfolded around him with timeless grace. Robert Powell walked the narrow, cobblestone streets of the town, his senses alive to the sights, sounds, and smells of a world both foreign and familiar. The honey-colored stone buildings, their shutters painted in soft pastels, reflected the Mediterranean sun, while the air carried the mingled scents of lavender, olive oil, and freshly baked bread. This was a place where history lived not in museums but in every corner of daily life.

As he approached the town square, the heart of Salon-de-Provence revealed itself in all its vibrancy. The square was alive with activity—a bustling market filled with merchants hawking their wares and townsfolk bartering for goods. Stalls overflowed with colorful produce: sun-ripened tomatoes, plump figs, and golden apricots that glistened in the light. Barrels of olives stood alongside wheels of pungent cheese and loaves of crusty bread dusted with flour. The sharp tang of vinegar mingled with the sweetness of honey as vendors offered samples to passersby.

In one corner of the square, a group of children played near the Fontaine Moussue, a moss-covered fountain that gurgled softly as water trickled from its spouts. Adults gathered nearby, some seated on wooden benches beneath the shade of trees, others standing in animated conversation. A street performer—a juggler dressed in vibrant patchwork—drew a small crowd as he tossed brightly colored balls into the air with practiced ease. Laughter rippled through the square as he performed an exaggerated bow after his act.

Robert lingered for a moment by a stall selling herbs and spices. Bundles of dried lavender hung from wooden beams alongside sprigs of rosemary and thyme. The merchant, a woman with weathered hands and a warm smile, greeted him in Provençal French. Her voice carried the lilting cadence of the region as she extolled the virtues of her wares. Robert responded carefully, his fluency allowing him to blend seamlessly into this world.

Leaving the square behind, he made his way toward the Church of Saint-Michel, its Romanesque architecture standing as a testament to centuries of faith and craftsmanship. The church's heavy wooden doors creaked open as Robert stepped inside, his footsteps echoing softly on the stone floor. The interior was cool and dimly lit, illuminated by shafts of sunlight streaming through stained-glass windows that depicted biblical scenes in vivid hues.

Robert paused before an alabaster statue of the Virgin Mary, its serene expression seeming to watch over all who entered. Nearby, votive candles flickered in their holders, casting dancing shadows on the walls. A priest moved quietly through the nave, his robes rustling softly as he attended to his duties. The scent of beeswax candles mingled with that of aged wood and incense lingering faintly in the air.

After offering a quiet moment of reflexional thought, Robert exited the church and continued his exploration. His path led him back to a market set up along one of Salon-de-Provence's winding streets. Here, artisans displayed their crafts—handwoven baskets, pottery glazed in earthy tones, and bolts of fabric dyed in rich colors.

One stall caught Robert's eye: a blacksmith demonstrating his trade. Sparks flew as he hammered glowing metal on an anvil, shaping it into tools and decorative pieces while onlookers watched with fascination. Next to him, a cobbler sat at his bench, stitching leather shoes with meticulous care.

The market was more than just a place for commerce; it was a social hub where townsfolk exchanged news and gossip as readily as they traded goods. Robert overheard snippets of conversation about local events—a wedding planned for next week, a dispute between neighbors over land boundaries—and even rumors about the weather they expected in the coming months.

As Robert moved through the market, he marveled at how seamlessly life here blended work and leisure. A baker offered samples of fougasse, a flatbread studded with olives or herbs; nearby, a vintner poured small cups of wine for potential buyers to taste. Musicians played lively tunes on lutes and flutes, their melodies weaving through the chatter like threads in a tapestry.

Everywhere he looked, Robert saw evidence of resilience and resourcefulness—qualities that had allowed this town to thrive despite the challenges of its time. From farmers selling their harvests to craftsmen plying their trades, each person contributed to the intricate web of community life.

As dusk began to fall over Salon-de-Provence, casting long shadows across its streets and squares, Robert found himself drawn back to the Fontaine Moussue. The fountain's moss-covered surface glowed softly in the fading light as townsfolk gathered around it once more—some filling jugs with water from its spouts, others simply enjoying its coolness after a long day.

For Robert Powell, this journey into 16th-century France was more than just an escape; it was an immersion into a world where history came alive in every detail. As he walked back toward the bar he had encountered earlier in the day, a sky painted with hues of pink and gold, he felt both humbled and inspired by what he had witnessed—a vibrant tapestry woven from countless lives across time.

As the day ended, Michel ventured beyond the village limits. The rolling hills called to him, adorned with vineyards and fields stretching toward the horizon. The scent of lavender wafted on a gentle breeze that whispered tales of Provençal beauty. It was here that Michel stumbled upon a modest farmhouse nestled among the hills. The air was filled with the symphony of crickets and the distant murmur of a stream. The farmhouse, with its weathered stone walls and tiled roof, radiated rustic tranquility.

Approaching the farmhouse, Michel saw a man tending to his fields. His hands—weathered and calloused from years of labor—worked with practiced precision. The man looked up from his tasks and met Michel's gaze with shrewd scrutiny. "Good day, stranger," he said in the lyrical tones of a Provençal accent. "What brings you to these parts?" Michel replied with practiced ease: "Greetings, kind sir. I have been traveling and have heard much about the hospitality of these lands. I seek nothing more than honest work and a place to rest my weary bones."

The farmer introduced himself as François and regarded Michel thoughtfully before replying: "Well, we always need an extra pair of hands here." He gestured toward his modest home. "If you're willing to work for your keep, you're welcome to stay."

Michel expressed his gratitude sincerely; their bond formed in that moment transcended words or elaborate introductions.

In the days that followed, Michel integrated into life on François's farm. The tasks were simple but demanding— tending crops, caring for livestock, and maintaining the property. Each day brought fulfillment as Michel embraced this visceral connection to land and labor—a stark contrast to his former life defined by technology and deadlines.

François shared fragments of his life during quiet moments: stories about generations who had tended these lands before him; reflections on seasonal cycles; and musings on Provençal resilience through history's trials. Michel listened intently—not just out of politeness but from genuine interest in immersing himself fully into this era.

As days passed, François began seeing Michel not merely as an extra set of hands but as an equal partner in rural life's symphony. Their growing camaraderie was tested one crisp morning when an unexpected crisis unfolded on François's farm—a challenge that would solidify their connection even further.

An unexpected, sudden storm, with winds carrying the scent of impending rain, threatened the harvest that François had toiled over for months. The lush fields of wheat, ready for reaping, stood vulnerable to the elements. Realizing the imminent threat, Michel sprang into action. With a shared sense of urgency, he and François raced against time to gather the crops and secure them in the barn.

As the rain poured down in relentless sheets, their efforts became a dance of synchronized movements amidst the rhythm of nature's percussion. Michel's modern knowledge of efficient farming practices, combined with François' deep understanding of the land, proved to be a formidable alliance. Together, they salvaged the harvest, ensuring that François' months of labor would not be lost to the tempest.

In the aftermath of the storm, as the sun broke through dissipating clouds, a mutual respect blossomed. François, his weathered face breaking into a rare smile, clasped Michel's shoulder in gratitude. The shared experience of overcoming adversity on the farm had woven a thread of trust between them, strengthening their bond beyond routine rural tasks. In that moment, amidst the glistening droplets on the harvested wheat, Michel became not just a temporary sojourner but an integral part of François' agricultural legacy.

The farmhouse, with its stone walls and weathered beams, became a sanctuary echoing with their shared laughter. One evening, as the sun sank below the horizon and cast a warm glow over the Provençal landscape, François invited Michel to share a meal with his family. The table, adorned with simple yet abundant dishes, became a gathering place where stories flowed as freely as the wine. Around it sat François' wife, Isabelle, and their children: Marie and Pierre. Their eyes—reflecting hues of the sunset—held the wisdom of generations rooted in the soil they cultivated.

Michel felt profound gratitude for their warmth and hospitality.

During dinner, he asked François if he knew anyone in the village versed in astrology, chemistry, or medicine. François replied in the negative: "The nearest doctor is more than two days' ride away," he explained. "In our village, we have only a healer."

Robert's heart quickened at the word healer. He leaned forward, his voice betraying a hint of urgency. "A healer? Who is this person? What do they practice?"

François shrugged nonchalantly. "She's a local woman—Marguerite. She knows herbs and remedies passed down through her family. People say she can cure ailments that even doctors can't."

Robert's excitement dimmed slightly at the mention of a woman healer. He had hoped to hear of Nostradamus, the famed apothecary and astrologer who had spent his final years in Salon-de-Provence. Still, the prospect of meeting someone with knowledge of Renaissance-era medicine intrigued him. Perhaps Marguerite could provide insights into the practices of the time—or even lead him to others with more specialized knowledge.

The next morning, Robert set off to find Marguerite's home, following François' directions through winding cobblestone streets lined with modest stone houses. The scent of lavender and rosemary wafted from small gardens as he passed, mingling with the earthy aroma of freshly tilled soil. When he arrived at her cottage on the outskirts of the village, he was greeted by a scene that seemed plucked from a pastoral painting. Marguerite stood outside, tending to rows of herbs planted in neat beds. She was middle-aged, her face weathered but kind, and her hands moved deftly as she clipped sprigs of thyme and sage.

Robert hesitated for a moment before approaching. "Madame Marguerite?" he asked in careful French.

She looked up, her expression curious but welcoming. "Yes? How can I help you?"

"I've heard of your skills as a healer," Robert began, choosing his words carefully. "I'm... a traveler with an interest in medicine and natural remedies. I was hoping to learn from you."

Marguerite studied him for a moment, her sharp eyes seeming to weigh his sincerity. Finally, she nodded and gestured for him to follow her inside.

Her cottage was small but orderly, its shelves lined with jars containing dried herbs and powders. A mortar and pestle sat on the wooden table alongside bundles of lavender tied with twine. The air was thick with the scent of chamomile and mint.

As Marguerite began explaining her methods—how she used poultices for wounds and teas for fevers—Robert listened intently, taking mental notes. Though disappointed that she wasn't Nostradamus himself, he couldn't deny her expertise or the value of her practical knowledge.

In that humble cottage, surrounded by the tools of her trade, Robert realized that history wasn't just shaped by famous figures like Nostradamus—it was also carried forward by everyday people like Marguerite, whose quiet work sustained their communities through times of need.

Michel wondered if he had chosen the wrong village but remained convinced that Michel de Nostradamus had lived somewhere nearby in medieval France.

Determined to uncover the truth, Michel decided to broaden his search to nearby villages. Over several days, he traversed rustic landscapes seeking local healers and wise folk who might possess skills attributed to Nostradamus. The quaint villages—with their thatched roofs and cobblestone streets—proved hospitable but yielded no trace of the legendary figure he sought.

Michel's quest became a pilgrimage through time and space. He listened to tales spun by village elders, sought counsel from herbalists, and consulted those known for their celestial knowledge. Yet no one seemed to match Nostradamus' enigmatic expertise in astrology, chemistry, and medicine. Michel's journey began in Saint-Martin-de-la-Brasque, a small village nestled in a valley surrounded by cultivated lands and dense forests. The villagers greeted him warmly, curious about the stranger who asked so many questions about healers and apothecaries. In the town square, bustling with activity, Michel approached an elderly man selling bundles of dried herbs. The man claimed to know of a healer who lived deep in the woods but warned Michel that she was as likely to curse as she was to cure.

Following the old man's directions, Michel ventured into the forest, only to find an abandoned hut overrun with ivy and moss. Disappointed but undeterred, he returned to Saint-Martin-de-la-Brasque and spent the evening at a local inn, sharing stories with farmers and craftsmen over bowls of hearty stew. Though they had little knowledge of healers, they spoke of their struggles with illness and their reliance on simple remedies—lavender for headaches, mint for stomachaches—passed down through generations.

The next day, Michel traveled to Simiane-la-Rotonde, a picturesque hilltop village known for its architecture and vibrant market. As he climbed the winding cobblestone streets toward the village square, he marveled at the honey-colored stone houses adorned with wrought-iron balconies and colorful shutters. At the market, he encountered a woman selling jars of honey infused with herbs. She claimed her remedies could cure anything from colds to broken hearts.

"Do you know of any healers who practice medicine or astrology?" Michel asked her in careful French.

The woman shook her head but pointed him toward a chapel at the edge of the village. "The priest there is said to have knowledge of healing prayers," she said. "Perhaps he can help."

Michel visited the chapel but found only a young acolyte sweeping its stone floors. The priest had left for another village days ago, the acolyte explained apologetically. Frustrated but polite, Michel thanked him and continued his search.

In Digne-les-Bains, renowned for its mineral-rich springs believed to have healing properties, Michel found hope renewed. The lavender fields surrounding the village stretched endlessly under the bright sun, their fragrance carried on a gentle breeze. He stopped at an outdoor café near the springs where locals gathered to drink water said to cure rheumatism and asthma.

Here, Michel overheard a conversation between two men discussing a healer who lived in Banon, another nearby village. "She's not like most healers," one man said. "She doesn't just use herbs—she reads the stars too."

Intrigued, Michel pressed them for details and set off for Banon that afternoon. The journey took him through rolling hills dotted with olive groves and vineyards until he reached another charming village perched on a rocky plateau. Banon's narrow streets were lined with shops selling artisanal cheeses and handmade crafts.

Michel followed directions to a small house on the outskirts of the village where he was told the healer lived. When he knocked on the door, it creaked open to reveal an elderly woman with sharp eyes and a knowing smile.

"You've come far," she said without introduction.

Michel hesitated before responding. "I'm searching for someone—a healer or astrologer who might understand… unusual remedies."

The woman invited him inside, her home filled with jars of dried herbs and books written in Latin and Provençal French. She spoke candidly about her work as a healer but admitted she knew little of astrology or alchemy.

"Your best chance is Salon-de-Provence," she said finally. "There's talk of a man—a doctor or apothecary—who has not yet flourished in his craft. He is to have knowledge beyond what most can comprehend."

Though it wasn't much to go on, Michel felt his spirits lift at her words. He thanked her sincerely before leaving Banon with questions in his mind about what he had just heard 'a doctor or apothecary—who has not yet flourished in his craft.'

Along his journey back toward Salon-de-Provence, Michel passed through Ménerbes—a quiet village perched along a ridge overlooking verdant countryside. Here he encountered an artist painting scenes of daily life: women washing clothes at a fountain; children chasing each other through narrow alleys; farmers tending their fields in the distance.

The artist paused his work when Michel approached and asked if he knew anything about healers or astrologers in Provence.

"I've heard whispers," the artist said thoughtfully as he wiped his brush clean. "But whispers are all they are."

Despite this cryptic response, Michel found comfort in the beauty around him—the timeless rhythm of life unfolding in these villages untouched by modernity.

As he neared Salon-de-Provence once more, Michel reflected on what he had learned—not just about healers but about humanity itself: resilience amid hardship; kindness offered freely; stories shared around firesides that connected people across time.

Though Nostradamus remained elusive for now, Michel felt certain his journey was far from over—and that every step brought him closer not only to answers but also to understanding what it truly meant to live within history's embrace.

The villagers he encountered were wise and skilled in their own ways but lacked Nostradamus' distinct blend of disciplines. The threads of time seemed to resist his attempts at weaving them into his envisioned narrative.

As days turned into weeks on François' farm, Michel found solace in rural life's routines. The harvest brought celebration—a testament to nature's generosity—and strengthened bonds between him and François' family.

Their connection became an enduring example of human warmth unburdened by modern complexities.

On quiet nights by the hearth light or beneath the skies painted with stars' brilliance, Michel reflected on choices that led him here: sacrificing his time for immersion into history; becoming part of humanity's essence rather than merely observing it.

Though uncertain about Nostradamus' whereabouts—or even existence—Michel resolved to continue searching while embracing life among Salon-de-Provence's people.

Doubt began to creep into Michel's mind. Had he misinterpreted the temporal threads? Was his childhood theory, nurtured by fascination and awe, merely a whimsical dream? Had time shifted as he made the trek to this specific moment and place? The absence of someone resembling Nostradamus challenged his belief's foundation. In quiet moments of reflection beneath starry skies or beside crackling hearths in humble homes, Michel pondered his journey's implications.

The villagers he encountered, while wise and skilled in their own right, lacked the distinct blend of astrology, chemistry, and medicine that had characterized Nostradamus' legendary abilities. The threads of time seemed to resist his attempts to weave them into the narrative he had envisioned. As the sun dipped below the horizon, casting long shadows over the medieval landscapes, Michel found himself at a crossroads. The search for a healer resembling Nostradamus had brought him to the brink of uncertainty. Yet, a resilient spark within him urged him to continue the quest—to unravel the mysteries that bound his present to echoes of the past. The quest for Nostradamus persisted, with time itself guiding Michel through an intricate tapestry of history.

The seasons passed, and Michel became an indispensable presence on François's farm. The harvest—a celebration of nature's generosity—brought a sense of achievement and shared joy. The bond between Michel and François' family became a testament to the enduring power of human connection, free from the complexities of the time Michel had left behind. On quiet nights, as he sat by the hearth, Michel reflected on the choices that had brought him to this moment. The sacrifice of his own time and immersion in a world untouched by modernity had become a pilgrimage to humanity's essence.

The simplicity of life in Salon-de-Provence, the genuine warmth of its people, and the lasting bonds forged in shared labor became threads that wove the fabric of Michel's existence.

Robert, blending carefully with the locals under his assumed identity, wandered through the narrow streets of the village. Weeks rolled by as he navigated life in 16th-century France. He interacted with locals, observed customs and traditions, and became a spectral presence in an era where his very existence defied natural order. The landscape changed with each passing day: seasons shifted, people lived their lives, and centuries unfolded in a tapestry of human experience. Immersing himself in the culture and events of this time, Robert became a silent observer of moments that would shape history.

Around him, the Renaissance unfolded—a period of intellectual and artistic flourishing. Political intrigues, cultural advancements, and daily life in 16th-century France became the backdrop to Robert's temporary sojourn.

Immersed in 16th-century life, Robert began to feel an overwhelming sense of loneliness. The people he encountered and events he witnessed became threads in a vast tapestry stretching across centuries. Sacrificing his own time for ethical innovation had become both his burden and legacy.

Meanwhile, back in the laboratory, Richard worked under direct orders from General Andrews' office. He had received no signal from Robert, and the encrypted files remained secure. The time machine—covertly hidden—stood as a silent testament to the sacrifices made in pursuit of ethical innovation.

Months passed as Richard monitored the encrypted data while feigning progress on reconstructing Robert's algorithms under military pressure. The weight of safeguarding their shared vision became his constant companion, aging him alongside his responsibilities. The encrypted files—repositories of temporal secrets—were testaments to their commitment to ethical resolution. Under General Andrews' directive, Richard delicately balanced feigned compliance with covert resistance, emphasizing the complexity of Robert's code while deliberately impeding reconstruction efforts.

With calculated frustration, Richard conveyed how intricate Robert's temporal algorithms were—a shield against unauthorized reconstruction that masked his deeper loyalty to their shared ideals. His obfuscation became both a sword and a shield: thwarting military ambitions without arousing suspicion.

Navigating these intricacies required precision; Richard knew their work's legacy depended on maintaining this delicate balance between duty and ethics. The Chrono-Field Generator tracking program remained inactive, a silent defiance against exploitation.

Outside, the Boston harbor, with its ships and seagulls, continued to dance with the tides, unaware of the echoes of sacrifice and innovation lingering in the silent halls of history. And so, the journey through time unfolded—a story etched into the tapestry of history, carried by temporal currents and guarded by a silent custodian of ethical innovation.

In the field near Salon-de-Provence, the covert time machine stood alone. The hills, fields, and village seemed unchanged by the passage of time. Robert and Richard's legacy, transmitted through the currents of history, resonated across the centuries.

As the months unfolded like the petals of a lavender flower, Michel found solace in the routines of rural life. The Provençal landscape, with its vineyards and olive groves, became a sanctuary where past and present coexisted in a harmonious dance. In moments of tranquility beneath a starry sky, Michel reflected on the legacy he had left behind.

The encrypted files from the laboratory, guarded by Richard with unwavering determination, held the key to their shared vision. The government's interest, once a sinister shadow, remained at bay, allowing their legacy of ethical innovation to endure.

By now, Michel had renovated the small storage shed that Francois had gifted him. It was now a fully functional small home near the main farmhouse. With its weathered beams and sturdy walls, the small hand-built house bore witness to Michel's journey through time. The laughter of François's grandchildren playing in the fields echoed with whispers of a past that had become a canvas upon which Michel painted strokes of his own existence.

And so, in Salon-de-Provence—where cobbled streets bore witness to the tranquil passage of time—Michel lived a life that defied the constraints of temporal understanding. The Provençal sun, with its warm embrace, cast long shadows over the hills as Michel, now an integral part of a world untouched by the relentless march of time, continued his journey through the annals of history.

Chapter 12: Life in Provençe

The covert time machine, hidden in the countryside near Francois' farm, stood as a silent sentinel in the tapestry of history. Michel, once Robert Powell but now fully immersed in the identity of a 16th-century laborer, approached the capsule with a mix of awe and acceptance. As he performed the anti-concealment procedure, temporal energies dissipated, revealing the familiar contours of the time machine. The hum of the Chrono Field Generator resonated across the quiet expanse, echoing through the hills as if recognizing the convergence of past and future within its metallic embrace.

The decision to enter the time capsule—to attempt communication with Richard in the future—hung in the air like a question mark. Michel, now an involuntary resident of the corridors of time, carried the weight of every choice that had brought him to this moment. With a steadying breath, he stepped inside. The interior, bathed in a soft glow of temporal energy, felt both familiar and otherworldly. The control panel, adorned with buttons and switches hinting at the complexities of time manipulation, awaited his command. Michel's fingers danced over the controls as he sought to establish a connection with the future.

The tablet, laden with 21st-century knowledge, became his conduit—a fragile bridge between past and future. He configured the temporal interface and sent signals into the quantum fabric of time, but only an unsettling silence responded. Understanding gripped him like a heavy shroud: communication with the future was impossible.

The isolation of the 16th century—its relentless temporal boundaries—cast Michel adrift in a sea of uncertainty. "Richard," he whispered, his voice heavy with resignation. "If you can hear me, you must know that I've tried. But it seems the currents of time have carried me beyond reach."

The silence inside the capsule mirrored Michel's growing loneliness. The time machine, with all its enigmatic potential, had trapped him in an era far removed from the familiar world he once knew. A decision crystallized within him: Michel could no longer linger in limbo between two worlds.

His only link to the future—the tablet—was both a lifeline and a burden. It held a repository of advancements, historical events, and modern complexities that would serve as his compass in this uncharted territory.

Michel's tablet was a masterpiece of 21st-century ingenuity, a device that encapsulated the pinnacle of human technological achievement. Sleek and lightweight, it was deceptively simple in appearance, yet its capabilities were nothing short of extraordinary. Its unbreakable screen, forged from advanced nano materials, could withstand impacts and scratches that would render ordinary devices useless. This durability made it a perfect companion for Michel as he navigated the rugged realities of 16th-century life.

The tablet's power source was equally revolutionary. Equipped with an unlimited battery capacity, it harnessed energy from sunlight or even dim daylight, ensuring it remained operational in any environment. A few minutes of exposure to natural light could sustain it for weeks, making it an unfailing lifeline in a world devoid of modern electricity.

Perhaps its most remarkable feature was its adaptive security system. Programmed exclusively for Michel as the administrator, the tablet's screen was visible only to him. If it detected another face through its advanced facial recognition software, it would instantly transform into a simple mirror, reflecting nothing more than the curious onlooker's image. This ingenious safeguard ensured that its treasure trove of knowledge—spanning science, history, art, and technology—remained hidden from prying eyes.

To Michel, the tablet was more than a tool; it was a bridge between eras, a silent witness to humanity's progress. In the solitude of his journey through time, it became his confidant and compass, a beacon of the future nestled discreetly in a past that could never comprehend its marvels.

Michel surveyed his surroundings within the capsule. Designed for temporal exploration, it had now become a cocoon for decisions that would shape his existence. He knew he couldn't carry all of 21st-century knowledge with him into this simpler age, yet he couldn't abandon it entirely either. The tablet represented a fragile thread connecting him to his former life.

Carefully concealing it within his clothing—fabric chosen to blend seamlessly with rustic 16th-century attire—Michel ensured its safety. The tablet became his secret companion: a beacon of knowledge hidden from prying eyes. As he emerged from the time capsule, weighed down by his circumstances, he reactivated its camouflage mechanism. Once again hidden from view, the metallic container vanished into obscurity.

The hills, fields, and nearby village remained oblivious to the enigma nestled in their midst. Carrying echoes of the future within his attire's folds, Michel resolved to embark on a journey entirely his own.

The Provençal landscape—with its vineyards and olive groves—became both backdrop and sanctuary for his pilgrimage through time. Navigating 16th-century life with newfound purpose, Michel found solace in small moments: tending fields alongside François's family or observing townspeople's simple yet profound lives.

The tablet remained hidden but ever-present—a source of comfort and connection to what he had left behind. Under cover of night or in moments of solitude away from watchful eyes, Michel would retrieve it. Its screen glowed softly under moonlight as it became a portal to knowledge transcending temporal confines: words and images from another era offering both solace and nostalgia.

Yet each passing day heightened Michel's awareness of discretion's necessity. To Salon-de-Provence's people, unaware of its origin or significance, such an object could disrupt their delicate world balance. Burdened by this responsibility, Michel vowed to protect its secrets at all costs.

The farm where Michel found refuge remained a sanctuary amid his journey through time. François and his family— blissfully unaware of their guest's enigmatic burden— embraced him as one of their own. For them, Michel had become far more than an industrious laborer. Michele was now an integral part of their lives.

Seasons changed, crops flourished and faded, and family bonds deepened in the steady rhythm of rural life. Over the months, Michel aged quietly in the shadow of Salon-de-Provence. The tablet, now a relic of a distant future, remained carefully concealed.

The Provençal landscape, with its timeless beauty, seemed to cradle Michel in an existence that transcended the relentless march of time. Amid the tranquility of the farm, surrounded by the love and camaraderie of François's family, Michel found a semblance of peace.

The once turbulent and unyielding temporal currents had softened into a gentle stream, carrying him through the ebb and flow of history.

The tablet, hidden yet ever-present, became a symbol of his enduring connection to both past and future. As its guardian, Michel carried the weight of knowledge that tethered him to the world he had left behind. His life now resonated with the daily events of the French Renaissance.

And so, in Salon-de-Provence—where cobblestone streets bore silent witness to the quiet passage of years—Michel lived out his days. The Provençal sun, casting its golden glow over rolling hills and vineyards, stood as a testament to the resilience of the human spirit in the face of uncertainty. The echoes of the future, tucked away within the folds of Michel's attire, remained silent witnesses to a journey that defied the boundaries of temporal understanding.

It was during one of these serene afternoons, as he sat beneath the shade of an olive tree overlooking the countryside, that Michel decided he needed to document his experiences.

The thought had lingered in his mind for weeks—a quiet urge to record not only the details of his life in 16th-century France but also the emotions and reflections that came with living outside his own time. He realized that his story, though deeply personal, was part of something much larger: a testament to human curiosity and resilience in the face of the unknown.

Michel reached into the satchel and retrieved his tablet. The device, a relic of his original era, was carefully concealed within a leather-bound cover designed to blend seamlessly with his surroundings. To anyone else, it would appear as an ordinary journal—a scholar's notebook filled with musings and sketches. But for Michel, it was a bridge between worlds—a tool that allowed him to preserve his thoughts without fear of losing them to time's decay.

He powered it on cautiously, ensuring no one was nearby to witness its faint glow. The familiar interface greeted him like an old friend, a comforting reminder of the life he had left behind. Using a stylus designed for precision, Michel began to write.

At first, his entries were simple—descriptions of daily life in Salon-de-Provence. He wrote about the bustling market square where merchants sold lavender and olives, about the church bells that marked the hours with solemn regularity. He described the people he encountered: farmers tending their fields, artisans crafting wares with practiced hands, children chasing each other through narrow alleyways.

But as the weeks rolled by, Michel's journal became more than just a record of events. It became a canvas for his thoughts and feelings—a place where he could wrestle with the complexities of his situation. He wrote about the loneliness that came with being untethered from his own time and the gratitude he felt for small moments of connection: a kind word from a villager, a shared meal under the stars.

He also used the journal to document discoveries that might one day benefit others. Michel recorded observations about 16th-century medicine and agriculture, noting techniques that had been lost or forgotten in his own era. He sketched diagrams of tools and machines he encountered, marveling at their ingenuity despite their simplicity.

As he wrote, Michel found solace in the act of creation. His journal became both a refuge and a compass—a way to make sense of a life lived between two worlds. Each entry was a reminder that even in uncertainty, there was meaning to be found in observation and reflection.

One evening, as twilight painted the sky in hues of orange and purple, Michel paused to review what he had written so far. The words on the screen seemed almost surreal fragments of a life that felt both immediate and distant. He realized then that this journal was more than just a personal record; it was a legacy.

Michel resolved to continue writing for as long as he could. Whether or not anyone would ever read his words didn't matter; what mattered was that they existed—that they bore witness to a journey through time and space that defied understanding yet celebrated humanity's enduring spirit.

And so, beneath the Provençal sun and among its timeless hills, Michel chronicled his new life—a story etched not on parchment but on pixels, carried forward by memory and hope into an uncertain future.

In the months that followed, Michel used his 'free' time to engage further with the people of Salon-de-Provence and the nearby villages. He decided to use his scientific and medical knowledge to help as many people as he could. While he had come to the 16th century with the intention of disappearing into history, he found it impossible to remain a passive observer. The suffering he witnessed—the untreated wounds, the fevers that took lives too soon, the ignorance of basic hygiene—stirred something deep within him. If he had the means to make a difference, how could he justify doing nothing?

Yet Michel's decision was not without its burdens. Every act of kindness, every cure administered, carried with it the shadow of the Temporal Paradox. What if his interference altered the course of history in ways he couldn't foresee? What if saving a life today meant endangering countless others tomorrow? These questions haunted him, but in the end, his humanity won out. He resolved to tread carefully, using his knowledge sparingly and only when absolutely necessary.

One evening, as Michel returned from the market with a basket of bread and cheese, a frantic woman approached him in the village square. Her face was pale with worry, her hands trembling as she clutched at his sleeve.

"Please," she begged in Provençal French, "you are learned, are you not? My son—he has been burning with fever for two days. The priest's prayers have done nothing."

Michel hesitated. He had tried to keep a low profile in Salon-de-Provence, presenting himself as a modest scholar rather than a healer or doctor. But the desperation in her eyes left him no choice.

"Take me to him," he said quietly.

The woman led him to a small stone cottage on the edge of the village. Inside, the air was thick and stifling, reeking of sweat and sickness. A boy no older than six lay on a straw mattress, his cheeks flushed red with fever and his breaths shallow.

Michel knelt beside him and placed a hand on his forehead—it was searing hot. He asked the mother about any other symptoms and quickly deduced that the child was suffering from an infection likely caused by untreated wounds on his legs. In his time, such an ailment would have been easily treated with antibiotics, but here in the 16th century, those were out of reach.

Instead, Michel relied on what he knew about natural remedies. He asked for clean water—though he knew it wasn't truly sterile—and boiled it over their fire before using it to clean the boy's wounds. From his satchel, he retrieved dried lavender and thyme—herbs he had gathered from local markets—and prepared an infusion to help lower the fever.

"It will take time," Michel told the mother as he applied cool cloths to her son's forehead. "But I believe he will recover."

Over the next few days, Michel returned regularly to check on the boy. Slowly but surely, the fever broke, and color returned to his cheeks. When he finally opened his eyes and smiled weakly at his mother, she wept with gratitude.

"You are a miracle worker," she said to Michel.

"No," Michel replied softly. "Just someone who knows a little about healing."

Word of Michel's success began to spread quietly through Salon-de-Provence and its neighboring villages. One afternoon, a farmer approached him while he was examining herbs at the market.

"Pardon me," the man said gruffly, holding out his bandaged hand. "I heard you helped young Pierre when he was sick. I've got this wound that won't heal—it's been weeks."

Michel unwrapped the cloth carefully and winced at what he saw: an infected gash running across the man's palm, swollen and oozing pus. Left untreated, it could easily lead to sepsis or worse.

"This needs immediate attention," Michel said firmly.

He led the farmer back to his modest lodgings where he kept some basic supplies hidden among more era-appropriate items. After cleaning the wound thoroughly with boiled water and vinegar—a common antiseptic of the time— Michel applied a poultice made from honey and crushed garlic. Both were known for their antibacterial properties even in this era.

"You'll need to keep this clean," Michel instructed as he wrapped fresh linen around the man's hand. "Change these bandages daily."

The farmer grunted in acknowledgment but looked skeptical. When Michel saw him again two weeks later at market, however, his hand was nearly healed.

"You've got strange methods," the farmer admitted with a wry smile. "But they work."

Not all of Michel's encounters involved physical ailments. One evening as he walked along a quiet path outside Salon-de-Provence, he came across a young woman sitting by herself near a stream. Her face was streaked with tears.

"Are you all right?" Michel asked gently.

She looked up at him with hollow eyes before shaking her head. "My father is gone," she whispered. "And now there is no one to care for our land."

Michel sat beside her and listened as she poured out her grief—how her father had died suddenly after falling ill; how their small farm was failing without him; how she feared being forced into servitude just to survive.

Though Michel couldn't bring her father back or save her farm outright, he offered what comfort he could: advice on crop rotation techniques that might improve their yield; suggestions for herbs that could ward off pests naturally; encouragement that she seek help from neighbors who might be willing to trade labor for goods.

"You're stronger than you think," Michel told her before leaving that night.

Months later when their paths crossed again at market, she greeted him with renewed confidence—and even managed a small smile.

While these acts of kindness brought Michel great satisfaction, they also weighed heavily on him. Each time he intervened in someone's life—whether by curing an illness or offering advice—he wondered what ripple effects might follow.

Would Pierre grow up differently because of those extra years granted by Michel's remedies? Would that farmer's healed hand allow him to harvest more crops than history originally intended?

Michel tried not to dwell too much on these questions; after all, no one could predict every consequence of their actions—not even someone who had traveled through time itself. Still, he resolved to remain cautious: helping only when necessary and always striving to leave as light a footprint as possible on history's fragile tapestry.

In helping others navigate their struggles in 16th-century France—whether through medicine or simple compassion—Michel found purpose amid uncertainty... even as shadows of paradox loomed quietly over every choice he made along this extraordinary journey through time.

Chapter 13: Life and Loss

Salon-de-Provence unfolded before Michel with the tranquil charm of a village tenderly embraced by time. Over the years, it became an inseparable part of his life as he seamlessly blended into the rhythms of Provençal existence. The villagers, recognizing Michel's knowledge of herbal remedies and his compassionate care, began to call him "Doctor." His humble abode, nestled at the foot of the hills, became a sanctuary for those seeking relief from ailments. Michel's days were marked by the rhythm of healing as he tended to the sick and dispensed herbal concoctions crafted with centuries-old wisdom.

The tablet, hidden in the sanctity of his home, remained a silent repository of knowledge, guiding his hands in the delicate art of alleviating suffering.

Beyond his role as a healer, Michel became increasingly involved in town affairs. Recognizing his intellect and literacy, the local government appointed him as a secretary. This new position immersed him further into the complexities of 16th-century life. Michel's duties as the town's government secretary were varied, ranging from drafting correspondence to managing records and assisting in the resolution of disputes. His role placed him at the heart of Salon-de-Provence's administrative and social life, offering him a unique perspective on the challenges and intricacies of governance in Renaissance France.

One of Michel's primary responsibilities was drafting letters and official documents on behalf of the town's leaders. In an era when literacy was a rare skill, his ability to write clearly and persuasively in French—and even Latin—made him indispensable. He composed everything from petitions to regional authorities to proclamations announcing market days or public festivals. Each document required careful attention to tone and language, as even minor errors could lead to misunderstandings or disputes.

Michel quickly became adept at navigating the formalities of Renaissance correspondence. He often worked late into the night by candlelight, penning letters with a steady hand while consulting reference materials he had brought with him from his own time.

His modern understanding of organization and efficiency allowed him to streamline processes that had previously been chaotic, earning him the respect of his colleagues.

Another critical aspect of Michel's role was maintaining the town's records. These included property deeds, tax rolls, and minutes from council meetings. Michel introduced a more systematic approach to record-keeping, creating indexes and cross-references that made it easier to retrieve information when needed. He also ensured that records were stored securely, protecting them from damage or loss.

The meticulous nature of this work appealed to Michel's analytical mind. As he pored over centuries-old documents, he felt a profound connection to history—a sense that he was not only living within it but also preserving it for future generations. At times, he couldn't help but marvel at how much of life in 16th-century France mirrored the bureaucratic challenges of his own era.

Michel's position often required him to mediate disputes among townsfolk. These ranged from arguments over property boundaries to disagreements about trade practices in the bustling market square. His calm demeanor and logical approach made him an effective arbitrator, earning him a reputation for fairness.

One memorable case involved two farmers quarreling over water rights for their adjacent fields. After listening carefully to both sides, Michel proposed a compromise: they would share access to the stream on alternating days, ensuring that neither was left without irrigation during critical planting seasons. The solution satisfied both parties and reinforced Michel's standing as a trusted problem-solver.

Michel soon discovered that his position came with its share of political intrigue. The town council was not immune to factionalism, with rival groups vying for influence over decisions ranging from tax policies to alliances with neighboring communities. As secretary, Michel often found himself caught in the middle of these power struggles.

While he tried to remain neutral, his intelligence and discretion earned him the trust of several key figures. They began seeking his advice on sensitive matters, valuing his ability to weigh options objectively and anticipate potential consequences. Michel tread carefully in these situations, aware that even well-intentioned actions could have unforeseen ripple effects on history.

Despite the demands of his official duties, Michel never lost sight of his commitment to helping others. His position gave him access to resources and information that he used discreetly to aid those in need. For example, when he learned of a family struggling to pay their taxes due to illness, he quietly arranged for their debt to be deferred until they could recover financially.

In another instance, Michel used his knowledge of agriculture and crop rotation—gleaned from both historical texts and modern science—to advise local farmers on improving their yields during a particularly harsh growing season. His suggestions proved successful, preventing widespread food shortages and further cementing his reputation as someone who genuinely cared about the community's well-being.

Throughout his tenure as secretary, Michel grappled with the ethical implications of his actions. He knew that every decision he made—whether drafting a letter or resolving a dispute—had the potential to alter history in subtle but significant ways. This awareness weighed heavily on him, but he resolved to always act with integrity and compassion. Michel often reflected on how his unique perspective allowed him to bridge past and future, blending modern insights with an appreciation for Renaissance values. By doing so, he hoped not only to serve Salon-de-Provence faithfully but also to honor the timeless ideals of justice and humanity.

To fulfill his duties, Michel needed documentation that could withstand scrutiny—a record aligning with the structure of the past.

In the solitude of his temporal refuge, Michel faced the culmination of years spent searching for traces of Nostradamus in medieval France. His fruitless quest had led him through picturesque villages and storied landscapes, yet the elusive figure remained a phantom of history. A bold decision began to crystallize in Michel's mind—a choice shaped by childhood dreams and temporal exploration.

With resolute determination, Michel embarked on a clandestine endeavor that blurred the lines between past and present. In his secluded sanctuary, he carefully crafted a birth certificate for himself, claiming December 1503 as his birthdate. Using information stored in the tablet, he fabricated names for his parents—anchors to this invented past. It was an audacious step into the unknown, mirroring the enigmatic essence of Nostradamus himself.

As the ink dried on the parchment, Michel felt a profound transformation within. The decision to become the man he had once studied as a child marked the convergence of two timelines. Adopting the mantle of Michel de Nostradamus symbolized a rebirth that transcended identity.

Embracing this persona, Michel immersed himself in pursuits that defined Nostradamus: astrology, alchemy, and medicinal practices. His studies mirrored those of the legendary healer as he meticulously recreated a life once sought but never found. In this quiet temporal sanctuary, Michel not only donned Nostradamus's cloak but also began writing a new chapter in history—one where observer and participant became indistinguishable.

The fabricated identity became both shield and tool—a necessary illusion in navigating 16th-century bureaucracy. As an employee of Salon-de-Provence's government, Michel walked a delicate line between authenticity and concealment. Every move was calculated with precision to protect his secret while fulfilling his duties.

As days, weeks and months passed, Michel's contributions transformed Salon-de-Provence into a more organized and prosperous community. His innovations in administration set new standards for efficiency while preserving the town's rich traditions. Yet despite these achievements, Michel remained humble about his role

Michel began compiling a detailed account of his experiences as secretary—a journal that combined practical advice with philosophical reflections on leadership and service. In doing so, he hoped to leave behind not just a record of what he had done but also an enduring reminder of why it mattered.

For Michel, being secretary was more than just a job—it was an opportunity to make a difference in ways both large and small while navigating the delicate balance between past and present... one carefully written word at a time.

Yet as Michel settled into this new life as "31 years old," an ache stirred within him—a longing for connection beyond Salon-de-Provence's confines. The tablet held a name buried deep in its archives: Henriette d'Encausse.

Driven by curiosity and yearning, Michel began searching for her. The tablet described her as vibrant as the Provençal sun—jet-black hair framing intelligent eyes.

Fate wove its threads into their lives when they crossed paths on a visit to Agen, a small town about 15 miles from Salon de Provence. An invisible bond emerged between them—a connection as ancient as time itself. Their courtship unfolded like a sonnet written in whispers of shared glances and unspoken understanding.

Michel orchestrated chance encounters at bustling markets where vendors hawked wares with medieval fervor. Each meeting deepened their bond through laughter and warmth exchanged like treasures. Inspired by romance's timeless charm, Michel composed verses that echoed through cobblestone streets while Henriette blushed at his heartfelt words.

Together they wandered fragrant orchards thick with blooming blossoms' scent. Michel presented Henriette handpicked flowers—tokens speaking a language only they understood. In her presence, he found solace; in their love, he discovered purpose amid time's relentless currents.

Picnics beneath the Provençal sun became a cherished staple of their blossoming romance. One afternoon, the sun shone bright over the rolling fields outside Agen, casting golden light on the couple seated beneath an old oak tree. Michel de Nostradamus spread a cloth over the grass, arranging bread, cheese, and a flask of wine. Henriette d'Encausse sat beside him, her dark hair catching the sunlight as she gazed into the distance.

Smiling softly, Henriette said "You always seem lost in thought, Michel. What is it you see when your mind wanders so far?"

Michel answered chuckling "The stars, perhaps. Or the mysteries they whisper. But today, I see only you." He paused, studying her face. "Tell me, Henriette. You've heard my stories of travels and studies. But what of your life? What shaped the woman before me?"

Sighing as she plucked a blade of grass, Henriette continued "My life has been simpler than yours, I think. I grew up in a small house near the river. My father was a merchant—honest but stern. My mother... she was softer, always singing as she worked. I suppose I inherited her voice more than her patience."

Leaning closer, Michelle whispered in her ear "And what did you dream of as a child? Surely not staying by the river forever."

Henriette, laughing lightly "No, never. I dreamed of seeing the world, of meeting people who spoke in strange tongues and carried stories from distant lands. But life had other plans." Her smile faded slightly. "When my father passed, it fell to me to care for my mother and our home."

Michel answered while gently taking her hand "And yet here you are, living those dreams in your own way."

Henriette, looking into his eyes asserted "Perhaps. And now... perhaps you are part of those dreams too."

The two sat in silence for a moment, the breeze carrying the scent of wildflowers as they shared a quiet understanding beneath the ancient oak.

Michel, with his keen sense of culinary artistry, curated feasts that celebrated the rich flavors of medieval France. Henriette, captivated by the fusion of aromas and tastes, discovered in Michel a kindred spirit who shared her appreciation for gastronomic delights. Their laughter rang out like a melody—a symphony of shared joy that transcended the boundaries of time.

As the sun dipped below the horizon, casting its golden glow across the landscape, Michel and Henriette found solace in quiet moments together. Candlelit dinners in rustic taverns—where flickering flames mirrored the dance of their intertwined destinies—became the backdrop for whispered confessions. Michel, his gaze locked with Henriette's, revealed the intricacies of his fabricated past, laying bare the tapestry of temporal secrets he carried.

Under a star-strewn sky, Michel and Henriette shared moments of intimacy that transcended the constraints of time. Their glances held unspoken promises, while stolen kisses whispered of a love that defied temporal and existential barriers. Their days together, steeped in the magic of a bygone era, became a testament to love's enduring power—a force that persisted through centuries.

Michel and Henriette walked side by side along the bank, their steps unhurried, their conversation light. The air was warm, carrying the faint scent of wildflowers and the soft rustle of leaves in the breeze. Michel seemed quieter than usual, his hands clasped behind his back as he occasionally glanced at Henriette, a thoughtful expression on his face.

Henriette noticed his silence and smiled. "You've been unusually quiet today," she said, her voice teasing but gentle. "What thoughts are you hiding from me?"

Michel stopped walking and turned to her, his face tender but serious. "Not hiding," he said softly. "Only searching for the right words."

Henriette tilted her head, her playful smile fading into curiosity. "Lost for words? This must be something worth hearing."

He reached for her hand, holding it gently as he took a step closer. The river murmured beside them, a quiet witness to the moment. "Henriette," he began, his voice steady but filled with emotion, "you've brought something into my life I never knew I needed. You've given me peace in a world that often feels chaotic. Your laughter, your kindness... they've become my anchor."

Henriette's breath caught as she saw the depth of feeling in his eyes. He continued, "I cannot imagine a future without you by my side. Will you marry me? Will you let me spend my life loving you?"

For a moment, Henriette was silent, her eyes glistening with unshed tears. Then she stepped closer to him and whispered, "Yes, Michel. Yes! There is nothing I want more."

Michel pulled her into his arms, their embrace warm and full of promise. Their lips met in a passionate kiss as the golden light of the setting sun enveloped them. The river flowed on beside them, its quiet song mingling with their unspoken vows, as if nature itself had blessed their union.

As they parted slightly, Michel rested his forehead against Henriette's, his voice soft but filled with conviction. "Henriette, I dream of a life with you—a home filled with laughter and love. A place where the walls echo with the voices of children, our children. I want to give them everything I never had."

Henriette smiled, her eyes shimmering with emotion. "And I will make that home a sanctuary for us all," she said, her voice steady and full of resolve. "I will care for it with my heart and hands, Michel. I'll tend the garden, fill the kitchen with warmth, and make sure it's a place where our children feel safe and loved."

Michel's grip on her hands tightened as he gazed at her with admiration. "You have such a gift for seeing beauty in the simplest things," he said. "I can already picture it—a little house by the river, perhaps, where we can watch them grow and teach them to marvel at the stars."

Henriette laughed softly, brushing a strand of hair from her face. "And you will teach them to dream," she said. "To look beyond what is seen and imagine what could be."

Michel nodded, his heart swelling at the thought. "Together, we'll give them a life full of wonder and love."

They stood there by the riverbank, hand in hand, dreaming aloud of a future yet to come—a future they would build together, minute by minute and moment by moment.

The tablet, hidden from prying eyes, stood as a silent witness to their love. Over time, Michel and Henriette married in a ceremony steeped in 16th-century traditions. Within the stone walls of the village church, they exchanged vows that resonated with the promise of a shared tomorrow. Michel de and Henriette's wedding was a celebration of love, tradition, and the vibrant culture of 16th-century France. The ceremony took place in a small stone church on the outskirts of Agen, its modest interior adorned with garlands of wildflowers gathered from the surrounding countryside.

Friends and family filled the pews, their faces glowing with joy as the couple exchanged vows under the soft light filtering through stained glass windows.

After the priest blessed their union with holy water and recited prayers in Latin and the local dialect, Michel placed a simple gold ring on Henriette's finger, following the custom of invoking the Holy Trinity: "In nomine Patris," he said as he slid it onto her thumb, "et Filii," as it moved to her index finger, "et Spiritus Sancti," before finally settling it on her ring finger. Their hands joined, they walked together to the altar for the final blessing, a veil held over them as a symbol of unity and protection.

The reception began just outside the church, where guests showered the newlyweds with petals and toasted their happiness with goblets of local wine. A procession led them to a nearby orchard, where tables were set beneath sprawling trees. The tables were laden with foods that reflected both rustic simplicity and French elegance: roasted duck, fresh trout from nearby rivers, hearty stews, and platters of cheeses paired with crusty bread. For dessert, a croquembouche—a tower of cream-filled pastries bound with caramel—served as an impressive centerpiece.

Music filled the air as minstrels played lutes and violins, their lively tunes encouraging guests to dance on the grass. Conversations flowed as freely as the wine; neighbors shared stories of past harvests, while Michel's scholarly friends debated philosophy and astronomy. Henriette's laughter rang out as she danced with children from the village, her flowered wreath slipping slightly from her hair. Later in the evening, as candles flickered in iron holders and torches illuminated the orchard, Michel stood to address their guests. "To my beloved Henriette," he began, his voice steady but full of emotion. "You are my guiding star, my anchor in this ever-changing world. Together, we will build a life filled with love, discovery, and hope."

Henriette rose beside him, her cheeks flushed from dancing. "And to you, Michel," she replied warmly. "You are my greatest adventure. I vow to make our home one of warmth and laughter—a place where our future children will thrive."

The crowd erupted in cheers as Michel pulled Henriette into an embrace. Their kiss was met with applause and laughter before the festivities resumed.

As night deepened, guests gathered around a bonfire for storytelling and song. The newlyweds danced beneath a canopy of stars while friends tied ribbons around them—a symbolic gesture wishing them unity and prosperity. The celebration continued until dawn when steaming bowls of onion soup were served to weary but contented revelers.

Michel sat across from François at the worn oak table, a goblet of wine in his hand and a contented smile on his face. The day's celebrations had left him weary but fulfilled. François, the farmer who had first taken Michel into his home years ago when he arrived in Salon de Provence, leaned back in his chair, studying the younger man with a knowing look.

"It was due time that you found love," François said, his voice steady but warm. "You are too good a man to spend your days alone."

Michel looked up, surprised by the farmer's words. He chuckled softly, swirling the wine in his goblet. "I've always been content with my books and my thoughts," he replied. "I never imagined that love would find its way into my life."

François shook his head with a faint smile. "Books and thoughts are fine company, Michel, but they can't warm a man's heart on a cold night or share his burdens when the world feels heavy. Henriette... she is your match. I see it in the way she looks at you, as though you've hung the stars themselves."

Michel's expression softened, and he glanced toward the doorway where Henriette had just passed moments ago, her laughter still lingering in the air. "She is remarkable," he admitted quietly. "I don't know what I did to deserve her." François leaned forward, resting his weathered hands on the table. "Deserve her? You've shown kindness to everyone you've met, Michel. You've healed strangers and shared your wisdom freely. If anyone deserves happiness, it's you." Michel smiled gratefully. "Thank you, François. Your faith in me means more than you know." It was a wedding that embodied not just their love but also the spirit of their time: joyous, communal, and deeply rooted in tradition. As seasons passed, their union was blessed with two children: Étienne and Amélie. The laughter of their children and the joy echoing within their home became a poignant reminder of life's fragility and beauty in Agen. Étienne, with his father's curious eyes and Henriette's infectious laughter, embodied youthful vivacity. Amélie, a reflection of her mother's grace and her father's contemplative spirit, brought an additional layer of warmth to their family. The pastoral rhythms of rural life in medieval France served as the backdrop for this growing tapestry of love and kinship.

Michel and Henriette embraced parenthood with earnest devotion that transcended temporal complexities. Mornings began with soft lullabies as Michel cradled Amélie in his arms while Étienne—his tousled hair and mischievous glint betraying his eagerness—awaited the adventures each day would bring.

The family's days were marked by shared activities that celebrated the simple joys of life. The orchards that had once witnessed Michel and Henriette's courtship now became a playground where Étienne and Amélie embarked on imaginary adventures. Henriette, with her patient guidance, nurtured a love for nature in their hearts, passing down the wisdom of the land that had sustained generations before them.

Picnics beneath the Provençal sun evolved into cherished family traditions, each meal a celebration of the bounties of their rural life. Henriette, her apron scented with homemade bread and freshly picked fruits, orchestrated feasts that brought the family together around a rustic table. Étienne and Amélie, wide-eyed with anticipation, listened intently to tales spun by their father—a harmonious blend of historical anecdotes and imaginative narratives.

The changing seasons became chapters in their family story. Summer days were spent chasing butterflies in meadows filled with birdsong and laughter. Autumn brought the harvest, a communal effort where small hands eagerly plucked ripe fruits under the watchful eyes of their parents. Winter nights unfolded by the hearth, where crackling flames cast a warm glow as Michel shared stories that filled their home with wonder.

Inspired by medieval craftsmanship, Michel began creating toys for Étienne and Amélie. Wooden horses, intricately carved puzzles, and dolls with hand-sewn dresses became cherished treasures—tokens of a father's love crafted with care.

These handmade creations symbolized the bond they shared as a family and embodied the spirit of the region.

The village, once merely a backdrop for Michel's temporal quest, now bore witness to the blossoming of a family deeply rooted in its essence. Michel and Henriette's legacy extended beyond their home; they became integral to the community through both their agricultural contributions and the unity and generosity they embodied. The laughter that once resonated within their home began to echo throughout the town—a testament to love's enduring power and the magic woven into life's fleeting moments.

But shadows soon crept into this idyllic tapestry. The plague—a silent specter that had haunted humanity for centuries—descended upon France with ruthless ferocity. Whispers of loss began as distant murmurs: a neighbor taken by fever, a friend succumbing to the illness that shrouded the village in mourning. As the tendrils of the plague drew closer, Michel felt an overwhelming sense of inevitability.

Amélie was the first to fall ill; her vibrant laughter was replaced by fevered silence. Michel, now a healer confronted by helplessness, tended to his daughter with desperate determination. Henriette stood steadfast at his side, her eyes reflecting both fear and hope as they clung to each other in an unspoken bond of grief.

Tragedy struck again when Étienne succumbed to the relentless grip of the plague. The once-vibrant home, where joy had danced like sunlight through leaves, transformed into a somber chamber filled with pain. While Michel worked tirelessly to attend to others in the village, Henriette's strength began to wane under the weight of loss. Shadows of sorrow enveloped their lives as one by one they lost neighbors, friends—and finally their own children.

The streets of the French Provence—once alive with bustling energy—now echoed with an eerie silence as death claimed its toll. In their home's fragile tranquility, Michel and Henriette faced the void left behind by those they loved most. The tablet, hidden like a silent companion, offered no solace against this unyielding reality. Its wealth of future knowledge could not shield them from fate's cruel hand.

Michel knew he could not alter time's flow; he had always known he would lose his wife and children to this plague. Yet this foreknowledge did nothing to soften the blow when it came.

As the specter of the Black Death tightened its grip on Agen, Salon-de-Provence, and other nearby towns, Michel faced his greatest challenge yet.

Armed with modern medical knowledge that could not change history but might ease suffering, he fought against despair with every tool at his disposal.

For Étienne and Amélie—now frail under the plague's unforgiving grip—Michel became a beacon of solace. With tenderness in his touch and love as his guiding light, he employed every remedy he could muster, herbal infusions brewed with care, poultices prepared from ancient recipes, and his soothing presence as balm for their pain.

Though powerless against fate itself, Michel's unwavering commitment offered comfort in their final days—a testament to a father's enduring love amidst unimaginable loss.

In the quiet moments by their bedside, Michel spoke words of comfort, weaving tales of courage and resilience. He held their frail hands, knowing that the warmth of human touch transcended the boundaries of time.

His knowledge of modern medicine offered only a slender thread of hope against the seemingly inevitable.

As the plague tightened its grip, Michel, tears staining his cheeks, shared stories of a world beyond their grasp—a future where disease was no longer a silent reaper and life was not overshadowed by the specter of death. He painted vivid images of a time when science had conquered the microscopic adversaries now wreaking havoc on their family.

The village, shrouded in death's shadow, bore witness to a father's unwavering resolve to bring solace to his children. Their home became a makeshift infirmary where Michel, fueled by love and knowledge, fought an unwinnable battle against the relentless plague.

Amélie, in the final throes of her illness, found refuge in her father's tender care. Michel's efforts—a beacon of hope in the darkness—offered relief, if not a cure. Surrounded by the scent of medicinal herbs and the warmth of her father's love, Amélie faced the inevitable with quiet courage.

As her final moments approached, Michel held her in a tender embrace, grief etched deeply across his face. The secrets of the future, once a source of wonder, now became a burden—a reminder of life's fragility. In the stillness that followed her passing, Michel contemplated time's unyielding passage and the enduring legacy of love that transcends mortality.

Étienne succumbed soon after. As he lay on his deathbed, his parents embraced him with a love that defied description—eternal and unbroken. Michel prepared a soothing herbal infusion to ease Étienne's pain, its gentle aroma filling the room.

In his final moments, surrounded by his parents' warmth and devotion, Étienne found peace. Michel's knowledge from another time became a compassionate salve, ensuring that Étienne's journey into the beyond was marked by tranquility and love.

Yet as grief settled over their home like an oppressive fog, an emotional storm brewed within Henriette. The solace Michel's knowledge provided clashed with the tempest of her anguish.

One evening, as shadows stretched across their humble abode, Henriette confronted him with eyes ablaze—a mix of sorrow and rage.

"Why couldn't you save them?" she demanded, her voice trembling under the weight of unspoken accusations.

Michel, worn down by grief and helplessness, met her gaze with eyes that mirrored her pain. "I tried everything within my power," he replied softly. "The plague's devastation was beyond our control."

Henriette shook her head in defiance. "You—armed with all your knowledge—couldn't change their fate? What good is this supposed wisdom if it can't shield us from destiny's cruel whims?" Her words cut through the air like daggers.

Michel struggled to explain what even he could barely comprehend: "Henriette, time is a tapestry woven with threads beyond our understanding. To challenge it risks consequences we cannot foresee."

Her grief flared into fiery defiance. "Consequences? What greater consequence could there be than losing our children?" Her anger burned brightly—a tempest that refused to be quelled by temporal logic.

In their shared sorrow, Michel and Henriette wrestled with the chasm between what could be known and what could not be changed. The knowledge Michel carried—once a beacon of hope—now stood as a painful reminder of humanity's limits in tampering with time.

As night unfolded, their voices rose and fell in a symphony of sorrow and frustration. Henriette demanded answers that even Michel's advanced wisdom could not provide. The clash between history's inevitability and their desperate yearning for another outcome created an irreparable fracture within their grief.

In the aftermath of this emotional tempest, silence enveloped them—a fragile truce forged in shared loss. Bound by sorrow yet divided by its weight, they found solace in fleeting moments of understanding. The corridors of time bore witness to love's intricacies and humanity's eternal struggle against fate.

Henriette's spirit eventually succumbed to grief and illness as the plague claimed its final toll on their family. Michel remained at her side until the end, their hands intertwined in one last act of shared humanity. In those heart-wrenching moments as mortality dimmed her light, their eyes spoke a language only they understood—a silent exchange carrying memories of laughter-filled days with their children and quiet moments of solace amidst life's chaos.

Amid the anguish, Michel's gaze sought Henriette's, a silent acknowledgment of their enduring love—one that transcended the temporal boundaries of life and death. Her eyes, though clouded by the torment of parting, held a reservoir of emotions too profound for words. It was a communion of souls, an intimate dialogue etched in the quiet spaces between their final breaths.

The room, heavy with the perfume of grief, bore witness to a love that defied the limitations of mortal existence. In the unspoken language of shared glances, Michel and Henriette found a sanctuary of understanding—a connection so profound that even time, with all its complexities, could never sever it.

The echoes of loss—the poignant melody of pain—became the funeral song that accompanied Michel through the uncharted territories of his sorrow.

After the plague subsided, Agen became a town shrouded in mourning. Michel, once a healer and now one of the afflicted, moved like a shadow through its streets, his heart weighed down by grief.

The tablet, its screen a silent testament to humanity's suffering, offered no answers to his lingering questions. The hills, fields, and stone houses that had borne witness to both joy and tragedy remained unchanged. Yet Michel, now an embodiment of loss, walked those cobbled streets with Henriette's memory and the weight of his children etched into his very being.

Michel's story—the journey of a temporal wanderer anchored in the embrace of the past—continued to unfold in Salon-de-Provence. After his family's demise, Michel felt it necessary to sell all his belongings and move back to where his story in this time had begun. It was a tale written in the language of love and loss, a testament to an indomitable spirit that persisted even in the face of the unknown.

Chapter 14: On Foreign Lands

In the late 1530s, Michel was accused of heresy after making a casual comment about a religious statue. Summoned to appear before the Inquisition, he wisely chose to flee Salon-de-Provence, embarking on years of travel through Italy, Greece, and Turkey. Michel de Nostredame's journey through Italy in 1538 was a transformative chapter in his life, one that shaped him into the figure history would come to know as Nostradamus. Fleeing persecution in France, Michel embarked on a six-year odyssey across the Italian peninsula, immersing himself in the vibrant intellectual and cultural milieu of the Renaissance. Italy, then the epicenter of art, science, and philosophy, offered Michel an unparalleled opportunity to expand his knowledge and refine his craft.

As he traveled through cities like Venice, Florence, and Rome, Michel encountered a kaleidoscope of sights that left an indelible mark on his soul. In Venice, he marveled at the intricate canals and bustling marketplaces where merchants from across the world traded goods and ideas. The grandeur of St. Mark's Basilica, with its shimmering mosaics and Byzantine splendor, inspired in Michel a sense of awe for humanity's creative potential. In Florence, he stood before Michelangelo's David and Botticelli's The Birth of Venus, absorbing the profound interplay of art and human emotion that defined the Renaissance spirit.

Michel's travels also brought him into contact with wise elders who shared their knowledge and philosophies. In Sicily, he studied the Mysteries of Egypt under scholars who preserved ancient texts from Alexandria. These teachings deepened his understanding of esoteric traditions and broadened his perspective on the interconnectedness of time, space, and human destiny.

In Naples, he met Sufi mystics who introduced him to The Elixir of Blissfulness, a text that explored spiritual enlightenment through meditation and introspection. These encounters not only enriched Michel's intellectual repertoire but also awakened within him a heightened sense of intuition—what some would later call his prophetic gift.

Throughout his journey, Michel honed practical skills that would serve him well in his later endeavors. He apprenticed with apothecaries in Milan and Bologna, learning to craft herbal remedies, perfumes, and even cosmetics. His meticulous notes on these practices would later form the basis of his book Traité des Fardemens. Michel also dabbled in alchemy during his time in Venice, experimenting with transmutation processes that symbolized the transformation of both matter and spirit.

During his travels through Italy, Michel de Nostradamus found himself at a quiet Franciscan monastery near Ancona. The monastery, nestled among rolling hills and olive groves, offered a serene refuge for the wandering physician and seer. It was here that he met Brother Felice Peretti, a young monk of humble origins who had once been a swineherd. Despite his lowly beginnings, Peretti exuded an air of quiet determination and intelligence that caught Michel's attention.

One evening, after a simple meal of bread, cheese, and wine shared with the monks, Michel and Brother Peretti strolled through the monastery's garden. The moonlight bathed the stone paths in a soft glow, and the scent of lavender lingered in the cool night air. Michel carried with him a small tablet—a tool he used to record his thoughts and visions. Earlier that day, it had revealed to him something extraordinary: this humble monk would one day ascend to the papacy.

"Brother Felice," Michel began, his voice measured but tinged with awe, "do you ever wonder what your purpose is in this world?"

Peretti chuckled softly. "Every day, Master Nostradamus. I am but a servant of God, tending to His flock as best I can. My ambitions go no further than these walls."

Michel stopped walking and turned to face him. "And yet, your path will lead far beyond these walls. I have seen it."

Peretti raised an eyebrow, intrigued but skeptical. "What have you seen?"

Michel hesitated for a moment before speaking. "I saw you dressed in white robes, seated upon the throne of Saint Peter in Rome. You will be His Holiness, the Pope."

Peretti laughed, though not unkindly. "Surely you jest! A former swineherd as Pope? The Church would never allow it."

Michel's expression remained serious. "The ways of God are mysterious, Brother Felice. Mark my words: your humility and faith will guide you to greatness."

Peretti fell silent, his laughter fading as he considered Michel's words. "If what you say is true," he said finally, "then I must pray for strength and wisdom to bear such a burden."

"You will have both," Michel assured him. "And when that time comes, remember this night and the promise it holds." The two men continued their walk in thoughtful silence, the weight of Michel's prophecy hanging between them like the stars above. Though Peretti could not fully comprehend the magnitude of what had been foretold, something in Michel's unwavering conviction stirred a spark of belief within him. Decades later, long after Michel's was gone, Felice Peretti would indeed ascend to the papacy as Pope Sixtus V. And on that day, he would remember the strange yet fateful conversation he had shared with a wandering seer under the moonlit skies of an Italian monastery—a moment that had marked the beginning of his extraordinary destiny. The moment that cemented Nostradamus's reputation as a seer.

As Michel wandered through Italy's storied landscapes—its rolling vineyards, sun-drenched olive groves, and ancient ruins—he reflected deeply on humanity's place within the vast tapestry of existence. These contemplations found expression in his burgeoning interest in astrology. Under star-filled Italian skies, he began charting celestial movements with newfound precision, seeing in them patterns that hinted at future events.

Michel's Italian sojourn was more than an escape from persecution; it was an initiation into the mysteries of time and existence. The knowledge he acquired during those years became the foundation upon which he built his legacy as Nostradamus—a temporal wanderer whose insights would echo through centuries yet to come.

Greece, with its rugged landscapes, ancient ruins, and vibrant culture, had long been a land of inspiration for scholars and seekers. Michel de Nostradamus had heard tales of its wisdom through the years, but it was a chance meeting with a Greek trader named Demetrios that planted the seed for his eventual journey to the cradle of philosophy and science.

It was a warm afternoon in Marseille's bustling port when Michel first encountered Demetrios. The trader, a man of middle years with salt-and-pepper hair and an air of quiet authority, was selling exotic herbs and spices from his homeland. Michel, ever curious about remedies and their origins, struck up a conversation.

As they talked, Demetrios shared stories of Greece—of its ancient philosophers who had unraveled the mysteries of existence, its astrologers who charted the heavens, and its physicians who healed with methods passed down through generations. "In Greece," Demetrios said, his voice rich with pride, "we see the world as a great tapestry woven by the gods. To understand even a thread of it is to glimpse the divine."

Michel listened intently, his curiosity piqued. "And do you believe these secrets are still alive today?" he asked.

Demetrios nodded. "They are alive in our monasteries, in the libraries of Mount Athos, and in the minds of those who have dedicated their lives to learning. But they are not easily given; one must seek them with humility."

That evening, as they shared wine at an inn overlooking the harbor, Michel confided in Demetrios about his own studies in medicine, astrology, and alchemy. He spoke of his desire to deepen his understanding of the cosmos and the human spirit. "I feel," Michel admitted, "as though I am standing at the edge of something vast—a knowledge that eludes me but calls to me nonetheless."

Demetrios smiled knowingly. "Then you must come to Greece," he said simply. "There is a monastery near Thessaloniki where I once traded goods for manuscripts. The monks there are guardians of ancient wisdom— philosophy, astrology, even medicine. If you seek answers, you may find them there."

Michel leaned back in his chair, gazing at the stars that dotted the night sky above Marseille. His mind raced with possibilities. The idea of walking in the footsteps of Aristotle and Hippocrates stirred something deep within him—a yearning to connect with a legacy that spanned centuries.

"Tell me more," Michel urged.

Demetrios leaned forward, his voice lowering conspiratorially. "The monks speak little but know much," he began. "They study texts older than Rome itself—works that speak of healing not just the body but the soul. And their astrologers… they see patterns in the heavens that most cannot fathom."

Michel's heart quickened as Demetrios spoke. He could almost see himself there: poring over ancient manuscripts by candlelight, learning from men who had devoted their lives to uncovering truths hidden from ordinary eyes.

By the end of their conversation, Michel had made up his mind. He would travel to Greece—not just as a physician or astrologer but as a seeker of wisdom. As he bid farewell to Demetrios that night, he felt a sense of purpose unlike any he had known before.

Little did Michel know that this decision would shape not only his understanding of the world but also his destiny as one of history's most enigmatic figures. For Michel, it became a land that he had to experience for himself. It would become a crucible of both physical endurance and spiritual awakening.

Traveling with a caravan of merchants through the mountainous terrain of northern Greece, Michel marveled at the remnants of ancient civilizations. The ruins of Delphi whispered tales of the Oracle who once communed with the gods, and the Parthenon in Athens stood as a testament to human ingenuity and devotion. Michel's curiosity was insatiable; he spent hours listening to the merchants recount stories of Greek mythology, philosophy, and history. These tales stirred his imagination and deepened his appreciation for the interconnectedness of past and present.

The caravan moved cautiously through the wilderness, aware of the dangers that lurked in the shadows. Bandits were a constant threat in these remote regions, preying on travelers who carried goods or wealth. Despite their vigilance, disaster struck one moonless night. As Michel rested under the stars, lulled by the crackling fire and the soft murmur of voices, chaos erupted. A group of robbers descended upon the caravan with ruthless precision.

The first warning was a blood-curdling scream from one of the sentries, followed by the clash of steel and the thundering hooves of horses. Michel jolted awake, his heart pounding as he scrambled to his feet. The robbers, their faces obscured by scarves, moved swiftly through the camp, their weapons glinting in the firelight.

Shouts and cries filled the air as travelers fought desperately to defend themselves. Shouts filled the air as men scrambled for their weapons; blades clashed, and panicked horses neighed in terror.

A merchant near Michel swung a staff at an approaching bandit but was quickly overpowered. Nearby, a woman clutched a dagger, her face pale but resolute as she shielded her young son. Michel grabbed a fallen branch and stood defensively, his mind racing. He was no warrior, but survival demanded action.

The robbers were relentless. They struck down anyone who resisted, their blades cutting through the night with brutal efficiency. Some travelers managed to fend them off briefly—an older man wielding a sword held his ground until two bandits overpowered him. A young woman hurled stones at an attacker before being dragged away, her screams piercing the chaos.

Michel found himself face-to-face with a bandit, his makeshift weapon trembling in his hands. Before the robber could strike, another traveler intervened—a burly man armed with an axe who drove the attacker back with a roar. "Run!" the man shouted at Michel before turning to face another foe.

Amidst the carnage, Michel spotted a wounded woman lying near an overturned cart. Her face was pale, and blood seeped from a gash on her arm. Without hesitation, he rushed to her side and dragged her behind a stack of barrels for cover. "Stay here," he whispered urgently before tearing a strip from his tunic to bind her wound.

The fight raged on around them. Flames from an overturned lantern began to consume one of the wagons, casting eerie shadows across the field.

Michel barely had time to react before a figure loomed over him. A flash of steel caught his eye, and pain seared through his lower abdomen as a knife found its mark. Staggering backward, clutching his wound, Michel's mind raced with thoughts of survival. He managed to grab his sling bag and slip away from the fray under cover of darkness, his breath ragged and his vision blurred.

The robbers pursued him relentlessly. Michel's strength waned as blood seeped from his wound, yet desperation drove him forward.

The shouts of his pursuers grew louder as he stumbled upon a precipice overlooking a rushing river below. Trapped between certain death at their hands or an uncertain fate in the waters below, Michel made a fateful decision. Summoning what little strength he had left; he leaped into the void.

The water enveloped him like a shroud, shocking his senses as he plunged into the river's depths. The current seized him with merciless force, carrying him downstream as consciousness slipped away. For several minutes he floated along the river's course, his body battered but alive—a fragile thread tethering him to existence.

When Michel finally awoke, it was to the sound of crackling firewood and the scent of herbs hanging in the air. His eyes fluttered open to reveal a small cabin nestled in a clearing surrounded by towering pines. The room was modest but warm, its walls lined with shelves filled with scrolls and jars of dried plants. A man sat nearby—a figure with a long white beard and piercing blue eyes that seemed to hold centuries' worth of wisdom.

"Ah, you're awake," said the man in a calm voice tinged with curiosity. "You've been through quite an ordeal."

Michel tried to sit up but winced as pain shot through his abdomen. The man gently placed a hand on his shoulder. "Rest," he said firmly. "Your wound is healing, but it will take time."

The man introduced himself as Elias, a hermit philosopher who had chosen solitude over society in pursuit of enlightenment. Over the next few days, as Michel regained his strength under Elias's care, he learned more about this enigmatic figure. Elias had once been a scholar in Athens but had grown disillusioned with worldly pursuits. He retreated to this remote cabin to study nature, meditate on life's mysteries, and seek harmony between body and spirit. Elias tended to Michel's wound with remarkable skill, using poultices made from wild herbs gathered in the forest. As they spent time together, their conversations delved into topics that ranged from philosophy and metaphysics to humanity's place within the cosmos.

Elias spoke with eloquence about concepts that resonated deeply with Michel—ideas about fate being both immutable yet influenced by human action; about time as an ever-flowing river where past and future coexist.

"You survived for a reason," Elias told him one evening as they sat by the firelight. "The river carried you here because your journey is not yet complete."

Michel listened intently as Elias shared insights gleaned from years of contemplation: how suffering could be a teacher; how wisdom often emerged from adversity; how even in chaos there existed an underlying order waiting to be understood.

During his time with Elias, Michel also learned practical skills that would serve him well in years to come. Elias taught him how to identify medicinal plants native to Greece—knowledge that expanded Michel's already impressive repertoire as an apothecary.

He also introduced Michel to meditation techniques designed to quiet the mind and sharpen intuition—practices that would later play a role in Michel's prophetic work.

One night under a canopy of stars, Elias handed Michel an ancient scroll containing fragments attributed to Heraclitus—the philosopher who famously declared that one could never step into the same river twice.

"Take this," Elias said softly. "You remind me of Heraclitus—always seeking truth amidst change."

After weeks at Elias's cabin, Michel felt himself transformed—not just physically but spiritually as well. The hermit's teachings awakened within him new perspectives on life's impermanence and humanity's capacity for resilience.

When it came time for Michel to leave, he did so reluctantly but with renewed purpose coursing through his veins like lifeblood restored after near-death experiences.

"Remember," Elias said as they parted ways at dawn near the edge of the forest clearing, "your path is yours alone to walk—but the wisdom gained here will guide you wherever it leads. Oh, I also must tell you…Your secret is safe with me." Elias winced at Michel as he walked toward the setting sun.

Michel bowed deeply in gratitude before setting off toward the next chapter of his journey across Greece—and ultimately toward his destiny. Michel's travels took him from the rugged hills of Greece to the bustling ports of Turkey. The transition from Greece's serene landscapes to Turkey's vibrant cities was striking. Here, in this cultural crossroads where East met West, Michel found himself immersed in a world teeming with ideas, philosophies, and spiritual traditions that challenged and enriched his understanding of humanity.

His first stop was Izmir, a city alive with activity. Merchants called out from their stalls in the bazaar, offering spices, textiles, and trinkets from across the known world. Michel wandered through the labyrinthine streets, marveling at the diversity of people and goods. It was here that he encountered a philosopher named Yusuf, who was delivering an impassioned lecture to a small crowd gathered in a shaded courtyard.

Yusuf spoke of the interconnectedness of all things, drawing on both Islamic mysticism and Aristotelian logic to weave his arguments. Intrigued, Michel approached him after the lecture and introduced himself as a traveler seeking wisdom. "Wisdom?" Yusuf said with a smile. "You'll find no shortage of it here in Turkey—if you know where to look."

The two men spent hours in conversation, discussing everything from metaphysics to medicine. Yusuf introduced Michel to the works of Ibn Rushd (Averroes), whose commentaries on Aristotle had bridged ancient Greek philosophy with Islamic thought. For Michel, these ideas resonated deeply; they spoke to his own desire to reconcile science and spirituality.

Yusuf also encouraged Michel to visit Konya, the city of Rumi, whose poetry and teachings had inspired generations. Following Yusuf's advice, Michel made his way inland to Konya, where he found himself drawn into the world of Sufism. The dervishes there welcomed him warmly, inviting him to witness their whirling dances—a physical manifestation of their devotion and search for divine truth.

One evening, after a particularly moving ceremony, Michel spoke with a dervish named Selim. Selim explained that their spinning was not merely an act of worship but a metaphor for life itself: "We turn because life is always in motion," he said. "To stand still is to deny the flow of existence."

These words stayed with Michel as he continued his journey. He began to see his own life as part of this eternal flow—a thread woven into the vast tapestry of time.

In Bursa, Michel encountered another figure who would leave a lasting impression: a self-proclaimed prophet named Ibrahim. Unlike Elias or Yusuf, Ibrahim was less concerned with philosophical discourse and more focused on practical guidance for living a virtuous life. He preached in marketplaces and town squares, urging people to care for one another and live in harmony with nature.

Though skeptical at first, Michel found himself drawn to Ibrahim's sincerity and compassion. One day, after listening to one of his sermons, Michel approached him with a question that had been weighing heavily on his mind.

"How do you reconcile helping others with the fear of unintended consequences?" he asked.

Ibrahim considered this for a moment before replying: "We cannot control what lies beyond our actions—but we can control our intentions. If your heart is pure and your purpose is just, then trust that you are walking the right path."

This simple yet profound answer gave Michel clarity. He realized that while he could not predict how his actions might ripple through time, he could ensure that they were guided by compassion and integrity.

As Michel traveled further eastward into Anatolia, he continued to encounter thinkers and visionaries who expanded his understanding of the world. In Ephesus, he visited the ruins of ancient temples and libraries—reminders of humanity's enduring quest for knowledge. In Cappadocia, he marveled at the underground cities carved into volcanic rock—testaments to resilience and ingenuity.

Each encounter added another layer to Michel's evolving worldview. He began keeping detailed notes in his journal—not just about the people he met or the ideas they shared but also about his own reflections on life's mysteries. These writings would later form the foundation for his prophecies.

By the time Michel reached Istanbul—the vibrant heart of the Ottoman Empire—he felt ready to embrace his destiny fully. The city's grandeur overwhelmed him: its towering minarets piercing the sky; its bustling streets filled with scholars, merchants, and pilgrims from every corner of the world; its palaces shimmering like jewels along the Bosphorus.

In Istanbul's libraries and coffeehouses, Michel delved deeper into astrology and alchemy—disciplines that sought to understand humanity's place within the cosmos. He conversed with astronomers who charted celestial movements with astonishing precision and chemists who experimented with transforming base metals into gold.

Through these experiences, Michel came to see prophecy not as mere prediction but as an art—a way of interpreting patterns within chaos and offering guidance for navigating life's uncertainties.

When it was finally time for him to leave Turkey and return westward toward France, Michel carried with him more than just memories; he carried wisdom gleaned from countless encounters across cultures and disciplines—a wisdom that would shape not only his own life but also those who would one day read his words.

As he boarded a ship bound for Europe under a setting sun that painted Istanbul's skyline in hues of gold and crimson, Michel felt a profound sense of purpose take root within him: he would write prophecies—not as declarations of fate but as invitations for humanity to reflect on its choices and strive toward its highest potential. The ship, a sturdy merchant vessel named Le Venturier, was laden with goods destined for Mediterranean ports, its crew seasoned by years of navigating the unpredictable waters of the Aegean and beyond. Michel took his place among the passengers, a mix of traders, pilgrims, and scholars, each with their own stories and destinations.

For the first few days, the voyage was uneventful. The sea stretched endlessly around them, shimmering under the sun by day and reflecting the stars by night. Michel spent much of his time observing his fellow travelers and jotting down thoughts in his journal. He felt a sense of calm as the ship steadily made its way westward, carried by favorable winds.

But that calm was shattered on the fifth night

It began with a distant rumble of thunder, low and ominous. The crew, ever vigilant, moved quickly to secure the ship as dark clouds gathered on the horizon. By the time the first drops of rain began to fall, the wind had picked up, whipping through the rigging with an eerie howl. The passengers were ushered below deck as waves began to rise, slamming against the hull with increasing force.

Michel remained near the entrance to the hold, watching as the crew worked tirelessly to keep the ship steady.

The captain barked orders above the roar of the wind, his voice cutting through the chaos like a blade. Sailors scrambled to reef the sails, their movements precise despite the slippery deck and lashing rain.

The storm intensified rapidly. Waves towered over the ship, crashing down with such force that Michel feared it might break apart. The air was thick with salt spray and fear. Passengers huddled together below deck, some praying aloud while others clung silently to whatever they could grasp.

Michel's heart pounded in his chest as he gripped a wooden beam for support. He had faced many challenges in his life—famine, war, even time itself—but this was different. This was nature at its most raw and unforgiving.

Despite his fear, Michel couldn't stand idly by while others struggled. He climbed back onto the deck, where chaos reigned. A sailor stumbled past him, clutching his arm where a jagged splinter of wood had torn through his sleeve.

"Let me help," Michel said loudly over the wind.

The sailor hesitated but nodded, leading Michel to a sheltered corner where he could examine the wound. Drawing on his medical knowledge, Michel quickly cleaned and bandaged it using strips torn from his own shirt.

"Thank you," the sailor said hoarsely before rushing back to his duties.

Michel then turned his attention to other tasks. He helped secure loose barrels that threatened to roll across the deck and assisted in bailing water from the hold as it seeped through cracks in the hull. His actions did not go unnoticed; several crew members nodded their thanks as they passed him amidst their frantic work.

At one point, Michel found himself beside the captain, who was gripping the wheel with white-knuckled determination.

"Can I do anything?" Michel shouted over the storm.

The captain glanced at him briefly before nodding toward a rope that had come loose from its mooring. "Tie that down—or we'll lose part of our rigging!"

Michel moved quickly despite the slippery deck and howling wind. His hands trembled as he worked to secure the rope, but he managed to knot it tightly just as another wave crashed over the ship.

Throughout the storm, Michel marveled at the courage displayed by those around him. The sailors worked tirelessly despite exhaustion and injury; their faces etched with determination. Even some of the passengers below deck found ways to contribute—passing buckets for bailing water or comforting those who were too frightened to move. Michel himself drew strength from their resilience. Though fear gnawed at him with every lurch of the ship, he refused to let it paralyze him. Instead, he focused on what needed to be done: tending to injuries, securing cargo, and offering words of encouragement wherever they were needed.

"You're doing well," he told a young sailor who was struggling to tie off a line. "Just keep steady—one knot at a time."

The boy nodded grimly and followed Michel's advice, managing to secure the rope just before another gust threatened to tear it free.

The storm raged through most of the night, battering Le Venturier with relentless fury. But as dawn broke over a turbulent sea, it began to subside. The wind lessened its grip on the sails, and the waves grew smaller with each passing hour.

By mid-morning, sunlight pierced through breaks in the clouds, casting golden rays over a battered but intact ship. The crew cheered weakly as they realized they had survived—and so had their vessel.

Michel stood at the bow, drenched and exhausted but filled with gratitude. He watched as sailors worked to assess damage and make repairs while passengers emerged cautiously from below deck.

The captain approached him then, clapping a hand on his shoulder. "You've got courage," he said simply. "We wouldn't have made it without everyone pulling together."

Michel nodded but said nothing. His thoughts were elsewhere—on how this experience had reinforced what Elias had told him: life's impermanence was both humbling and inspiring. The storm had tested not only their physical endurance but also their capacity for courage and cooperation.

As Le Venturier resumed its journey toward Europe under calmer skies, Michel returned to his journal. He wrote about what he had witnessed—the fear that threatened to overwhelm them all and the bravery that ultimately carried them through.

He realized then that storms came in many forms: some external like this one at sea; others internal like doubt or despair. But in every case, survival depended on resilience—and on finding strength in unity.

This lesson would stay with him long after he reached France... shaping not only his life but also his prophecies for generations yet unborn.

They docked in Marseille at five in the morning on a Wednesday. Michel learned of this from the captain, who had become a friend during the voyage. They said their goodbyes, and Michel stepped onto the bustling docks of Marseille, the city still shrouded in the pale light of dawn. The air was thick with the scent of salt and fish, mingling with the earthy aroma of goods being unloaded from ships. Determined to reach Salon-de-Provence, Michel wasted no time. He found the first caravan headed in that direction and negotiated a price for the journey. By early afternoon, they were on their way.

The caravan consisted of three horse-drawn wagons carrying goods and a handful of passengers like Michel— merchants, travelers, and a family relocating to a nearby village. The road to Salon-de-Provence stretched approximately 65 kilometers (about 40 miles), a journey that would take two days at a steady pace. The wagons moved slowly but steadily, their wooden wheels creaking against the packed dirt road as the horses trotted along.

The countryside unfolded around them in a patchwork of olive groves, vineyards, and fields of lavender. The late summer sun cast a golden glow over the landscape, and Michel found himself captivated by its beauty. Yet he remained vigilant; his experiences in Greece had taught him that bandits often preyed on travelers along such routes.

As evening approached, the caravan stopped near a small stream to rest the horses and allow everyone to eat. The travelers gathered around a makeshift fire while one of the merchants prepared a simple meal of bread, cheese, and dried meats. Michel contributed some herbs he had purchased in Istanbul, which added flavor to an otherwise modest fare.

The group shared stories as they ate, their laughter mingling with the crackling of the fire. Michel listened intently, learning about local customs and legends from his fellow travelers. One merchant spoke of Salon-de-Provence's famous healer, Nostradamus, whose reputation had reached even distant villages.

Michel remained silent about his true purpose but felt a flicker of anticipation at hearing Nostradamus' name spoken so casually. He wondered if fate had truly brought him here or if it was merely coincidence.

After dinner, they set up camp for the night. The wagons were arranged in a circle for protection, and blankets were spread out on the ground for sleeping. Despite their camaraderie during dinner, there was an unspoken tension among the travelers as darkness fell. Everyone knew that bandits often struck under cover of night.

To ensure their safety, they decided to take turns keeping watch. Michel volunteered for one of the shifts, knowing he wouldn't be able to sleep soundly anyway. Armed with a sturdy staff he had carried since Greece; he sat near the fire and scanned the surrounding shadows for any signs of movement.

The night was eerily quiet except for the occasional rustle of leaves or distant howl of a wolf. Michel's thoughts wandered as he kept watch—he reflected on his journey so far and what lay ahead in Salon-de-Provence.

When his shift ended, Michel woke another traveler to take his place and lay down to rest. Sleep came fitfully as he remained half-alert to every sound around him.

The next morning brought relief as sunlight dispelled the shadows that had seemed so menacing during the night. The travelers packed up their belongings quickly and resumed their journey, eager to reach their destination before another night on the road.

As they traveled through rolling hills dotted with cypress trees, Michel noticed signs of human activity—small farmhouses nestled among fields and occasional shepherds tending flocks of sheep. These glimpses of rural life reassured him that they were nearing Salon-de-Provence.

By late afternoon on the second day, they crested a hill and saw Salon-de-Provence spread out before them—a picturesque town with its stone buildings glowing warmly in the setting sun. The sight filled Michel with both relief and anticipation; after weeks of travel by sea and land, he had finally arrived at his destination.

The caravan entered through one of the town's gates, where guards greeted them with nods but little fanfare. The streets were lively despite the hour—merchants hawked their wares in the market square while children played near fountains adorned with moss-covered statues.

Michel bid farewell to his fellow travelers as they dispersed into different parts of town. He stood for a moment in the square, taking it all in—the sounds of laughter and conversation, the scent of freshly baked bread mingling with lavender from nearby stalls.

His journey had been long and fraught with challenges, but as he stood there amid Salon-de-Provence's vibrant life, Michel felt a renewed sense of purpose. Among the many reasons for his return, visiting his old friend François was foremost in his mind. With directions from a local merchant, Michel set off toward François' farm on the outskirts of town.

The familiar path brought back memories of shared meals and long conversations under the Provençal sun. But when Michel arrived at the modest stone farmhouse, he was greeted not by François but by his wife, Marie. Her expression softened when she recognized him, though her eyes carried a weight of sadness.

"Michel," she said quietly, "you've come too late. François passed two years ago."

The words hit him like a blow, and for a moment, he could only nod in silence. Marie insisted he stay for lunch— "François would not have had it any other way," she said— and soon they were seated at the wooden table where Michel had shared so many meals with his friend.

As they ate bread and vegetable stew, Marie spoke of François' final days—how he had worked tirelessly despite his failing health and how he had often spoken fondly of Michel. "He would have been so happy to see you again," she said softly. Michel thanked her with a heavy heart, vowing silently to honor François' memory in whatever way he could.

The firelight flickered across Michel's face, now marked by the passage of more than 20 years. His once-youthful features had grown weathered and lined, his skin bearing the creases of countless sleepless nights spent studying the stars or tending to the sick. A long beard, streaked with white, obscured much of his face but could not hide the wisdom and weariness in his piercing gray eyes. His hair, unruly and cascading past his shoulders, was almost entirely white now, save for a few stubborn streaks of its original dark hue. Michel's presence carried an air of quiet authority, tempered by the humility of a man who had seen both triumph and tragedy. His robes were simple yet dignified, their edges stained by travel and work. Though his body moved slower than it once had, there remained a vitality in him—a mind ever sharp, filled with questions about the heavens and humanity alike.

As Marie spoke on, Michel stared into the fire, his thoughts drifting between memories of the past and the mysteries still waiting to be unraveled in his future.

And so began another chapter in Michel's extraordinary journey—a journey that transcended borders both temporal and geographical... one guided by an unyielding quest for understanding amidst life's infinite complexities.

Resuming his role as a healer, Michel offered comfort to those who sought refuge in his knowledge. The grateful villagers regarded him with reverence and curiosity. Once a temporal wanderer tethered to the 16th century, Michel had become an integral part of Salon-de-Provence's tapestry

Chapter 15: Love Returns

Michel first encountered Anne Ponsarde on a balmy summer evening in 1547, during the Fête de la Saint-Jean, a lively festival celebrated in the heart of Salon-de-Provence. The town square was alive with the sounds of music, laughter, and the crackling of bonfires that illuminated the cobblestone streets. The air was perfumed with lavender and rosemary, mingling with the aroma of freshly baked bread and roasted meats from nearby stalls. It was a celebration of life, community, and tradition—a moment where time itself seemed to pause in homage to joy.

Michel, now back in Salon after years of wandering and healing work, found himself drawn to the festival. Still carrying the weight of his past losses and the burden of his knowledge, he sought solace in the simple pleasures of communal life. As he wandered through the bustling square, his eyes caught sight of Anne.

She stood near a group of women laughing and chatting, her hazel eyes sparkling in the firelight. Her auburn hair was loosely braided, adorned with small wildflowers that seemed to mirror her natural grace. She wore a simple yet elegant dress that swayed gently as she moved to the rhythm of the music. To Michel, she seemed like an embodiment of Provençal beauty—earthy yet radiant, grounded yet ethereal.

For a moment, Michel hesitated. His heart quickened as he considered approaching her. Though he had faced plagues and perilous journeys, this felt like an entirely different kind of courage. Summoning his nerve, he stepped forward just as musicians began playing a galliard—a lively Renaissance dance known for its spirited leaps and intricate footwork.

"Would you honor me with a dance?" Michel asked, his voice steady but tinged with vulnerability.

Anne turned to him, her smile warm and inviting. "I would be delighted," she replied.

As they joined the other couples on the town square's dance floor, Michel felt an unfamiliar lightness in his heart. The galliard's vigorous steps required precision and energy, but Michel found himself buoyed by Anne's laughter and grace. Her movements were fluid yet playful, her joy infectious. For those moments, under the glow of bonfires and starlight, Michel felt as though he had stepped out of time's relentless march into a realm of pure connection.

After the dance ended, they retreated to a quieter corner of the square where they could talk. Michel learned that Anne was a widow who had inherited her late husband's olive groves and vineyards. Despite her losses, she spoke with resilience and warmth about her life in Salon-de-Provence. She admired Michel's work as a healer and was intrigued by his travels and knowledge.

Their conversation flowed effortlessly, punctuated by shared laughter and moments of quiet understanding. As the festival wound down and lanterns replaced bonfires, Michel walked Anne home through Salon's winding streets. The town felt transformed in the soft glow of candlelight—its medieval ramparts and honey-colored buildings bearing silent witness to their budding connection.

In the weeks that followed, Michel found himself seeking opportunities to see Anne again. He would visit her olive groves under the pretense of offering advice on medicinal herbs or stop by her vineyard during market days to share stories over glasses of wine. Anne welcomed his presence with open-hearted kindness that gradually deepened into affection.

Their courtship unfolded against the backdrop of Salon's pastoral rhythms: picnics amid lavender fields; strolls through olive orchards where sunlight filtered through ancient trees; evenings spent under starry skies sharing dreams and fears alike. Anne admired Michel's intellect and compassion while he marveled at her strength and wisdom—qualities forged through life's trials yet softened by an enduring hopefulness.

By autumn, their bond had grown undeniable. On a crisp evening as they walked along the banks of the Durance River, Michel paused beneath a canopy of poplar trees. Taking Anne's hands in his own, he spoke from his heart.

"Anne," he began, his voice steady despite the emotions welling within him, "I have walked many paths in my life—some filled with light, others shadowed by loss—but none have brought me greater joy than walking beside you. Will you do me the honor of becoming my wife?"

Tears glistened in Anne's eyes as she smiled warmly. "Yes," she replied without hesitation.

Michel could hardly contain his joy as Anne's affirmation echoed in the quiet evening air. Her "yes" carried with it a warmth that seemed to melt away the shadows of his past, leaving only the glow of their shared moment.

Taking her hand gently in his, Michel led her toward his modest home nestled on the outskirts of Salon-de-Provence. The walk was filled with quiet anticipation, their fingers intertwined as the soft hum of cicadas serenaded them under a canopy of stars.

When they arrived, Michel opened the door to reveal a cozy interior illuminated by the flickering glow of candles. The scent of herbs and freshly baked bread lingered in the air, mingling with the faint aroma of lavender from a vase on the wooden table. Michel had prepared a simple yet thoughtful dinner—roasted vegetables, fresh bread, and a bottle of wine from Anne's own vineyard. They sat together at the table, sharing stories and laughter as they savored each bite. The intimacy of the evening grew with every passing moment, their connection deepening through unspoken glances and the gentle brush of hands.

As the meal concluded, Michel poured them each another glass of wine before leading Anne to the sitting area by the hearth. The fire crackled softly, casting dancing shadows on the walls as they settled onto a plush bench draped with a woolen throw. Michel turned to Anne, his gaze steady yet tender.

"Anne," he said softly, brushing a strand of auburn hair from her face, "I never imagined I could feel this way again—so alive, so whole. You've brought light into places I thought would remain forever dark."

Anne's hazel eyes glistened as she placed her hand over his. "And you," she replied, her voice barely above a whisper, "have shown me that love can be both healing and transformative."

The space between them seemed to dissolve as Michel leaned in, their lips meeting in a kiss that was both tender and charged with emotion. Time itself seemed to pause as they lost themselves in each other's embrace.

Michel's hands moved to cradle Anne's face; his touch reverent as though she were something sacred. Anne responded with equal fervor, her fingers tracing the contours of his jawline before tangling in his dark hair.

Without breaking their kiss, Michel stood and gently guided Anne to her feet. Their movements were unhurried yet purposeful as he led her toward his bedroom—a space filled with bookshelves, soft linens, and an open window through which moonlight streamed. The cool night air mingled with the warmth radiating between them as they stood together at the foot of the bed.

Michel paused for a moment, searching Anne's eyes for confirmation. She smiled and nodded, her trust and affection evident in every gesture. What followed was an expression of their love that transcended words—a union marked by vulnerability, passion, and an unspoken promise of forever.

In that quiet room under the Provençal moonlight, Michel and Anne began not just a new chapter but an entirely new story—one written in shared breaths, whispered confessions, and the rhythm of hearts beating as one.

Their wedding was a modest, yet joyous affair held at Salon-de-Provence's Church. Friends and neighbors gathered to celebrate their union with music, feasting, and heartfelt blessings.

As they exchanged vows beneath vaulted ceilings echoing centuries-old prayers, Michel felt an overwhelming sense of gratitude—not only for Anne but for this new chapter in his life.

Michel de Nostradamus and Anne Ponsarde built a life together in the charming town of Salon-de-Provence, a place that became the heart of their shared journey. Their marriage was one of mutual respect and deep affection, a partnership rooted in love, intellect, and purpose. Together, they created a home that was both warm and vibrant, filled with the laughter of children and the quiet hum of Michel's scholarly pursuits.

The mornings in Salon-de-Provence began with the golden light of the Provençal sun spilling through the shutters of their modest home. Michel was often the first to rise, his mind already buzzing with ideas for his work. Quietly, so as not to disturb Anne, he would slip into his study.

The room smelled faintly of ink and herbs, and its shelves were lined with books, astrological charts, and medical texts. Here, Michel would spend the early hours poring over manuscripts or drafting his latest quatrains.

Anne woke shortly after him, her movements graceful yet purposeful. She had a natural rhythm to her mornings—opening the shutters to let in the fresh air, checking on their six children, and preparing breakfast. Their home was modest but well-kept, with wooden beams overhead and walls adorned with tapestries she had chosen herself. The scent of freshly baked bread often wafted through the house as Anne worked alongside their eldest daughter, who had taken an interest in cooking.

By the time Michel emerged from his study, the family would gather around the table for breakfast. It was a lively affair filled with chatter and laughter. The children spoke excitedly about their plans for the day while Anne gently reminded them to eat their porridge or help with chores. Michel listened quietly, offering advice or sharing an amusing anecdote from his youth.

After breakfast, Michel often left for town to see patients or consult with locals seeking his guidance. His reputation as both a healer and a prophet had grown over the years, drawing people from far and wide to seek his counsel. Anne sometimes accompanied him on these visits, especially when they involved families she knew personally. Her presence brought comfort to those in need; her kind eyes and soothing words complemented Michel's expertise.

While Michel worked in town, Anne managed their household with skill and care. She oversaw everything from tending their small garden to teaching their younger children how to read and write. Education was important to both Michel and Anne; they wanted their children to grow up curious about the world and equipped to navigate its challenges.

The Nostradamus household was alive with energy thanks to their six children—three boys and three girls—each with unique personalities. Their eldest son, César, was studious like his father and showed an early talent for art. He spent hours sketching scenes from daily life or copying illustrations from Michel's manuscripts.

The younger boys were mischievous by nature, often getting into scrapes that left Anne shaking her head but laughing, nonetheless. They loved exploring the countryside around Salon-de-Provence, returning home with treasures like smooth stones or wildflowers for their mother.

The girls were equally spirited. The eldest daughter shared Anne's practicality and often helped her manage the household. The middle daughter had a gift for music; she could often be heard humming melodies as she worked or playing a small lute that Michel had purchased for her on one of his trips. The youngest girl was still small but already fiercely independent—a trait that both amused and occasionally exasperated her parents.

Afternoons were often spent outdoors when weather permitted. The family loved walking through Salon-de-Provence's cobblestone streets, greeting neighbors and stopping at market stalls where Anne picked out fresh produce while Michel chatted with merchants about local news or celestial events.

On special occasions, they ventured into nearby fields of lavender or olive groves. The children ran freely through the countryside while Michel and Anne enjoyed quiet moments together under the shade of ancient trees.

Back at home during quieter afternoons, learning became a family activity. Michel took great pleasure in teaching his children about astronomy, medicine, and philosophy. He spread out charts on the dining table or demonstrated how certain herbs could treat ailments. His children listened intently—though some were more interested than others—and peppered him with questions that sparked lively discussions.

Anne supported these lessons wholeheartedly but ensured practical skills weren't neglected. She taught her daughters how to sew and cook while encouraging all her children to treat others with kindness—a value she held dear.

Evenings by the Fire

As evening fell over Salon-de-Provence, supper brought everyone together once more around a hearty meal of stews made from vegetables grown in their garden or roasted meats seasoned with Provençal herbs. Conversation flowed easily as everyone recounted their day's adventures or asked Michel questions about his work.

After supper came moments of quiet reflection by the firelight. Michel sometimes read aloud from one of his manuscripts or told stories about his travels before settling into more contemplative discussions about life's mysteries. Anne would sit nearby embroidering while listening intently; even as her hands worked on delicate patterns, her attention remained fully on him.

On clear nights when stars blanketed the sky above Salon-de-Provence like scattered diamonds, Michel took his children outside to gaze at constellations he knew so well. He explained how ancient civilizations used them for navigation or storytelling—a magical experience that left his children wide-eyed with wonder.

Anne watched these interactions with quiet pride; she knew how much Michel's work meant to him but also saw how deeply he cared for their family—a balance that only deepened her love for him.

Life in Salon-de-Provence wasn't without its challenges—illnesses swept through towns unpredictably; crops sometimes failed—but together Michel and Anne faced every difficulty head-on as partners bound by love.

For Anne especially, Salon-de-Provence wasn't just where they lived—it was home: where she raised her children alongside Michel while supporting both his prophetic work & healing endeavors alike—a legacy rooted firmly within love itself.

Anne became not only Michel's anchor but also his muse—a source of inspiration that infused his writings with humanity's enduring spirit even as they grappled with time's mysteries.

Though challenges arose—as they inevitably do—their love remained steadfast through it all: a testament to resilience forged through shared joys and sorrows alike.

Chapter 16: Writing The Future

For Michel de Nostradamus—physician turned prophet turned husband—the encounter with Anne Ponsarde at that fateful town festival was more than serendipity; it was destiny weaving its intricate threads into a tapestry richer than any quatrain could capture fully. Their union, steeped in the traditions of the time, added a new dimension to Michel's identity. Together, they navigated married life in their home nestled before the hills cradling Salon-de-Provence—a haven filled with love and shared dreams.

Anne, the daughter of a wealthy family, brought not only companionship but also stability to Michel's life. Her family's riches meant that Michel no longer had to worry about making a living through his medical practice or other pursuits. This newfound freedom allowed him to focus on his intellectual passions, and Anne encouraged him to embrace them wholeheartedly. She saw in Michel not just a husband, but a man destined for greatness—a thinker whose words could shape the world.

"You have a gift, Michel," she would often say as they sat together by the fire in the evenings. "The way you see the world; the way you understand things that others cannot—it's extraordinary. You must share it."

Michel would smile at her words, sometimes brushing them off with modesty. "I'm just a man trying to make sense of what I see," he would reply. But Anne was undeterred. She believed in him with an unwavering conviction that became the foundation of their life together.

Their home in Salon-de-Provence became a sanctuary for Michel's work. With Anne's support, he transformed one of the rooms into a study—a quiet space filled with books, manuscripts, and astrological charts. The walls were lined with shelves holding volumes on medicine, philosophy, and astronomy, while a sturdy wooden table stood by the window overlooking their garden.

Anne took great pride in creating an environment where Michel could thrive. She ensured that he had everything he needed—whether it was rare texts from her family's connections or simple comforts like fresh ink and parchment. "If you're going to write," she would say with a playful smile, "you need to do it properly."

Michel often found inspiration in their shared life. Anne's warmth and optimism balanced his introspective nature, grounding him when his thoughts drifted too far into abstraction. She had an innate ability to see beauty in the everyday—a quality that reminded Michel of the importance of connecting his lofty ideas to the lives of ordinary people.

It was Anne who first suggested that Michel compile his observations and reflections into written works. While she didn't fully understand what form these writings would take—whether they would be medical treatises, philosophical essays, or something else entirely—she was certain that they would leave an impact.

"People need guidance," she told him one evening as they walked through their garden under a canopy of stars. "You've seen so much, learned so much—why keep it all to yourself? Write it down so others can benefit."

Michel hesitated at first. The idea of putting his thoughts into writing felt daunting; he worried about how they might be received or whether they would even matter in the grand scheme of things. But Anne's encouragement gave him courage.

"Even if only one person reads your words and finds comfort or understanding," she said gently, "it will have been worth it."

Her faith in him became a driving force behind his work. Over time, Michel began to see writing not just as an intellectual exercise but as a way to fulfill what he increasingly felt was his purpose: to offer insights into humanity's struggles and aspirations.

Their home became a hub for intellectual exchange as scholars, philosophers, and astrologers visited from across France and beyond. These gatherings enriched Michel's understanding of diverse perspectives while providing material for his writings.

Anne managed their household with grace and efficiency, ensuring that guests were well cared for while allowing Michel the freedom to focus on his work. She also handled much of their social obligations, using her charm and connections to protect Michel from distractions or conflicts that might impede his progress.

"You're building something important," she would remind him whenever he expressed guilt about leaving practical matters to her. "Let me take care of the rest."

While Michel worked on his manuscripts, Anne dreamed alongside him. She imagined a future where their children— if they were blessed with them—would grow up surrounded by books and ideas, inheriting both their father's intellect and their mother's resilience.

Though life brought its share of challenges—including periods of illness and political unrest—their partnership remained steadfast. They supported each other through every trial, finding strength in their shared vision for what could be achieved through knowledge and creativity.

Anne often joked that she was Michel's first reader and fiercest critic. Whenever he completed a draft or formulated a new idea, he would share it with her first—not just out of respect but because he valued her perspective.

"You make me think differently," he admitted one day after she pointed out an inconsistency in one of his arguments. "You see things I don't."

"And you see things no one else does," she replied with a smile.

As Michel delved deeper into astrology and esoteric studies, Anne remained his steadfast supporter—even when others dismissed such pursuits as frivolous or dangerous. She understood that these disciplines were not ends in themselves but tools for exploring larger truths about human existence.

"People may not understand you now," she said one evening as they sat by the fire, "but someday they will."

Her words proved prophetic in their own right. Though Michel faced skepticism during his lifetime—and even accusations of heresy—his writings would eventually earn him enduring fame as Nostradamus: author of cryptic quatrains that continue to fascinate readers centuries later.

By 1550, Michel's life took a significant turn that would forever alter his legacy. The villagers began whispering about his growing interest in the occult—a shift marked by his decision to write an almanac for the year. This compilation of astrological predictions, weather forecasts, and practical guidance represented Michel's first foray into writing—a departure from his role as a healer.

The first almanac written by Michel, drew considerable attention in Salon-de-Provence. The townspeople, intrigued by its astrological predictions and cryptic verses, began to see Michel in a new light. The epithet "Doctor" now shared space with another name whispered through the cobblestone streets: Nostradamus. Encouraged by its success, Michel embarked on an annual tradition. Each year, he scrutinized the celestial tapestry, weaving threads of perception into quatrains that hinted at events yet to unfold.

One night, seated at his worktable under the soft glow of candlelight, Michel reflected on his path forward. The tablet, hidden within the sanctity of his home, remained a silent witness to the temporal secrets that defined his existence.

Michel sat alone in his dimly lit room, the flickering glow of a single candle casting shadows that danced across the walls. Before him lay a blank sheet of parchment, his quill poised above its surface.

The air was thick with the scent of ink and dried herbs, remnants of his dual life as both healer and seeker of truths beyond the veil of time. Tonight, however, he was neither physician nor apothecary. Tonight, he was something else entirely—a chronicler of the future, a messenger to generations yet unborn.

He closed his eyes and allowed his mind to drift into a meditative state. Michel had developed a method to write what he believed were glimpses of the future. He would light candles around the room. He grabbed his 21st Century tablet and powered it on. As he gazed into the tablet, he would enter a trance-like state, his mind flooded with the vivid images—scenes of people and events that unfolded before him like a living tapestry.

These visions were his past and his future. Michel understood that they were not meant to be interpreted literally but rather as symbols—metaphors for larger truths hidden within the flow of time. He would jot down these impressions in rough notes, later refining them into quatrains: four-line stanzas that encapsulated the essence of what he had seen. The quatrain form, with its balance of brevity and rhythm, allowed him to convey complex ideas while leaving room for interpretation—a necessity in an era when too much clarity could invite persecution.

After Michel reviewed the images and text that displayed on the tablet, he dipped the quill into the ink and began to write. His first quatrain emerged slowly; each word chosen with care:

"Beneath the shadow of the crescent moon,
The lion's roar shall echo through the land.
Two brothers torn by fire's consuming bloom,
The eagle weeps where towers used to stand."

He paused, reading over what he had written. The lines were deliberately ambiguous, their meaning layered with symbols that could resonate with readers across different times and contexts.

The "crescent moon" might evoke thoughts of Ottoman power or celestial influence; the "lion's roar" could signify strength or conflict; "two brothers" hinted at division or tragedy; and "the eagle" carried connotations of empire or freedom lost.

Michel understood that his audience—the people of 16th-century France—needed these prophecies to be relatable yet enigmatic. By weaving his visions into poetic language rich with allegory, he not only protected himself from accusations of heresy but also invited readers to engage with his work on a deeply personal level. Each interpretation would be shaped by their own experiences, fears, and hopes. Satisfied with his first attempt, Michel leaned back in his chair. This was only the beginning—a single thread in what would become an intricate tapestry spanning centuries. With each quatrain he wrote, Michel sought not just to predict events but to provoke reflection, urging humanity to consider its choices and their consequences within the vast labyrinth of time.

Determined to navigate the delicate balance between revealing and concealing truths, Michel chose quatrains—a poetic form that veiled mysteries within layers of ambiguity. This decision weighed heavily on him; he understood the tightrope he walked between temporal delicacy and revelation. The burden of transcendent knowledge etched lines of contemplation on his face.

As quiet Provençal nights unfolded, Michel immersed himself in transcribing glimpses of the future onto parchment. His inked quill moved with purpose as he chronicled tales of caution: the rise and fall of empires, echoes of wars reverberating through time, and humanity's fragile dance with its world. His words sought to guide without imposing fate's shackles.

Michel understood that altering destiny carried consequences rippling across ages. By candlelight's hushed glow, each stroke became a bridge spanning temporal realms—linking his era with epochs yet unknown.

His writings warned of plagues, political upheavals, and environmental perils while urging future generations to tread mindfully through existence's labyrinth.

The inked pages stood as silent testaments to Michel's dual role: healer and prophet; man of his time and harbinger of epochs to come. In these moments of quiet labor, he grappled with time's paradox—illuminating paths forward while remaining anchored in the present.

Yet Michel's resolve faced its sternest test when love entered the equation. As he chronicled history's unfolding tapestry, his quill hesitated over pages where Henriette's memory lingered. Grappling with moral quandaries about influencing personal connections, Michel made a conscious choice: certain pages would remain blank—a veil shrouding their shared journey in uncertainty.

To Michel, love was sacred—a tapestry woven spontaneously through unguarded moments rather than preordained fate. He believed decisions about affection should remain untouched by external influence—a sacred prerogative for those traversing humanity's enigmatic landscape.

As Michel inscribed warnings and wisdom into history's annals, he reflected deeply on responsibility woven into every action. The future—once an unwritten symphony—now bore imprints shaped by both restraint and foresight. As guardian navigating inevitability's currents, Michel recognized humanity's delicate dance between guidance and free will.

In concluding his chronicles, Michel left behind an enduring message for those inheriting his legacy: wield knowledge with reverence; understand that destiny's threads—while woven with foresight—remain inseparable from human agency.

Michel's decision echoed through the epochs, resonating with the gentle cadence of time's passage. His writings, a testament to the intricacies of temporal stewardship, invited reflection on the delicate balance between revelation and the sanctity of the unknown.

In the quiet Provençal nights, Michel became a beacon for those seeking to navigate the labyrinth of time, armed not only with foresight but with timeless wisdom that cloaked the future in mystery.

The almanacs, taking shape under the careful strokes of his pen, became vessels of foresight—an offering to humanity walking the thin line between revelation and concealment.

The tablet, with its encrypted secrets, remained Michel's silent confidant in this dance with destiny. As his almanacs were printed and distributed beyond Salon-de-Provence, they generated both admiration and skepticism. The quatrains—steeped in Nostradamus's mystique—became a source of fascination for those eager to decipher time's enigma.

A rumor began to circulate. Someone claimed to have seen Michel one night alone at his table, illuminated only by candlelight. The story described him gazing into a "piece of glass" as if in a trance. The villagers embraced this tale, convinced that Michel could peer into the future.

The decision to embrace his role as a seer—to use his pen as a bridge between past and future—marked Michel's transformation into Nostradamus. The shadows of destiny, cast by flickering candlelight on that fateful night at his kitchen table, became the ink that flowed through his prophetic words.

Yet even as Nostradamus navigated his new identity, the burden of temporal knowledge remained ever-present. The tablet, hidden deep within his home, held the key to secrets that shaped his destiny.

Michel's delicate dance with the future—expressed through quatrains and celestial intuitions—reflected his determination to traverse time's labyrinth with grace.

The people of Salon-de-Provence, enchanted by Nostradamus's mystique, regarded him with a mixture of awe and reverence. His almanacs, filled with cryptic verses and celestial guidance, became beacons that transcended the boundaries of the 16th century. Nostradamus—the temporal wanderer now rooted in Provençal life—continued to walk destiny's tightrope as his quatrains echoed through the corridors of time.

The year was 1553, and the warm Provençal sun bathed the town of Salon-de-Provence in golden light. Life in the Nostradamus household had been peaceful, filled with the hum of daily routines, Michel's writings, and Anne Ponsarde's care for their six children. She was the heart of their home—a woman of quiet strength and unwavering devotion. Michel often marveled at her ability to balance the demands of their family while supporting his work as a physician and astrologer. But fate, as it often does, had plans that would shatter their tranquil existence.

One crisp autumn morning, Anne was tending to the garden outside their home. She loved the rhythm of her work—gathering herbs for Michel's remedies, pruning the lavender bushes, and ensuring their home always smelled of life and growth. As she reached to pluck a sprig of rosemary from a high branch, her foot slipped on the damp stone path. She fell hard onto the ground, striking her head against the edge of a low wall.

The commotion brought Michel rushing from his study. He found her lying still among the herbs, her face pale but conscious. "Anne!" he cried, kneeling beside her. She opened her eyes weakly and tried to speak, but her words were slurred. Michel's heart sank as he recognized the signs—her fall had triggered a stroke.

He carried her inside with trembling arms, laying her gently on their bed. For days, he refused to leave her side. His knowledge as a physician guided him as he prepared herbal tinctures and poultices to ease her pain and reduce swelling. He massaged her limbs in an effort to restore movement and whispered words of encouragement into her ear. "You are strong, my love," he said softly. "You will recover."

But Anne's condition worsened with each passing day. Her speech became more fragmented, and she struggled to move even her fingers. Despite Michel's tireless efforts, he knew deep down that she was slipping away from him.

One evening, as the fire crackled softly in their bedroom, Anne managed to speak clearly for the first time in days. "Michel," she whispered, her voice faint but steady. "You have done everything you could... more than anyone could ask for."

Tears welled in Michel's eyes as he clasped her hand tightly in his own. "I cannot lose you," he said, his voice breaking. Anne smiled weakly. "You will not lose me," she replied. "I will always be with you—in your heart, in our children... in everything you do."

Her words broke something inside him, but they also gave him strength. He stayed by her side through that long night, holding her hand as she drifted between wakefulness and sleep.

As dawn broke over Salon-de-Provence, Anne took her final breath. Michel sat with her still form for hours, his grief too deep for words. When he finally rose, he vowed to honor her memory by continuing his work—healing others and sharing his knowledge of future events—just as she had always encouraged him to do.

Michel sat alone in the dim light of his study, the heavy wooden chair creaking beneath him as he leaned forward, his head buried in his hands. The fire in the hearth had burned low, casting flickering shadows across the room, but Michel paid it no mind. His thoughts were elsewhere—tangled, restless, and unrelenting. Anne was gone. The woman who had been his anchor, his partner, his love, had died in his arms just hours ago. Her absence was a void so vast he could scarcely comprehend it. And now, as grief clawed at his heart, another question gnawed at the edges of his mind: what was he to do next?

He lifted his head slowly, staring at the cluttered desk before him. The quills and parchment seemed foreign now, relics of a life that suddenly felt hollow. His gaze shifted to the small device hidden beneath a pile of papers—the pad that provided inspiration. It was his only link to the twenty-first century, the time he had left behind when an accident had flung him into this distant past.

Michel exhaled deeply and leaned back in his chair. "What am I doing here?" he muttered aloud to himself, his voice hoarse and raw from hours of weeping. "What is my purpose now?"

The room offered no answers, only the faint crackle of dying embers. But Michel's mind was relentless, and soon he found himself speaking again—this time not as a lament but as a conversation with himself.

"You've built a life here," he said softly, as though addressing another version of himself sitting across the room. "You've helped people—healed them, guided them. You've written prophecies that will echo through the ages. Isn't that enough?"

He paused, waiting for an answer that would not come.

"And yet…" he continued after a moment, "what if it isn't enough? What if there's more I'm meant to do? What if I've abandoned something greater by staying here?"

His thoughts drifted to Richard—the friend and colleague he had left behind in the twenty-first century. Richard had been there when they first tested the Chrono-Field Generator. He had been there when everything went sideways, when Michel was pulled into the currents of space-time. Did Richard think him dead? Or worse—did Richard blame himself for what had happened?

Michel rubbed his temples as conflicting emotions warred within him. "If I go back," he mused aloud, "what will I find? Decades have passed here… but how much time has passed for them? Days? Weeks? Years?" He shook his head. "And what if I return to find nothing? What if Richard is gone? What if everything I knew is gone?"

The thought sent a shiver down his spine. Returning to the twenty-first century might mean facing a world that had moved on without him—a world where he no longer belonged.

"But staying here…" Michel's voice faltered as he glanced toward the empty chair where Anne used to sit while she read or embroidered by the fire. The sight of it sent fresh waves of grief crashing over him. "Staying here means living with this pain every day for the rest of my life."

He stood abruptly, pacing the room like a caged animal. His long robes brushed against the stone floor as he moved back and forth, his hands gesturing wildly as though arguing with an invisible opponent.

"You're a coward," he spat at himself suddenly. "Afraid to face what lies beyond this moment—afraid to take a step forward because you don't know where it will lead."

He stopped pacing and gripped the edge of the desk tightly, staring down at the Chrono-Field Activator buried beneath the papers.

"But what if going back is not about me?" he asked quietly, almost pleadingly. "What if it's about something greater? What if I'm meant to return—not for my sake but for theirs?"

The idea gave him pause. He thought of all he had learned during his years in medieval France—the knowledge of medicine, astrology, and philosophy he had painstakingly acquired and refined. Could that knowledge serve a purpose in the twenty-first century? Could it help Richard—or anyone else—understand time itself in ways they never could before?

Michel closed his eyes and took a deep breath, trying to calm the storm raging within him. When he spoke again, his voice was steadier but still tinged with uncertainty.

"If I go back," he said slowly, "I may lose everything I've built here... but if I stay, I may lose myself."

The words hung in the air like a verdict waiting to be carried out.

He turned toward the window and gazed out at the darkened streets of Salon-de-Provence. The town was quiet now, its people asleep and unaware of the turmoil their healer and prophet wrestled with alone in his study.

"Anne," Michel whispered into the silence, his voice breaking once more. "What would you have me do?"

He imagined her answer—not in words but in her gentle smile and steady gaze. She would tell him to follow his heart wherever it led him—to trust himself as she always had.

Michel nodded slowly as though hearing her voice in his mind. He returned to the desk and carefully uncovered the ever patient tablet. The device felt cool and solid in his hands—a reminder that even amidst chaos, some things remained constant.

"I will decide," he said firmly to himself. "Not tonight... but soon."

With that resolution made, Michel placed the device back on the desk and extinguished the fire in the hearth. As he climbed into bed alone for the first time since Anne's passing, he felt no closer to an answer—but for now, it was enough that he had asked the question.

Michel sat in his study, the room dimly lit by the flickering light of a single candle. The air was thick with the scent of aged parchment and the faint aroma of dried herbs hanging from the beams above. His quill rested on the desk beside an unfinished quatrain, its ink still fresh. He leaned back in his chair, staring at the tablet he had hidden beneath a cloth in the corner of the room. It had been a while since he last used it, and many years since he had been flung into this time, far from the twenty-first century and his friend Richard.

His life in Salon-de-Provence had become one of routine and purpose. He was a husband, a father, and a healer to those who sought his aid. His prophecies had brought him fame, and his almanacs were eagerly read across France. But tonight, as he sat alone in his study, he felt the weight of time pressing upon him—not just the time he lived in, but all time.

He picked up a quatrain he had written earlier that day and read it aloud to himself:

"The great machine shall hum beneath the stars,

Through time's veil it will pierce afar.

Two friends divided by centuries' wall,
Shall meet again when fate does call."

The words echoed in his mind, stirring memories of Richard and their work together in the twenty-first century. They had been close partners in an experiment that pushed the boundaries of science. The Chrono-Field Generator had been their shared dream, a device meant to explore the mysteries of time itself. But everything had gone wrong when General Andrews showed up, and Michel had been forced to travel to this distant past.

At first, he had been consumed by despair. The world of the sixteenth century was alien to him, its people suspicious of his knowledge and methods. But over time, he had found a place here. After he married Anne Ponsarde, a kind and intelligent woman who became his anchor in this strange new life. Together they built a home filled with love and laughter, raising six children who brought him joy beyond measure.

Yet even as he embraced this life, a part of him remained tethered to the world he had left behind. He often wondered what had become of Richard. Had his friend continued their work? Had he tried to bring Robert back? Or had he given up entirely, assuming he was lost forever?

Michel stood and walked to the field where the Chrono-Field Activator lay cloaked. He uncovered it slowly, running his fingers over its smooth surface. The device was patiently waiting all this time, but it still worked—The fusion engine that powered it would last hundreds of years, maybe more. He knew that much.

"Should I try?" he whispered to himself.

He paced. If he activated the device again, there was a small chance that it would not start as planned. What if it would not take him back to Richard or even to the twenty-first century. After all these years, might it fling him further into the past or into some unknown future? What is the program had become corrupted after all this time? And what of their children? Could he leave them behind?

But then another thought struck him: what if Richard needed him? What if their work held answers that could change not just their lives but the course of history itself?

Michel sat down again and placed his head in his hands. "What is my purpose?" he asked aloud.

The question lingered in the air as memories flooded his mind—memories of treating plague victims in Provence, of writing quatrains late into the night while Anne slept beside him, of holding his newborn children for the first time. His life here was meaningful; it mattered deeply.

But so did Richard.

He thought back to one of his most famous quatrains:

"From depths of West shall wisdom rise,
A union forged beneath strange skies.
The past will meet where futures blend,
A journey begun shall find its end."

Had he written those words with Richard in mind? Was this prophecy meant for them?

Michel stood once more and approached a window overlooking Salon-de-Provence. The town was quiet now, its streets bathed in moonlight. He could hear faint sounds from neighboring houses—the laughter of children, the murmur of voices—reminders of all that tied him to this place.

And yet…

He turned back to the Time Machine. If he used it again, it would mean risking everything: his family, his home, even his life here in this time. But if he didn't try, if he let fear hold him back... would he regret it forever?

Michel took a deep breath and reached for a piece of parchment. He began writing furiously—a letter to his children explaining everything: who he truly was, where he came from, and why he felt compelled to try returning to Richard.

"My dearest children," he wrote, "you have given me more than I ever thought possible: love, family, purpose. But there is another part of my life I cannot ignore—a part that calls to me even now."

As he wrote, tears blurred his vision. He loved them deeply; leaving them would break his heart. But they deserved to know the truth.

When he finished the letter, Michel placed it on his desk alongside one final quatrain:

"Through fire's gate or water's flow,
The path ahead none can know.
Yet bonds unbroken shall endure,
A love eternal ever pure."

He looked at the tablet one last time before covering it again with its cloth.

"Not tonight," he said softly to himself. "But soon."

For now, Michel returned to his desk and picked up his quill once more. There were still prophecies to write, still lives to touch through his words.

And somewhere out there—perhaps across centuries—Richard waited for him.

Michel would find him again... when fate deemed it so.

270

Epilogue

The hills of Salon-de-Provence remained unchanged, cradling the secrets of centuries in their silent embrace. As the Provençal sun cast its golden glow over the picturesque village, Michel—now a 60-year-old man known as Nostradamus—felt the weight of time descend upon him like a familiar cloak. The covert time machine, hidden in the countryside near Salon-de-Provence, awaited his return. Its fusion engine's 0 a marvel of temporal engineering, still vibrated with latent energy, ready to power the enigmatic craft. The hills, fields, and stone houses bore witness to a moment that transcended the ordinary limits of the 16th century.

With a contemplative gaze, Michel approached the time machine. Memories flickered in his mind: joys and sorrows intertwined with the quatrains that had woven his legacy as Nostradamus. The life he had built in Salon-de-Provence—the healing, the love, and the loss—felt like a distant dream as he stepped into the capsule. The familiar hum of the Chrono Field Generator enveloped him like an old friend. The control panel, adorned with buttons and switches, greeted him with its timeless familiarity. Now standing at the intersection of past and future, Michel paused to reflect on the extraordinary journey that had brought him to this moment.

With a steady breath, Michel activated the communication module. A longing stirred within him—a desire to reconnect with Richard, his friend from the 21st century. Hidden within his attire was the tablet containing encrypted secrets from a life that had defied temporal understanding. "Anyone there?" Michel's voice resonated through the capsule as he sent his message across time's vast expanse. "Richard?" A heavy silence followed—a pregnant pause that seemed to echo through temporal corridors.

Then, as if awakening from slumber, the Communication Unit crackled to life. A voice emerged on the other end—tinged with curiosity and disbelief. "Hello? Who is this? Where are you calling from? Hello?"

Michel felt a wave of emotion surge within him as he responded. "This is Robert—Michel—or Nostradamus, as they call me here," he said with measured calmness. "I'm calling you from the 16th century, Richard. It's been a long journey through time, my friend. Are you there? Can you hear me?"

The silence that followed stretched like an eternity before another voice broke through—a younger voice filled with both reverence and urgency. "Michel… or Nostradamus," it began cautiously. "You're speaking to Richard Jr., my father's son."

Michel's heart sank at this revelation. Richard Jr., carrying both curiosity and apprehension in his tone, continued: "My father vanished after your journey to the past. We believe he was abducted by military forces after delaying construction of another time machine. He insisted he didn't have all the details—that you had taken the critical plans they needed. They wanted those secrets."

The weight of Richard Jr.'s words fell heavily on Michel's shoulders as he absorbed this unexpected twist in his story. The confirmation of Richard's disappearance sent shivers down his spine—a chilling reminder of how fragile timelines could be.

"I promised myself I'd continue his work," Richard Jr. admitted after a pause. "He left behind encrypted notes— details about time travel hidden in layers of secrecy only I could decipher. But I've always wondered about you—the man my father spoke so highly of—the one who ventured into the past."

As their conversation unfolded across centuries, Michel shared fragments of his story while listening intently to Richard Jr.'s account of resilience and determination. The younger man's commitment to unraveling time travel's mysteries painted a picture of hope amidst uncertainty—a torch passed down from father to son.

"The encrypted notes," Richard Jr. explained, "have guided me for years. They're more than just instructions—they're a testament to my father's sacrifice and belief in something greater."

The two men—separated by centuries yet united by destiny—found themselves forging an extraordinary bond across time itself. Their dialogue became a bridge between past and future: Michel offering wisdom gleaned from his journey while Richard Jr., driven by his father's legacy, sought answers that could reshape history.

As they exchanged stories through crackling transmissions, Michel reflected on how their shared mission transcended individual lives. The encrypted notes left by Richard Sr., now illuminated by his son's dedication, became threads weaving together narratives across epochs—a testament to human perseverance in unraveling life's greatest enigmas.

"Richard," Michel said finally, his voice steady yet tinged with emotion, "your father was the smartest man I ever knew. He would have hidden the encryption key in a very safe place—somewhere only he, and someone like you, would know to look."

Richard's eyes gleamed with excitement. "Michel, now that you say that I think I know where the key might be hidden. When I was a kid—around the time you left—we were working on an adventure program together. I wonder if that's where he hid the code."

Michel nodded thoughtfully. "That sounds exactly like something your father would do. How long do you think it will take to find out?"

"Give me seven days," Richard Jr. replied confidently. "I'll need to deconstruct the game's code, but once I do, I'll know for sure."

"Perfect," Michel said with a hint of optimism in his voice. "I'll contact you again in seven days. In the meantime, be careful. You never know who might be listening…"

The Communication Unit crackled faintly as if acknowledging this profound connection between two eras—a bridge forged by shared determination to navigate time's intricate dance.

Michel leaned back in his seat within the capsule, the weight of past decisions mingling with a newfound sense of purpose coursing through him like an unbroken current flowing between centuries.

As he prepared for what lay ahead—for conversations yet unfinished and paths yet untrodden—Michel felt anchored not only by memories but also by hope: hope carried forward by those who dared to explore beyond the boundaries imposed by ordinary existence.

Made in United States
Cleveland, OH
25 February 2025

14626019R00154